FIXED ASSET

DISCOVER OTHER TITLES BY RILEY EDWARDS

Hollow Point

Playing with Lies

Playing with Danger

Playing with Love

Playing with Forever

Takeback

Dangerous Love

Dangerous Rescue

Dangerous Games

Dangerous Encounter

Dangerous Mind

Dangerous Hearts

Dangerous Affair

Gemini Group

Nixon's Promise

Jameson's Salvation

Weston's Treasure

Alec's Dream

Chasin's Surrender

Holden's Resurrection

Jonny's Redemption

Red Team: Susan Stoker's Universe

Nightstalker

Protecting Olivia

Redeeming Violet

Recovering Ivy

Rescuing Erin

Gold Team: Susan Stoker's Universe

Brooks

Thaddeus

Kyle

Maximus

Declan

Blue Team: Susan Stoker's Universe

Owen

Gabe

Myles

Kevin

Cooper

Garrett

Silver Team

Theo

Easton

Smith

Jonas

The 707 Freedom Series

Free

Freeing Jasper

Finally Free

Freedom

The Next Generation (707 Spinoff)

Saving Meadow

Chasing Honor

Finding Mercy

Claiming Tuesday

Adoring Delaney

Keeping Quinn

Taking Liberty

Triple Canopy

Damaged

Flawed

Imperfect

Tarnished

Tainted

Conquered

Shattered

Fractured

The Collective

Unbroken

Trust

Stand-Alone Titles

Romancing Rayne

Falling for the Delta (cowritten with Susan Stoker)

FIXED ASSET

RILEY EDWARDS

This is a work of fiction. Names, characters, organizations, places, events, and incidents are either products of the author's imagination or are used fictitiously. Otherwise, any resemblance to actual persons, living or dead, is purely coincidental.

Published by Montlake, Seattle
www.apub.com

EU product safety contact:
Amazon Media EU S. à r.l.
38, avenue John F. Kennedy, L-1855 Luxembourg
amazonpublishing-gpsr@amazon.com

ISBN-13: 9781662532764 (paperback)
ISBN-13: 9781662532757 (digital)

Cover design by Hang Le
Cover image: © JooLaR, © Leigh Prather, © phiseksit / Shutterstock; © Wander Aguiar Photography

Printed in the United States of America

To my family—my team—my tribe.
This is for you.

Chapter One

"Have you lost your goddamn mind?"

The caller needed no introduction. I knew that growly voice.

I hadn't heard from him in nine months, but who was counting? Not me. Nope. I was not ticking off the days since I'd last seen Jack Donovan. I wasn't still dreaming of our time in Las Vegas or all the times he'd made me laugh.

"Hello, Jack. How have you been?" I kept my voice low, not wanting to draw attention to myself in the café. Even with my hair dyed dark brown and my clothes purchased from the local mall, I didn't blend in. An American was easy to spot.

"I asked you a question, Catarina."

Another growl, this one feral. A shiver ran up my spine despite the heat and lack of air-conditioning in the small restaurant.

God, he had such a great voice—full of gravel with a hint of rugged edge.

Right, had I lost my mind?

Probably.

Just being a woman in Honduras was dangerous. An American woman eating lunch in a café in the gang-controlled Barrio Guadalupe was akin to a death sentence. But Jack shouldn't have known where I was.

"Why would you ask that?"

"Catarina."

Sweet Jesus, I loved hearing him say my name. I wasn't proud to admit I'd fantasized about how it would sound falling from his lips while he moved inside me. But I had. Jack Donovan had starred in every self-induced orgasm in the last nine months.

"Jack."

"Is everything a game to you?"

That was an interesting question. One I didn't need to think all that hard about. Life was a game. Nothing more than a series of choices—some choices moved you forward, some sideways, and some backward. The trick was knowing the game, who your opponent was, and what moves they were going to make. My problem was, I never could figure out Jack's next move. He was too smart to show his hand.

"Yup," I answered honestly.

"What the hell are you doing?"

I glanced down at my forgotten bang bang chicken, then slid my gaze around the room. One could say that in the US, the health department would've closed this establishment on a variety of violations that had nothing to do with the old, chipped tables or the missing chunks of mortar between the bricks that made up the walls. Though I was a tad bit worried the building was going to crumble at any moment.

"Eating lunch."

I left out the "taking my life into my own hands by eating bang bang chicken off a plate that doesn't look like it's actually been washed since the last person used it" part. Call me crazy, but I didn't think he'd find my comment amusing in his current mood.

"Jesus fuck, woman—"

The sound of rapid gunfire out on the street had me diving for the dirty floor. The glass shattering all around made me curl up in a tight ball with my hands covering the back of my head. I'd been in Tegucigalpa for three days. This was not the first time I'd heard shots fired. It was, however, the first time I'd been minding my own business eating lunch and become an active participant in the festivities.

The gunfire stopped. The café was eerily quiet; no one was screaming or scrambling to make an escape. There was no panic coming from my fellow patrons—not that there were many of them—and no one made a fuss. A drive-by was a normal occurrence in the gang-infested neighborhood.

I lifted my head and pulled up on my knees to have a look around. The front windows were toast. New bullet holes peppered the wall behind me. A man at a corner table was still sitting in his chair eating, unbothered there'd just been a shoot-out. A few people were getting to their feet. One man was helping a young boy off the floor.

I spotted my phone, snatched it up, righted the chair I'd been occupying, then hefted myself to my feet.

Right. This might've been an everyday occurrence for the people of Barrio Guadalupe, but I'd lost my appetite. I didn't know if or when the police would show up, but I *did* know I didn't want to be here if they did. They could tip off the wrong people. I wanted to be seen, but I was in this particular neighborhood for a reason—the gang that controlled the area was a step down from the viciousness of the rival gang two streets over. And that step down could mean the difference between merely being kidnapped or taken to the killing field and murdered.

With that in mind, I fished some money out of my wallet, tossed a few bills on the table. Swung my backpack over my shoulder and secured it in front of me. The pack would do nothing to shield me from the next round of bullets, which could fly at any moment, but wearing it backward would stop thieves from snatching it off my back.

Glass crunched under my feet as I exited. It would be easy to call the situation insane. The normalcy of a drive-by that didn't set off a panic was absolute lunacy. But in truth, it was tragic.

Once outside, I hustled east, back to the relative safety of the Central District municipality. I didn't dally and take in the sights as I had during my stroll to the café—not that the sights were your typical vacation points of interest. Unlike the modern buildings and high-rises near the US Embassy—and the Centro Morazán, with its gleaming, blue-tinted glass rising forty stories above the busy, clean street and shopping boutiques on the bottom levels—Guadalupe reeked of desperation and fear. The buildings were dilapidated and rough. As with any major city, only blocks separated the different areas, the juxtaposition mind boggling. Two kilometers divided shopping malls, nice cars, a Popeyes, and a KFC from the dangerous slums.

A turn down the wrong street could mean death—literal death. Thus, I was paying attention to where I was going. My hotel next to the embassy should've been a little over a two-kilometer trek, according to Google Maps. However, my alternate route carefully skirting Mara Salvatrucha gang territory added twenty minutes to the walk.

A door to my right swung open. I quickly sidestepped the stumbling, drunk man coming out of the liquor store. A few meters ahead of me, a woman was yelling in rapid-fire Spanish at an older man—which was dangerous. The woman was speaking too fast for me to pick up more than a few angry words. The traffic on the street was busy. The cars did not stop for pedestrians here, but I'd rather take my chances playing *Frogger* and dodging cars than risk getting caught up in the domestic dispute up ahead. I'd had enough adventure for one day. I just wanted to get back to my hotel, study the maps my contact at the CIA gave me, and plan tomorrow's outing.

I stepped closer to the curb, waiting for the traffic to clear enough that I could make a mad dash across the two lanes. Scooters, bicycles, rusted trucks, and cars in varying states of disrepair sped by.

One foot was on the crumbling curb, the other on the garbage-covered asphalt. I was getting ready to make a break for it when I caught a white van barreling down the road at a high rate of speed, narrowly missing a man pushing a cart.

I was on my back foot, preparing to jump out of the way, when someone came up from behind and hooded me. In an instant, everything went dark. Two arms banded around me, immobilizing me.

It was too soon.

This wasn't supposed to happen here.

Not yet.

Not now.

I struggled and screamed, but the arms tightened. I heard tires screech. The smell of rubber and diesel mixed together.

The second I was lifted off the ground, I kicked out. My foot made contact with something solid; there was a grunt but no other sound. I was being attacked on a busy street. There were people all around, and not one person came to my rescue. Not one person shouted for my attacker to let me go.

Not a single soul helped.

My ankles were grabbed and, with quick precision, secured together. I twisted the best I could to get free until I heard the scraping of metal followed by a bang as the door closed, and I felt the van moving.

The whole abduction—from the hooding to getting me into the vehicle—took seconds. I hadn't even had time to register how hard my heart was thumping in my chest. Fight-or-flight had kicked in, but the fear trailed behind. Now that I was in the back of a moving van, terror ripped through me.

My plan had looked good on paper—risky but necessary.

Now I was at the mercy of men who wouldn't bat an eye at killing me—or worse—and I saw my mistake.

Jack had been right. I'd lost my mind.

The fight drained from my body, my muscles locked, and my training kicked in. Now wasn't the time to try to escape while I was in a confined space with an unknown number of assailants. Now was the time to listen, gather intel, think, and plan.

I didn't need my life to flash before my eyes—or to think about all the things I'd never done, never accomplished—to know if I died, I'd go to my grave with a mountain of regret. I'd leave this world never knowing what it felt like to be in love.

A flicker of a memory of Jack teasing me before everything had turned to shit. I'd convinced myself I'd fallen for him. I'd believed I meant something to him. Right up until those blue eyes of his—so dark they were navy, and unless you were in the light, they looked black—turned cold and he walked away from me.

I pushed the wayward thoughts of Jack out of my mind and focused. I'd been trained by the best, spent years attached to the First Special Group. I knew my way around a hostile interrogation—both in practice on the battlefield and in the classroom. I'd played hide-and-seek with my SERE instructors and survived—twice. My first go-around with my Human Intel class was easy, the second time not so much. SOCOM didn't screw around when it came to training their soldiers.

Deep breath.

The van took a hard right, my body pitched to the side, but strong arms kept me in place.

Something wasn't right.

I took another breath, this one more of a sniff.

Clean.

No body odor, no smell of booze or pot. All of which I'd smelled in abundance since I'd arrived in Honduras.

I didn't think gang members cared all that much about freshly laundered clothes before they snatched a woman off the street. But that didn't mean the Bratva hadn't heard about an American woman roaming the streets unprotected and decided to make a play in rival territory. Though the Russians mostly kept to Ecuador, I'd been warned they were still operating in Honduras.

I wasn't sure which was worse—the Russians or the Hondurans. One of those groups would have me in a shipping container headed to the Mother Country before anyone knew I was missing. The other would likely enjoy torturing me before help could arrive.

The van came to an abrupt stop. Hands wrapped around my secured ankles. But instead of being yanked from the vehicle, I was lifted.

I turned my head toward one of the arms locked around me and sniffed again.

Tide.

Did I smell Tide?

Chapter Two

I was going to spank the ever-loving hell out of Catarina Keys. Peel her jeans down her legs, bend her over my lap, and redden her delectable ass.

The woman had no sense.

None.

I'd died a thousand deaths since I'd met her.

The problem was, she was smart as fuck, and her risky behavior paid off. At least it had when she was undercover in Las Vegas pretending to be a ditzy bombshell on the prowl for a sugar daddy. Our target had zeroed in on Cat's gleaming blonde hair, blue eyes, tight body, and gorgeous face, and took the bait. Then for the next few weeks, I had to watch her cozy up to a rich scumbag who made his money by selling women. Not only selling them outright to other rich, sick fucks but renting them out by the night.

Each time she'd tricked herself out for a meeting with Martin Jackson, my gut had churned. Every night she had been with him, worry had set in until it burrowed deep and turned to fear. One wrong move would've been the end of her. It wasn't just our target but also his entourage of guards she'd had to fool.

In reality, there was nothing sweet, soft, or compliant about Catarina. Yet she'd expertly pulled it off. All the way to the very end, when, during the takedown, Cat had beaten the absolute shit out of Martin.

I couldn't say the man hadn't deserved it, but the rage behind it was what had worried me. I'd seen the way Martin had touched her.

How his hand had rested on her thigh while the motherfucker made her sit on his lap. That beating said something other than takedown—it screamed of retribution.

The last time I saw the woman was on the veranda of a mansion—dress torn, barefoot, with blood coating her hands along with splatters on her face, neck, and forearms.

And there she was, once again putting her life in danger. This time without the full support of the Sex Offender Investigation Branch of the US Marshals Service. She didn't have the FBI as backup. She didn't have my old boss, Wilson McCray, and my old team to watch over her.

This time, she was alone in a country known for femicide. And she was there, *alone*, eating lunch in a café in an area of town that was a hotbed for kidnapping and murder.

Oh yeah, I was spanking her ass. Then I was demanding answers. I was done playing games with this woman.

My teammate, Mason Hughes, lifted Cat's feet and stepped out of the van. I hadn't zip-tied her wrists—something I'd have to think about later—but the lack of restraints meant I'd had to keep her back pressed tightly to my chest the short drive to the warehouse. I wasn't exactly sure if I wanted the excuse to keep her in my lap or if hooding her and tying her ankles together was as far as I was willing to go in my 'scared straight' ploy.

Once we had her in the middle of the room, I jerked my chin to Mase. He slowly lowered her feet.

My mistake was thinking since she'd been docile in the van, she'd stay that way. I should've known better—she was trained and highly skilled.

The moment I relaxed the band my arms around her formed, she quickly bent her knees and dipped down while just as quickly lifting her arms, breaking loose. Her elbow caught me in the right kidney. Even blind, her aim was perfection.

Before I could stop her, she spun to face me and threw a right jab to my gut, then a left hook aimed for my jaw. I easily dodged the hook, grabbed her wrist, and twisted it behind her back. In a stupidly brave maneuver, she used my momentum and launched herself backward.

Not wanting to dislocate her shoulder or break her arm—which was what I would've done had she been anyone else—I eased off the arm hold and controlled our fall. But just because I didn't want to hurt her didn't mean I didn't have a point to make. I twisted, rolled her facedown on the concrete, rolled again so I was on top of her, and pinned her with my weight.

"God," she huffed. "You win, Jack."

My body froze.

"What's with all the drama?" she continued. "You couldn't just roll up, say hello, and offer me a ride like a normal person?"

Mase's chuckle echoed throughout the cavernous space. Saint 'Pete' Young wasn't far behind with his laughter.

"That's it?" Pete asked. "I thought you had at least one more round in you."

"If you're talking to me," Cat wheezed, "I'm smart enough to know when to tap out. And two hundred pounds of muscle, I have no chance of moving." To punctuate her statement, she shoved her ass into my groin. I stifled a groan by grinding my molars. "Unless I do damage to his testicles. And as a thank-you for not popping my shoulder out of its socket, I've decided to spare him the pain of a twist and pull."

My second error related to my first mistake—I'd lost focus and hadn't paid enough attention to her shifting under me. What felt like her wiggling in order to breathe while I gave her most of my weight was, in reality, her worming her hand down between her legs. With a shift of her shoulder and a lift of her hips, she awkwardly found her target.

She could get a handful, but to make her point, her fingertips grazed my crotch.

I dropped my chin until my mouth brushed the burlap still over her head and whispered, "Careful, Catarina, you break 'em, you buy 'em."

Harder this time, her fingertips made another pass.

"With the stunt you pulled, you've already earned yourself a red ass," I warned. "Maybe you should stop while you're ahead."

"What stunt?"

Her question came out as a breathy whoosh, and I wondered if it was the lack of oxygen or something else.

Then stronger this time with, "You can't blame me for hitting you. Surely you didn't expect me not to put up a fight."

"The café," I reminded her. "No, rewind—you being in Tegucigalpa, wandering the streets."

"Hey, Mr. and Mrs. Smith, you wanna share with the class what you two are talking about?" Pete asked.

Cat took that as an opportunity to grind her ass harder into my crotch.

"Warning, baby. No one in this room will stop me from dragging you out of here."

"Clearly. Seeing as they're all accomplices in my abduction."

"I didn't accomplice anything," Fallon Harris joined in. "Or is it assist? Either way, I was sitting here minding my own business when Jack tore out of here on his K-and-R mission."

"Good luck with the *R* part of that," Cat said from under me. "No one cares about me enough to pay a ransom."

I frowned at her response.

"There was no *R*," Mase interjected. "Just the *K*."

"You wanna roll off me, big guy? It's getting hard to breathe with this hood on."

No, I didn't want to roll off her. If I did, I'd lose my excuse for touching her. Not that I wanted to be horizontal with her in front of my team. But once the hood came off and I saw her fathomless blue eyes, it would be harder to remind myself Catarina Keys was off limits.

One could say I had a type—feisty, smart-mouthed, witty women did it for me. Hair color, eyes, height, body shape . . . didn't matter to me as long as the woman was top-tier funny and smart. Catarina had the feisty down. Her wit was razor sharp. She was intelligent as fuck.

Gorgeous face, prettiest eyes I'd ever seen, a body that made my mouth water, and hair that made me fantasize about wrapping it around my fist while my tongue was in her mouth.

But she was careless.

Careless with her personal safety—totally unconcerned. She took dangerous risks without a thought, which contradicted her intelligence.

With that as a good reminder, I rolled off Cat, got to my feet, hauled her up, and tossed her over my shoulder.

It was a short walk to the makeshift lounge we'd set up. When I bent to set her on the ratty-ass couch, her hands went to my belt.

"I'm not going to drop you," I told her.

"I can't see," she hissed.

Right. The hood.

"Let go so I can set you down."

She let go. I got her settled on the couch and pulled the burlap bag off her head.

Brown hair tumbled around her shoulders. Irrational irritation flared.

The dye job was professional, the brown locks were shiny, healthy, and she'd taken a few inches off since I'd last seen her. The dark hair made the blue of her eyes stand out, the contrast stunning. However, she was a natural blonde. That was how I'd met her, and that was how she came to me in my dreams—thick, glossy, sun-kissed golden hair.

Cat lifted a hand and demanded, "Knife."

I fished my PSK out of my pocket and handed it over.

With deft movements, she flipped off the lock, slid her thumb to the stud, and flicked the folder open. She bent forward to cut her ankles free while saying, "Your pivot screw needs to be tightened." A moment later, she continued to bitch. "When was the last time you sharpened this? It's criminal how dull your blade is. I should call Benchmade and report this blasphemy, have them recall your right to purchase—or better, confiscate her and restore her to her original glory."

"I think I like this chick," Fallon quipped.

I chanced a look at my teammate. A risk I hoped didn't end bloody, now that Cat was armed. I wouldn't put it past the crazy woman to stab me to prove a point.

Fallon, Pete, and Mase formed an arc off to the side—identical poses, arms crossed over their chests, boots planted shoulder-width apart. To complete the pose, they all had matching grins.

The peanut gallery.

Great.

Fallon's lips quirked, and my gaze quickly skidded back to Cat.

My knife was no longer visible, the plastic ties discarded on the concrete. Cat pushed off the couch, lifted a foot, and rolled her ankle.

"Which one of you zipped my feet?" she asked.

"With that elbow and right hook you've got, not sure you're gonna get a confession," Mase told her.

Catarina smiled. Not the kind that was toothy and wide and conveyed happiness. No, this smile was a barely there smirk, but it lit her eyes. It was the kind of smug smile that made a man want to kiss the arrogance off her lips, taste the magnificence of her self-satisfaction.

Truth be told, I wanted to see that smile aimed my way when I fucked her. Then and now, I wanted her with or without the smirk. The bottom line of it was, nine months ago when I'd met her in Vegas, I'd needed to fight the pull of her. I even went so far as to not be alone with her. Our banter had turned flirtatious, and I hadn't trusted myself not to take that further and see how she'd respond to openly filthy.

My guess? She'd give it back in spades, and she'd do it with this same smug smile. Thus started the fantasy of wanting to plant her astride me and watch that smile turn into awe.

Jesus fuck, less than thirty minutes in her presence and I was already back to mentally getting her naked. Technically, I hadn't even clapped eyes on her in person before my palms started itching to touch her. That shit started when I caught her on CCTV bopping down Boulevard Morazán.

Then reality hit. She was taking a stroll in one of the deadliest cities in the world. And something else had kicked in—the need to get her safe. Not just safe, but under my protection.

I couldn't deny I was a man with a strong need to protect and serve, skills I'd spent my adult life honing and fine-tuning. However, that essential part of me had never extended to any one person—it had always been for the mission, for the greater good, for the men and women who served with me. But there was something about Catarina that kicked those instincts into hyperdrive.

The thought of her being in danger sent my blood pressure skyrocketing to unreasonable heights.

And that was why she was off limits.

The woman loved putting herself in danger.

The fuck of it was, nine months ago, I'd fallen in love with her. Then in an effort to do the right thing, to allow her to be who she was without me dragging her down, I walked away.

I had a feeling the second time around was going to be even harder.

Chapter Three

The struggle was real, but I managed to peel my gaze from Jack to the other three men in the room.

One of these men had to be Mia Keniston's brother, Saint 'Pete' Young. My guess was the tallest one, who shared Mia's brown hair and brown eyes, but more than that, they had the same high cheekbones. On Mia they looked striking, on Pete they looked chiseled.

I moved to the side where the men were standing and took my chances, offering my hand.

"I'm Catarina Keys. Saint, right?"

The man took my hand in a firm grip. No smile. Assessing gaze of a former Team Guy.

"Pete," he corrected, offering his nickname. "Nice to meet you."

When Pete released my hand, the man next to him lifted his in offering.

"Mason Hughes," he introduced.

This man smiled and his grip wasn't quite as firm. I'd bet he charmed the panties off many a woman with those green eyes and that mop of sandy-blond hair. But it was the devilish grin that stated plain he was up for a good time, however that good time came to be.

"Good to meet you."

"Fallon Harris," the last man greeted.

He was shorter than the others, but what he lacked in height—not that he wasn't tall, just not as tall as the giants in the room—he made up for in width. The guy's biceps looked larger than my waist, and his shoulders were so broad I wondered if he had to turn sideways to walk through a doorframe.

"Now that that's out of the way," Jack interjected, "let's talk about why you're here."

I ignored Jack.

"Please excuse Mr. Supremely Bossy Pants. He seems to have forgotten his manners," I told Fallon. "It's good to meet you too."

Fallon's extremely large shoulders started shaking. "I think we have a winner." He chuckled. "Mr. Bossy Pants just rolls right off the tongue."

Jack made a rude sound, clearly not liking the nickname.

Oh well. That's what he gets for snatching me off the street.

"Why. Are. You. Here?" Jack enunciated each word.

With a sigh, I turned to face him. Unfortunately, I forgot to brace for the wallop his good looks packed. Jack had the whole Henry Cavill thing going on—minus the cleft in the chin—with Ryan Gosling's smile and the body of Mark Wahlberg circa his underwear modeling days. It was a mash-up that had a powerful effect on my lady parts.

"Why are *you* here?" I returned.

A dark brow lifted, and not even his clenched jaw could stop the muscle in his cheek from jumping.

I was trying his patience. It wasn't the first time, and it certainly wouldn't be the last. Jack found me exasperating. I found it fun to poke the beast.

When he didn't answer, I matched his brow lift and added a hand to my hip.

"Why don't we head back to the office? We can sit and talk this out," Pete suggested.

"Or, we can stay here and see if they challenge each other to a duel at dawn. My money's on Miss Catarina Keys. Something tells me she's got some tricks up her sleeve," Mason added as an alternative scenario.

"The only thing she has up her sleeve is my knife," Jack huffed.

"Oh, ye of little faith. I see you still don't trust that I know what I'm doing."

"No, I think you know exactly what you're doing. It's your judgment I question."

Ouch.

"Ah, right, now I remember." I stopped to make a show of snapping my fingers. "It's Jack's way of thinking or it's the wrong way of thinking."

"My way of thinking doesn't land you on some asshole's lap, with his hand up your dress and his eyes on your tits," Jack ground out. "Neither does it put you in a position of being forced to endure that fucker's hands on you in the name of mission success."

My body locked tight. Not at the familiar refrain but the vehemence behind it.

When I'd met Jack in Las Vegas, he worked for an outfit called Takeback. His team was being used as a force multiplier to take down a high-profile sex trafficker. After an eighteen-month joint investigation with the SOIB and FBI, we'd finally gotten a lock on Martin Jackson. For some reason, a man who'd managed to keep his name clean by using front men and women decided to come out of the shadows and throw a weekend-long, sick-as-fuck sexathon preview party in his hotel suite before he'd personally hosted an auction.

A weekend I had spent at his side while working undercover.

The part I'd never understood was that, at first, Jack didn't make a peep about me going in with the sole purpose of catching Martin's attention. Only after Martin took notice did he have a change of heart and start questioning the precautions I was taking and insisting on more safety protocols.

But it wasn't until after we had verification that the auction was actually taking place that he lost his mind and demanded for me to stay behind.

I defied his order. Not that it was in his power to order me to do anything. Actually, I'd outranked him during that operation. My bosses at the SOIB had cleared me to attend; the Marshals Service tended to frown on sex-trafficking twats and had been counting on me to help the FBI and Takeback, to make sure no one left without a pair of metal bracelets.

All of that to say—I'd heard Jack's opinion on my judgment before, but I'd never heard him express it with anger tinged with hurt.

"I had it under control," I reminded him.

"Are you talking about Vegas?" Pete asked.

"Yes," I answered. "Jack has a problem with my work ethic."

"Is that what you call putting yourself in danger?"

I drew in a breath in an attempt to keep a handle on my temper. "No, Jack, that's what I call doing my job. I didn't seek employment with the Marshals Service to sit behind a desk and sip coffee while gossiping with my workmates. I signed up for the fieldwork." I waved my hand around the open space. "Which, just to point out, you yourself have a very similar job."

The tight line of his body and his frown indicated I'd scored a hit with that, but I wasn't done.

"Either you see me as an equal or you don't. Either you trust me to know myself, my limitations, and believe I'm damn good at keeping myself safe, or you don't. In other words, your thoughts on the matter are not my problem, they're yours. Obviously, I'm here working, same as you. Your kidnapping stunt was amusing until it wasn't. Now, I have an assignment to get back to. If someone would please take me back to my hotel so I can get on with my day, I'd appreciate it."

When I was done, three men were staring at their boots, and one looked like his head was going to explode.

Any guesses on which one looked ready to have a coronary?

"You're right, it's not my business."

Good Lord, that hurt.

I didn't want it to, but it did, all the way down to that place I pretended didn't exist. The place that Jack had occupied for a few weeks, until he'd made it clear I wasn't who he wanted, then it went back to being empty.

"Great." I fake smiled. "Anyone up for giving me a ride or should I walk?"

And where the hell did my backpack go? I'd been so caught off guard with the hooding, I'd lost track of everything else.

As if reading my mind, Jack tipped his head to the side. "You're not gonna ask, are you?"

His cheap shot pissed me off; so much so, I lost my temper.

Jack was no farther away than the length of the three-seater couch that looked like it had been dragged in from the dump. That meant I didn't have far to go before I was in his face, which was unfortunate, because the minimal distance hadn't allowed me to get a lock on my anger.

I rolled up on my toes, slammed my palms on his chest, and angrily clipped, "What's your problem?"

"Me?" he smoothly rumbled. "I'm not the one—"

"Cut the shit, Donovan."

His hands came up, circled my wrists, and tugged me closer. Mere inches separated our mouths. So close I could feel his exhales dance across my lips. Closer than we'd ever been, yet still not close enough.

How was it possible I wanted to kick him in his balls and beg him to finally kiss me at the same time? Well, not the same time. I wanted to kick him in his balls first, then after I had that satisfaction, I wanted to beg him to kiss me.

"You drive me insane," I spat.

"Welcome to my world, woman."

"I think I've seen a few X-rated films start like this," Mason mused.

"Only you would call porn a film," Pete muttered.

"If Mase starts talking about popping a boner, I'm out," Fallon joined in.

Throughout this exchange, Jack's gaze stayed locked with mine. There was something working behind those dark-blue orbs. Something I couldn't make out. But whatever he was contemplating would remain a mystery.

"To answer the question you're too stubborn to ask, Mase took your pack right before he zip-tied your ankles."

I thought back, and I didn't remember being divested of the bag, but I was struggling and wiggling, trying to regain my freedom, so anything was possible. I mean, obviously it was, because I no longer had my backpack.

"Way to throw me under the bus," Mason mumbled.

"The answer to your other question is, no one is taking you back to the hotel until after we talk."

Talk?

What the hell was there to talk about?

"A lot," Jack answered my unasked question.

"Stop reading my mind."

"Baby, your every thought is playing across your face."

That wasn't true. I had an excellent poker face.

One side of Jack's mouth hitched up.

I narrowed my eyes, leaned closer, and inquired, "What am I thinking now?"

What was supposed to be an act of defiance backfired. I knew this when what I'd meant to sound snotty instead came out breathy.

"Do you really want me to answer that, Cat?"

"If your answer is anything other than me wanting to punch you in the face, you'd be wrong," I lied.

Jack made a tsking sound. He lowered his head, veering to the side before his lips touched mine, but I felt them ever so gently whisper across my temple before his mouth was at my ear and he quietly said, "Such a pretty liar."

He pulled back, leaving my brain scrambled. Since I was incapable of speaking, I stared mutely as he released my wrists, only to pry one of my hands off his chest and use it to pull me around the dingy couch.

"Excuse us."

We were crossing the threshold of a doorless doorway when I found my voice. "Where are we going?"

"To work this out."

Jack threatening to spank me immediately sprang to mind. My hand in his involuntarily spasmed.

"Not that way, Cat. But I like the way you think."

Goodness gracious, the dude was the master of mixed signals. One second he looked like he wanted to throttle me and was telling me I was a pain in his ass, the next he was whispering sexy things in my ear.

"What is this place? And where is it?"

"Palmira."

Well, that explained the short van ride. This neighborhood was only a few blocks from where I'd been eating lunch.

"Are you insane? Palmira is controlled by Adrián Lopez."

"No crazier than you walking down the street with a neon sign flashing above your head announcing: BEAUTIFUL AMERICAN, PLEASE TAKE ME. And I'm impressed you've done your homework."

I yanked my hand, trying to free it from his grasp. Unfortunately, this did nothing. His grip was ironclad.

"Just so you know, your insult canceled out your compliment."

We'd only made it a few feet down the corridor when I heard a sharp whistle.

Jack jerked to an abrupt halt and turned his head to look behind me. I craned my neck to see what had stopped us.

Pete was standing at the open doorway. Right hand up, index finger extended, circling the air.

"What's—"

"We have company," Jack irately announced.

"What kind of company?"

"The bad kind."

Well, shit.

This couldn't be good. Jack and his buddies were in Lopez's territory. I highly doubted they asked the gang leader for permission. I was equally sure if they had, Lopez would've killed them on the spot. His numbers weren't as high—those numbers being members, not kills—as some of the other local gangs. I'd been warned to stay clear of Lopez and the Calaveras. Lopez was known to be ambitious. That ambition was shrouded in brutality. There was only one way for the Calaveras to claim neighborhoods that were already controlled by a rival—war.

The Calaveras had earned their name honestly by keeping the severed heads of the rival leaders when they acquired a neighborhood.

I didn't want my skull to be Lopez's newest keepsake.

"Our talk's gonna have to wait."

I bit back my 'no shit, Sherlock' retort and opted for something more relevant.

"I'm unarmed."

Jack pivoted, his strides now urgent as he towed me behind him back into the large warehouse.

"Cat needs kit."

I heard Mason chuckle before he peeled off and disappeared behind the van.

Pete was glaring at a tablet. Fallon already had an M4 carbine hanging across his chest from a sling and was shoving a handgun into his thigh rig.

"Four tangos C-side," Pete started, then swiped his thumb over the tablet screen. "Six coming up on A." Another swipe. "B and D are clear."

I glanced at Jack for an explanation.

"Side A." He pointed to the large bay doors. "Clockwise around the building."

In other words, side A was the front, C was the back, and B and D were the sides.

"Got it."

"Yo, Cat," Mason called. "You want the Beretta PX4 GS-D or the Rugger-Magpul RXM collab?"

"Is the PX4 the Langdon Tactical edition or the compact?" I asked.

"Compact."

"I'll take the RugPul."

Next to me, Fallon snorted.

"What?"

"Just surprised."

Now I was getting annoyed. "That I know the difference between an RXM and PX4?"

Fallon's eyebrow winged up.

"Fuck no. I'm just surprised you have shit taste like your boy in platforms. The RXM is a total Glock knockoff. I took you for someone who would appreciate a G-type decocker."

"We got ten heavily armed men converging on us; maybe you two gun nerds should wait to debate striker fire versus hammers after we put them down," Pete suggested.

"Sorry," I mumbled.

Mason was coming my way with two rifles slung over his shoulder, a vest in one hand, and the RXM in the other. Gone was his sexy-beach-bum persona as he morphed into untouchable warrior.

"Here. It's gonna be big on you but it's better than nothing. Mag pouches are full." He held out the vest. I took it and quickly put it on.

I ran my hands over the pouches, getting a feel for where my reloads were. The vest was set up differently from how I normally kept mine, but there was no time to reorganize. I pulled the straps on the sides as far as I could, but it was still huge.

"This isn't going to work. It'll bounce around when I run."

I was pulling back a Velcro strap when Jack's hand knocked mine out of the way, and he refastened the cummerbund.

"It stays on."

"Jack—"

Suddenly we were nose to nose.

"It . . . stays . . . on."

The tiny pauses between each word with the added enunciation left no room for argument.

"Fine. But if a thirty-round mag busts my lips, I'm blaming you."

"You bust your lip, I'll kiss it better. You take a round to the chest without a plate, I'll be pissed."

"They breached the fence. Time to roll out," Pete commanded.

Jack stepped back.

Mason handed me the RXM, shoved my arm through the tactical strap of the M4, and told me, "They're both chambered."

"Locked and loaded and ready to go," Fallon called out.

As a team, the men made their way to the van with Pete leading the way. I was sandwiched between Fallon in front of me and Jack behind me.

Jack was helping me into the van when it dawned on me . . .

"Where's your kit?"

"Guns are already in the van."

"Where's your vest?"

"You're wearing it."

With that, he slid the metal door closed in my face.

You're wearing it.

Jack gave me his vest, which meant he'd left himself unprotected.

Damn.

Chapter Four

By the time I got my ass planted in the passenger seat, Pete had the engine running.

"Hold tight," he warned.

I looked over my shoulder to make sure Cat was secure, or as secure as someone in the back of a van kitted out for transport, not passengers, could be.

She was eyeing her pack behind Pete's seat. I bet she was still trying to puzzle out how Mason had gotten it off her while I'd had her arms pinned to her sides.

She reached out, grabbed a strap, and had her answer.

"You cut my straps," she muttered.

"I'll buy you a new one," Mase told her.

Pete hit the gas. Fallon grabbed Cat by the back of my vest as she pitched to the side.

"Might want to brace, he's taking out—"

Fallon didn't finish, mainly because Pete crashed through the garage door, rendering his warning moot. The van veered right and Pete corrected. I turned to face forward and grabbed my RXM from the glove box, leaving my M4 wedged between the center console and the seat as my last resort.

"I've got four at our nine," I said, calling out the four men to the left of the vehicle.

Pete would have to take care of them. I couldn't shoot across him. He swerved the van to the left, gunned the engine, and played chicken with four Honduran gang members who would rather be run over than go back to Lopez and explain how they pussied out and ran for cover.

I scanned to the right, found the two others, and engaged, sending warning shots instead of taking them out.

"Brace," I called back to the team.

A second later, Pete hit the chain-link gate. Mangled metal scraped the side of the van as he drove through.

I pulled the barrel of my RXM back into the vehicle and out of sight. The road was empty of pedestrians, but in this neighborhood, that didn't mean shit. Lopez had scouts everywhere, peeking through dirty windows, sitting in cars, on the rooftops . . . Anywhere someone could hide, they did.

"One of you call in to Shep. Have him run the footage and catalog. We also need a new safe house," Pete instructed.

"Shepherd Drexel?" Cat asked.

I clamped down on my molars in an effort not to growl my frustration and focused on watching the road.

I wasn't surprised Cat knew who Shepherd Drexel was. Shep was a well-known hacker. He also skirted the boundary between morally gray and morally bankrupt. It wasn't that the man didn't know right from wrong—he did. He just lived by the code of: by any means necessary. Whereas most people had lines they wouldn't cross, Shep would back up and take a running start before he leaped over them.

So Cat knowing who Shep was wasn't what had me struggling to keep my attention on my surroundings. It was the wonder I heard that was borderline giddy. The last person Catarina Keys needed to have contact with was Shepherd Drexel. The two of them together would do my head in.

"Yeah," Fallon answered. Now I wanted to turn around and punch my teammate. "He runs intel for us."

"Seriously? I thought he—"

"We got a tail," Pete thankfully cut in. "White Honda."

I glanced in the side mirror and spotted the old hooptie.

"Driver and passenger," I confirmed. "I can't see if there's anyone in the back."

Pete made a sharp left, narrowly missing an oncoming car, taking us closer to the end of Lopez's territory.

One of the unusual things about Tegucigalpa was the pockets of gang presence. Some of these pockets were only separated by a street. You could cross over into a rival gang's area simply by crossing the intersection. The city was a maze of violence, some areas worse than others, some relatively safe if you stayed in the center city by the malls. *Relatively safe*, meaning it was relative to the daily murder count that happened in the barrios. Safety also depended on if you were a man or a woman.

Women were never safe in the Northern Triangle of Central America.

"One block until we're clear."

As soon as the words left Pete's mouth, bullets peppered the back of the van.

"Motherfucker," Mason groused. "You had to say it."

More bullets peppered the side of the van.

"Hit the floor, Kitty. The van's not bulletproof," Fallon informed Cat.

Jesus fuck, I was totally punching my friend in the mouth when we got out of the van.

"Should we be shooting back?" Cat asked.

"This is just the Calaveras boys' way of asking us nicely to leave," Mason informed her.

More rounds popped off.

I heard the familiar *whiz-crack* of a projectile snap past my head right before the windshield spiderwebbed.

The high-pitched ringing started immediately. I heard loud but muffled sounds and couldn't make out words over the painful buzzing. I reached up to touch the side of my head, ear, neck. Nothing felt sticky.

More loud pops, these coming from inside the van. I turned to look into the back and died another thousand deaths, courtesy of Catarina.

She was on her knees at the back of the van, and I could tell by the jerk of her shoulders she was returning fire, along with Mason.

"Pull her the fuck back," I shouted.

Either no one could hear me over the ringing in their ears, the gunfire, or both, or they were ignoring me.

I was getting ready to crawl into the back and remove Cat from the direct line of fire myself when Pete made another turn, and the shooting stopped.

"Driver's out," Mason yelled, or at least that's the best I could interpret.

The silence that ensued only exacerbated the incessant ringing that I knew from experience we'd be suffering for at least the next hour, if not two.

There was a tap on my shoulder. I glanced over to find Fallon shoving his phone at me. I grabbed the device, looked at the screen, and read the message on the opened Notes app.

Texted Shep. Waiting to here back.

If it hadn't felt like an ice pick had punctured my eardrum, I would've made fun of him for his typo. I'd file that away for later. I kept reading.

Your woman's a badass. I think we should keep her.

I was going to need dental work when I got back to San Diego, or I was going to give myself TMJ from the jaw clenching.

I shoved the phone into Fallon's waiting hand and looked for a landmark.

Mas X Menos supermarket, next to a sketchy-looking auto repair station. We were officially in a gang-free zone. Or, an area that wasn't fully controlled by a gang. The US Embassy was two blocks down. The politicians weren't the only ones who played politics in Honduras.

Just because the gang leaders were ruthless criminals didn't mean they weren't smart. They'd agree to keep the area around the embassy neutral for a payoff.

Fallon shoved his phone back through the space between the seats. I glanced at it and felt a headache blooming.

Three words that had me wanting to scrap the mission until I could safely escort Cat home.

San Pedro Sula—the hub of drug trafficking.

If there was one city in all of Honduras I didn't want to take Cat to, it would be San Pedro Sula. If Shep was sending us there, that meant he'd located our target. And of course, Berta 'the Angel of Death' Lanza *would* be in San Pedro Sula. Where else would a woman on the warpath be?

Good Christ.

I jerked my chin. The phone disappeared. I pulled mine out of my pocket, opened the Maps app, and put in the city name. It was a minimum of a five-hour drive to the northern coast, closer to six if we avoided the toll roads. Not to be confused with traditional toll roads like the Jersey Turnpike or bridge tolls. These tolls were nothing more than a money grab from the police. They'd set up checkpoints for the sole purpose of extorting a few bucks.

The problem wasn't the money, though it was annoying as fuck to have to stop every twenty kilometers to pay off another cop; it was that each time we got stopped, we courted an issue with our documents. Not that they wouldn't hold up under scrutiny, but getting hauled in for questioning was out of the question. It was better to take the long route, avoid the tolls and possible side-of-the-road battles.

Traffic was a nightmare in this part of the city. Instead of silently showing Pete the map on my phone, I told him where we were going. I saw him wince, then jerk his chin in recognition.

One problem solved.

Next up, Cat.

I turned in my seat.

I don't know what I thought I would find her doing, but sitting on her ass, knees cocked up, leaning up against the side wall of the van next to Fallon with her head bent to his phone and smiling, shards of broken glass littering the scarred and dirty floorboards, was not it.

I glanced at Mason. His position was the same, but his legs were stretched out, ankles crossed, armed folded over his chest, eyes firmly on Catarina, checking her out.

I knew that look. I'd spent the last nine months with my new team. Six of those months were spent training at Pete's compound in the Jamul Mountains south of San Diego. It wasn't battle tactics we practiced. We all had the same training from the SEAL Teams. The six months were spent team building, learning how to work together in flawless synchronicity, learning how to read each other, learning strengths and weaknesses. I'd studied them, and they'd studied me.

To the average observer, Mase looked like he was checking out a hot chick, but the once-over had nothing to do with her good looks.

Just because I didn't see it didn't mean I didn't know that when Mason deemed it was time to return fire, Cat scrambled—maybe even shoved Fallon out of the way—to get into a firing position.

That was Catarina, always in the mix. Brave, skilled, fearless, and bold. Damn fine qualities—if she'd learn to protect herself.

I let out a sharp whistle. Three heads turned my way. I pointed at Cat and crooked my finger, motioning her to come to me.

The squinty-eyed gesture in return was lethal and hot. I wondered how she'd respond to the demand if she was naked. If I ordered her on her hands and knees and told her to crawl across the bed, would she throw attitude or would she be a good girl?

Knowing her, she'd make me work for it. There was no chance Catarina would bend unless the man in her bed had earned it. And the thought of bending Cat to my will never failed to make my cock hard. The fuck of it was, it had more to do with earning her than getting her to submit.

Submission was easy. I didn't want compliance. I wanted Cat's surrender. I didn't want to just fuck her, I wanted to fuck her until the rest of the world was erased and I owned her—body and soul. I'd never met a more frustrating woman. A woman who, if given the chance, would own *me*.

I watched Cat push away from the wall. Mason shifted his legs out of her way. And either to tease me or infuriate the hell out of me, she crawled—*fucking* crawled—the short distance to the front seats. I glanced at Mason, then to Fallon. Both men had their eyes glued to her ass.

I felt the rumble in my chest, though it didn't register over my ringing ears, but I knew the men heard the unhappy sound. Mase looked up and smirked. Fallon smiled and went back to looking at his phone. Cat held on to the back of the seats and pulled up on her knees, bringing herself to my eye level.

"You summoned?"

I was going to do a lot more than summon her if she pulled that shit again.

"Do me a favor and don't swing your ass in front of my team."

Lethal and hot morphed into fatal. A lesser man would've withered to dust under her stare. Unfortunately for me, it was a turn-on.

"You know, telling me not to do something is only going to make me want to do it more," she informed me.

I'd already lived that nightmare, so I was well aware Cat did shit out of spite. If my ears weren't throbbing I would've pointed out the idiocy of her statement.

"Do you have anything important in your hotel room?"

I didn't miss the small grimace; no doubt her ears hurt worse than mine.

"No."

"Nothing? Electronics? Files? Passport?"

"I know what important means, Jack. I don't need an itemized list," she sassed.

Good Christ, I wanted to kiss that attitude off her lips.

"We're headed to San Pedro Sula," I told her.

"Why?"

"Do you want to have this conversation now, or wait until the buzzing's stopped?"

Cat thought for a moment, undoubtedly weighing the pain in her ears against her impatience.

"Wait."

With that, she pushed away from the seats, swiveled on her knees, and crawled back to her spot next to Fallon. Her ass was on display, her hips were swaying, my dick was getting harder by the second.

Goddamn woman was going to be the death of me.

Chapter Five

My poor ass was not made for this.

Some of us had never taken a transatlantic flight in the cargo hold of a C-130.

Me. I was that someone.

All my deployments to Europe and central Asia had been aboard a C-17. One could say the Air Force had it going on. The Globemaster was luxury compared to the Hercules. Or so I'd been told by bellyaching sailors.

And the hard metal of the van's loading bay made a Hercules look like first class. My ass was officially numb. That, and my back was killing me from being jostled around. Fallon and Mason didn't look like they had an ache or a pain. Mason had tipped his head back and closed his eyes. He must have been awake, unless he possessed some special skill that gave him the ability to chew gum and sleep at the same time. Fallon was scrolling through sports headlines on his phone and had been since he'd stopped showing me memes he had saved on his cell. I was now in possession of the useless knowledge that he favored Florida sports teams. This would come in handy if one day there was a Fallon trivia night. He also got sidetracked a lot and fell for clickbait headlines.

When I couldn't take it a second longer, I scooted away from the wall and crab-crawled to the front of the van. It must be noted, the crab-crawl was due to the aches and pains. If I could've managed to get to my hands and knees without whimpering and showing weakness, you could bet your ass I would've. Fallon barely glanced in my direction before he went back to his phone.

I was nearly to the front when Jack turned and took me in.

The grin on the bastard's face had me wanting to bite his lip and see if he was still smiling after I drew blood—especially when the grin turned lopsided and one side of his mouth pulled up in the sexiest freaking smirk.

I think at this point in my life I'd suffered from too many concussions. There was no other explanation for my attraction toward a man who'd made it clear he wasn't interested—though he did want to spank me. Which merited contemplation, at least by the part of me that was turned on. But only after I puzzled out why I was attracted to a man who infuriated me.

He only infuriates you because you want to bang him.

Yup. I needed to see a head doctor. I was now talking to myself.

"You okay?" he asked.

"I need to hit the head."

Jack blinked and stared like I was speaking in a foreign tongue.

"The bathroom," I clarified.

"I know what the head is."

That's what she said.

"Great. Then can we pull over so I can use it?"

Jack's gaze slid to the windshield. Mine followed. Nothing but beautiful green trees with a gentle slope of a hill on the right.

"I'll take a bush," I told him.

"Can you wait thirty minutes?"

I thought about my bladder demanding relief and shook my head. "Not without courtin' a UTI."

"I'll pull over," Pete rushed to say.

After the hours of silence my ears had thankfully stopped ringing, but the faint buzzing hadn't subsided. "Thanks."

"Are we taking a piss . . . um, pit stop?" Mason inquired.

I didn't know if he heard or if he felt the van slow.

"Yeah," I called back.

"Thank fuck. I was getting ready to pull out the Gatorade bottle and ask Kitty to close her eyes," Fallon put in.

"Kitty? You couldn't come up with something . . . better?"

Before Fallon could answer, Mason beat him to it.

"Gatorade? Dude, you don't need a wide mouth—"

"Not all of us are you, Mase. No need to brag." Pete shocked the hell out of me by joining in.

I mean, I didn't know the man, but he had an air of stoicism about him. I didn't know the hierarchy of the team, but I'd guess Pete was the team leader.

The van rolled to a stop. Jack pinned me with an unhappy expression and commanded, "Wait for me to open the door."

"You know, I normally require dinner and a little foreplay before I follow demands."

There was utter silence in the van, followed by a sputtered laugh from behind me, then the cabin filled with roaring hilarity.

Jack didn't laugh, he didn't even crack a smile, but his dark eyes flared. He leaned close to quietly tell me, "Keep it up, Catarina. I got a good memory, baby, and the stamina to make it so you never forget."

I really wanted him to tell me more about this stamina, or better yet, show me. But, sadly, I could hear the men behind me moving around.

Jack turned around, breaking the spell, yet I didn't move until I felt a big hand land on my shoulder and smelled minty-fresh breath.

"My money's on you," Mason told me.

The big side door slid open, Mason stepped out, Fallon followed, then Jack was there holding out his hand to help me down.

I glanced at his hand, and it wasn't the first time I'd noticed how big his hands were, how he had long, thick fingers.

"Yes, it's true what they say," Jack rumbled.

I glanced up at him and asked, "*Who* are they? And *what* do they say?"

"About big hands."

"Oh, right, big hands, big feet. I think there's a name for that."

Jack cracked a smile—a real, honest-to-God smile—and I swear it felt like I'd won a prize.

"Come on, Cat." He reached for my hand.

My pulse kicked up. Now that I wasn't in the midst of a kidnapping, hooded, or being shot at, his touch registered in a big way. Just like in Vegas, my body responded to him in ways that should've been criminal. An innocent touch from Jack did more for me than any other man had managed. Not that I'd had a lot of experience, but neither was I a virgin. Sex for me had always been bland. I knew that was on me. My personality and sex didn't mix. Hell, my personality and relationships didn't mix.

I was strong willed; a type A, if you will. It would take a strong man and a whole lot of trust for me to loosen the reins of control. My problem was, until Jack, I'd never met a man who was strong enough to take me on without being a dick.

Yet, proving my theory correct, my personality was *still* too much for a man like Jack. He could be attracted to me, he could threaten to spank me, participate in some back-and-forth banter that could be construed as flirting, but he'd never want me. Maybe for a night or two, which I was thinking might be my best course of action at this point. Propose a night of sex and get it out of our systems. We could test his stamina, and, with any luck, it'd be hot and wild and I could finally have an orgasm that wasn't self-induced.

Jack's smile faded, and that's when I realized I'd been staring at his mouth, fantasizing about what it would feel like between my legs, on my breasts, my neck. I shivered at the thought and glanced up, only to have my fantasy explode in vivid detail when my gaze connected with Jack's dark, smoldering eyes. The cool, fresh air of the countryside did nothing to chill the heat blistering between us.

Jack's hand spasmed, or was it mine? I couldn't decipher which with the sizzling electricity coursing through me, turning my body into a live wire—my nipples pebbled, my breasts felt heavy, my panties dampened. Jack looked like he wanted to shove me back into the van, close the door, lock his team out, and fuck the hell out of me.

Oh yeah, I'd been doing this sex thing all wrong. Never had I wanted to have sex so badly in my life. It had never been an ache, a need so strong that I felt if I didn't have it, I would die.

"Clear," Mason called out.

The cold slap of reality intruded.

Instantaneously, Jack's expression cleared, the heat between us evaporating, leaving me cold and wanting.

"Come on." Jack tugged me out of the van.

As soon as my sneakers hit the dirt, he let go of my hand.

A new kind of cold settled over me, the kind that left me feeling desolate and a little lost.

I knew Jack thought I was reckless, but I wasn't. I was calculating. I weighed the risk against the consequences. If there was a reward to be had, I contemplated the moves I'd need to make to claim my victory. I never put reward over risk. I never took a chance whose consequences I wasn't willing to live with.

But standing next to Jack, I wondered if he was right. Was I being reckless? Would a night with him leave me with consequences I couldn't live with? Would I get a night of orgasms but a lifetime of wishing I was a different kind of woman? A longing for a man I could never keep, because I was me and couldn't change who I was, nor did I want to?

Probably.

Yet, I couldn't stop myself from wanting him.

I walked into the heavily treed forest, found a bush, did my business while mentally waxing poetic how lucky men were. They'd never understand what a pain in the ass it was for a woman to drop trou on the side of the road.

When I was done, I made my way out of the woods and found Pete and Jack standing next to the van, heads bent, looking at a tablet.

Mason was leaning against the back, eyes on the road, keeping watch. Fallon was nowhere to be seen.

"We're waiting on Fallon, then we'll roll out," Pete told me when I got close.

Jack did a top-to-toe scan like I'd just gotten back from war and he was checking for injuries.

With some effort, I ignored Jack and took in my surroundings. It was beautiful out here, far away from the congestion of the city. Peaceful. But that peace was an illusion. From the road we were traveling, to the beauty of the hills, to the thick forest, we were smack in the middle of a drug-trafficking route.

I glanced back to the trees. How many bodies had been dumped in those woods, never to be found? The good, honest people of Honduras had no peace. The gangs and corruption prevented them from enjoying the beauty of the country where they'd been born. I'd been to a lot of places, I'd seen evil, I'd felt the desperation of people who simply wanted to live without the fear of death, but I'd never felt fear like I felt in Honduras. It wasn't my fear that had leached into my skin; it came from every person I'd passed on the street. It flowed from the women and children I'd come into contact with at the shopping mall. It was everywhere.

I wasn't dumb enough to think I could put a stop to it or even make an impact. But if I could make a difference in one person's life, save one woman from the hell she was living, then this trip would be a win. With any luck, when I found my target and gave her my intel, the Angel of Death would help the masses.

But this side trip to San Pedro Sula would delay those efforts. So would Jack. No doubt he'd be a pain in my ass and try to derail my mission.

"Ready?" I heard Jack ask.

I spun to face him. Seeing as he was speaking to me, I nodded.

"You get the front," he told me.

I wasn't going to argue. My aching back and ass had had enough for one day.

"Thanks," I said when he opened the door.

"Should've switched with you earlier," he mumbled, not looking at me.

So that was how he was going to play it—no eye contact. The cool detachment of a warrior. Unfortunately for him, he'd forgotten he wasn't the only one who knew the game.

And that two could play.

Chapter Six

After stopping to fuel up and Mason taking the opportunity to stock up on snacks, Cat had directed Pete to the safe house. I'd spent the remaining hour of the drive with my eyes closed, wrestling with my thoughts.

That meant when we got to the safe house, I was in no mood for lighthearted banter between my team and Cat. Moreover, I was in no mood for her giving me the cold shoulder while she was warm and friendly with Fallon and Mason, and to a lesser degree with Pete. It seemed she hadn't gotten a lock on my team leader yet.

It would've amused me how incorrectly she'd pegged Mason if I hadn't been using all of my energy to wrangle my body's reaction to Cat under control. She had no idea that out of all the men I worked with, Mason was by far the deadliest. Pete had the patience of a saint, which was apropos of his name. But Mason—when that switch was flipped, you could kiss his good-natured disposition goodbye. He turned into a single-minded beast who stopped at nothing until all threats were eliminated—and that switch was easy to flip on.

"This place is nicer than my condo in Prescott," Cat said as she walked into the kitchen from the living room.

Arizona?

"I thought you lived in DC."

"I did. Now I don't." Cat's attention diverted to Mason, and she mumbled, "I hate you."

"What?" he said around a mouthful of chocolate bar. "I offered to share."

I watched her roll her eyes to the ceiling. When they rolled back, she shook her head.

"There are times being a woman sucks," she started. "Like when we need to urinate outside or, say, in a public restroom. Then there are times like this, when a fit man without an ounce of body fat offers to share his chocolate like the calories magically don't stick due to the Y chromosome. While my double Xs soak them up, then store them in all the places I'd rather they not."

Mason crushed the candy wrapper in his hand and shoved it in his pocket while smiling. "You mean all the right places," he corrected. "One day women will figure out men don't like pointy bags of bones. We like curves, and soft, and something to grab ahold of."

He wasn't wrong, but I had a bad feeling about the direction of this conversation.

I knew I was right when Mase aimed his action-hero smile at Cat and added, "But it's good to know all my hard work in the gym has paid off. I can show—"

"No, you can't," I cut Mase off.

"What can't Mase do?" Fallon asked as he rounded the corner, coming into the kitchen from the dining area opposite where Cat entered.

"Show Cat my workout routine," Mason supplied.

This was not my first shit-talking huddle, where jabs and digs were exchanged with the sole intent of getting under the skin of a bud. However, this was the first time those digs were aimed my way.

"You have a workout routine that includes clothes?" Fallon returned.

Mason smirked his answer.

I tipped my head back to stare at the ceiling.

"You know it's not fun if you don't participate," Mason noted.

I ignored Mase's jab and belatedly felt guilty for giving my brothers at Takeback shit when each of them was getting to know their women.

Not that Cat was my woman.

Catarina, being the smart-ass she was, latched onto Fallon's question. "Naked workouts sound dangerous. The treadmill must be murder."

Christ.

"You have no idea," Mason drawled.

I lost the battle.

"Honest to God, I'm gonna punch you in the throat."

Catarina broke first and busted out laughing. Fallon and Mase weren't far behind. Thankfully, Pete joined us, and I had a reason to put a stop to their stupidity.

"Time to lay your cards on the table, Catarina," I said through their amusement.

"I don't have cards," she quipped.

"Jack's right. It's time we had a chat. Let's take this to the dining room."

Fallon and Mason heard Pete's tone and immediately switched from idiots to the professionals they were. It was obvious that Pete had spent his time upstairs not inspecting the bedrooms to assign sleeping arrangements but talking to Shep. Which meant he'd been fully briefed on Cat's background. Something I was privy to, seeing as my old boss, Wilson McCray, was thorough in his investigation of anyone who worked closely with Takeback.

Catarina turned wary.

Interesting.

Further from that, what was more curious and annoying was she didn't have a quick and ready comeback for Pete.

I followed Cat and the team into the dining room, commandeering the chair farthest away from the one Cat chose.

Pete cut straight to it. "Why'd you leave the Marshals Service?"

Now, *that* was a tidbit I was unaware of.

"Is that the real question you want to ask?" Cat shot back.

"For starters. Then we'll move to why, after years of the CIA approaching you while you were in the Army, then while you were with Homeland, and again while you were with the Sex Offender Investigation Branch, you finally decided to take them up on their offer."

Cat shrugged. "I was bored."

Her tone made her sound just that—bored and uninterested.

"You seem to get bored a lot, the way you jumped from command to command. Didn't stay on a team for more than a workup."

"Or alternately, my skills were in high demand and the Army moved me where they needed."

"I could see that," Pete conceded. "It's not every day the Army finds themselves a human lie detector with your powers of persuasion."

What the hell was Pete talking about? That wasn't in the original dossier I'd read back in Nevada.

"Is that what your source told you? Sorry, but they oversold my skills. I'm observant, not a lie detector. And I didn't have to persuade—that was always the problem. Our military forgot just because cattle are treated better than women in most of the countries we were in, doesn't mean they weren't valuable. All I had to do was ask nicely, show some kindness, and they talked. You know the sad part? They didn't want the money. They couldn't risk being caught with it. All they wanted was to feel seen, heard, valued. Once I gave them that, they gave up their men."

Well, fuck.

"Your intel took out a lot of terrorists."

"I know," Cat said proudly.

"Is that why you left the SOIB? The CIA offered to send you to Honduras to try your hand at turning women into informants?"

"Nope."

She was lying. I saw the same small twist under her left eye I'd seen back in Vegas, when she'd told me she'd wait until we had backup in place before she headed to the auction at the mansion. News flash, she hadn't waited. Instead of making an excuse about why she was going to be late and driving herself there, she'd gone with Martin and his lackeys.

"Friends don't lie to friends, Catarina," I told her.

"Friends? I was unaware we'd all become friends. In that case, tell me, old buddy, why are *you* in Honduras?"

"We're here to find a woman named Berta Lanza. She's a Lenca woman who has managed to assemble a collective of Indigenous women who've built a network of safe passage for women and children to flee the country."

When I was done, Catarina was staring at me with her lips parted, clearly surprised I'd be forthright and end the subterfuge. Now was not the time for a long, drawn-out game of battle chess.

I dipped my chin to indicate it was her turn.

"The Angel of Death," she muttered.

"You've heard of her?" Pete asked.

"No. I mean, yes, I've heard of her. She's why I'm here."

And . . . *fuck* again.

"What does the CIA want with Berta?" Fallon joined.

"Nothing. I'm here to give her intel."

Pete blew out a frustrated breath and leaned back in his chair.

"What's the intel?" Mason inquired.

"Why do you want her?" Cat volleyed.

"Oh, no, friend, Jack went first last time. Your turn to give up the goods first."

Catarina raised a brow and remained silent.

It was then that something hit me square in the chest. Cat had no idea where Berta was. She could've been in the city waiting on word of a location like we were. But the CIA had no idea where Berta was or they would've sent Cat directly to her or sent a local source to deliver a message.

The Agency needed Cat to find the Angel of Death.

And there was a way to get Berta's attention.

"You were going to use yourself as bait," I ground out.

Cat's gaze slowly glided around the table before finally landing on me with a defiant lift of her jaw.

Motherfucker.

"Have you lost your fucking mind, woman?"

"I believe you've already asked that. And we established—"

"The only thing we've established is that you're goddamn insane," I growled, and pushed back from the table, taking to my feet but bending forward to plant my palms on the tabletop. "You're in a country where nearly four hundred woman are murdered every year. That's one a day, sometimes two or more. And you're setting yourself up to be taken in *hopes* Berta gets word an American woman was taken, and she herself swoops in to save you or she sends her people. The problem with that is, hope isn't a fucking plan. Hope doesn't mean shit when those animals can violate you in ways you'd wish they'd killed you. And they can do that within minutes of your abduction. They could do that shit to you in broad daylight on the sidewalk, and as you've seen, no one would come rolling to your rescue."

Catarina calmly sat there with a mask of bland interest on her gorgeous face. A hundred different horrific scenarios sped through my mind, each worse than the one before. All of the foul ways her beautiful body could be violated. All the ways I would kill any man who dared to touch her, harm her, take her against her will.

Fuck this.

I pushed up from the table, glanced over at Pete, and as soon as he gave me a dip of his chin, I made my way across the room. I stopped at the archway and turned back to Catarina.

"You were wrong," I told her.

"What was I wrong about?" she snottily asked.

"About no one caring enough to pay your ransom." I poked my chest with a finger. "I care. I'd pay it. And just so we're clear, I'll lose my goddamn mind if you continue with this bullshit."

There was no heat or attitude when she probed, "More than you are now?"

"Baby, this is me keeping my cool. You'll watch the world burn before I stand by and watch you pull this shit for a second time. Vegas was careless; this is lunacy."

The woman didn't know when to quit—her shoulders squared, her jaw lifted, exposing more of her delicate throat. I watched her swallow, then heard her lie. "I had it covered."

She did not.

I turned and left the room without dignifying her asinine statement. If she'd had cover or backup, I wouldn't have been able to snatch her off the street. If the CIA had a man close, she wouldn't, right now, be sitting in a house two hundred and eighty kilometers from where she'd been taken.

The last hour had done nothing to touch my anger. Not the two-mile run I'd taken around the block to blow off steam, which also provided a good cover to surveil the neighborhood. The beautiful mountains behind the house did nothing to quiet the voices in my head. My shower proved frustrating when visions of Catarina joining me—naked, wet, and soapy—filled my mind.

Every damn thing revolved around the frustrating woman.

I opened the door to the bathroom, and speak of the devil. There she was, sitting on the side of the bed with her bare feet up on the wood frame and her hands in her lap, looking deceptively innocent.

"Now's not a good time."

I stopped at what I hoped was a safe distance and tightened the towel around my waist.

It was like I hadn't spoken. She didn't move—not her gaze from my bare chest, not her legs to take her out of the room, not a muscle.

"Catarina." I growled her name, unable to keep my impatience in check.

I needed her to leave before what was left of my control slipped.

Her eyes flew up along with her hands, palms facing me in surrender.

"I'm not here to argue."

That was unlikely. I wouldn't've been surprised if her middle name was Scrappy, the way she loved to squabble.

"You need to leave."

She pushed to her feet and took a step in my direction. I took a step back, which put me in the doorway.

"Please, Jack. We need to talk."

The woman didn't possess an ounce of self-preservation, but I knew she had situational awareness. How she thought now was a good time was lost on me.

"For the love of God, Catarina, just once pull up whatever survival instincts you have, recognize the danger, and get the hell out."

Her eyes turned squinty, and she advanced.

"I'm in no danger from you."

Was she crazy?

Scratch that—asked and answered with a resounding *hell yes*.

"Catarina."

"Jack."

My cock twitched.

"You need to leave now."

"We need to talk."

I sucked in a breath, grabbed ahold of what was left of my restraint—which was now limited to holding my body perfectly still—and warned, "If you stay in this room, we won't be talking."

I saw the hunger bloom in her eyes, and the corresponding tremble—no, that wasn't a tremble, it was a full-body quake that made my dick weep with need. I was two seconds away from snapping and not above pleading.

"Please, I'm begging, Cat, stop fucking around and get out."

"Do I scare you?"

There was that smart-ass mouth of hers that never failed to drive me crazy.

"No. I'm scared of what I'm going to do to you."

She closed the remaining distance between us, stopping so close that if I moved an inch in her direction, her tits would be on my chest. Dark and dangerous thoughts flooded. Snatches of fantasies flew through my mind, all the things I'd dreamed of doing to her, all the ways I wanted her.

Cat lifted her hand, but I quickly caught her wrist before it hit its destination.

"You don't want to do that."

"Don't tell me what I want, Jack," she scolded.

And why did that turn me the fuck on?

Then, in a moment of weakness and insanity, I released her hand. She didn't go for the towel and pull it off like I thought she would.

Instead, she found the opening and shoved her hand through it, then fisted my cock.

Heat coiled in my balls, and before I knew what I was doing, my hips jerked forward into her palm. Cat's thumb brushed over the head, smearing precome over the crown. A catlike smile curled her lips up.

"Hmm," she hummed.

The damage was done. Catarina Keys was stroking my dick. It was too late to second-guess my foolishness.

"Is this what you wanted, Cat, to give me a hand job?"

Her hand tightened around my shaft, pulling a grunt out of me. The silence stretched a beat, then two. When she didn't answer, I blinked away the haze of lust she was creating and studied her expression. The woman was so ballsy and bold, it would've been easy to miss it—the shyness lingering just under the surface.

She wanted it, she just didn't know how to ask for it.

"Take off your pants, Cat."

Relief mixed with desire. But she still didn't move.

"*Now*, baby. Pull your pants off."

Her hand released my dick, went to her pants, unsnapped the button, pulled the zipper down, peeled the jeans over her ass, and she shimmied them down her thighs. After she kicked them away, I hooked her around the back of her neck and yanked her to my chest.

"Eyes, Catarina." She lifted her gaze to mine. "You sure?"

Her eyes started to narrow.

My hand on the back of her neck squeezed.

"No sass, no attitude. Tell me you're sure. I need to hear you say it."

Cat rolled up on her toes, and with her lips a breath away, she nearly spat, "I'm sure."

That was all I needed.

But it wasn't me who made the first move.

Catarina attacked.

Her mouth hit mine, her tongue invaded, and fucking *finally* I had the taste of her I wanted.

My hands went to her ass, I hauled her up, my towel fell away, and I walked with her wrapped around me back into the bathroom. One of her hands slid around the back of my neck, then up into my hair. Her short nails dug into my scalp. She kissed like she did everything else, bold, aggressive, no holding back.

Christ, phenomenal.

Better than I imagined.

I set her ass on the vanity top, shifted my hands—one going between her legs, the other going under her tee to cup her tit. Catarina whimpered and used those strong thighs as leverage to grind her pussy into my hand. She might've been shy with her words, but her body had no problem asking for what it wanted.

I moved the material of her panties to the side, slid a finger through her excitement, and pushed inside. So damn wet, she was drenched.

My dick pulsed with need.

Catarina shifted again, tore her mouth from mine, and groaned, "Now."

This close, I could see all the different shades of blue in her beautiful eyes. Clear blue filled with arousal.

A sudden wave of tenderness hit me. All the feelings I'd buried came rushing to the surface. Nothing had changed since Vegas. If anything, it was worse now. But I could no longer fight it. If nothing else, I'd take her back and keep her safe until her mission was over. Then I'd let her go again. I'd let her be free to be who she needed to be without me standing in her way. But right now, for as long as I had her, I wasn't going to hold back, at least not physically.

I released her breast, pulled my other hand free, hooked my fingers under the strings at the sides of her panties, and yanked. The flimsy material ripped easily.

Cat's eyes rounded, her lips quirked, and through a sultry smile she breathed, "Smooth."

I took my dick in hand, rubbed the head over her clit, and warned, "It's about to get rough."

With no further warning, I drove my hips forward. Catarina's yelp of surprise turned into a low, throaty groan. I held still, relishing the feel of her tight pussy hugging my dick.

"Yo, Jack!" My name was accompanied with two loud raps on the bedroom door.

Fuck.

Catarina jolted. Her inner muscles squeezed my cock; the movement had my balls tightening.

"Ten minutes, we're rolling out," Mason yelled through the door.

In my moment of indecision, Catarina shook her head.

"Don't you dare." She growled her demand.

"It's cute you think you're in charge," I told her as I moved my fingers to her clit and circled.

"Oh God."

I drew back, drove in, and watched her eyes go hooded.

"More," she pleaded.

"Unlock your legs."

Catarina immediately loosened her legs. I hooked one leg behind her knee, hitched it higher, and on my next drive slid in deeper.

Her pussy rippled—so tight, so wet, my mind blanked. No mission. No ten-minute warning. No danger. Just us, our bodies—her cunt, my cock, and the driving need to feel her fall apart. The need to hear her call out my name. The need to claim, to mark her as mine, to tie her to me.

"Jack."

There it was.

My name falling from her lips.

"Give it to me," I demanded.

With a rough pinch of her clit, she gave. Her body locked tight, her pussy clamped down, and I followed her over the edge into the darkness and exploded.

"Fuck, baby," I snarled.

White-hot pleasure clawed at my chest. My dick jerked with each rope of come that forcefully spilled. This wasn't an orgasm, it was an out-of-body experience I never wanted to end. Buried deep in Catarina. Finally. I closed my eyes and let the euphoria pull me under.

Chapter Seven

I was still swimming up from the best orgasm I'd ever had in my whole life. My one and only that was not given to me by my own hand.

Holy *wow*.

"Baby?"

I blinked away the haze and focused on Jack's handsome face.

"Huh?"

His hand came up and cupped my cheek, the touch so gentle I nuzzled into his palm.

"You okay?"

"Oh yeah."

I was more than okay, I was stupendous. The area between my legs was gloriously sore. My mind was filled with memories of Jack's rough thrusts, which came in second place only to the hungry look in his eyes as he fucked me. The look won out only because it made me feel powerful, wanted, so desired Jack couldn't hide it. I'd never forget that look or the feeling.

"Fucks me to say this, but we only have a minute before someone comes knocking again."

Shit, how had I forgotten?

Because you had a hot guy banging you with his hot-guy big dick, giving you a mind-erasing orgasm.

Right, that was why.

For all my bravado when I was hot and bothered and worked up, now that I was post climax, I had no idea what I was supposed to do.

Jack did. He slid out.

I whimpered at the loss of him—then he froze.

"What's wrong?" I asked when he didn't move.

He glanced down between my legs. A sudden bout of shyness hit, and I tried to close my legs. This didn't work for two reasons—first, his hips were in the way, second, his hands went to my thighs and kept them spread.

His gaze drifted back up. My belly did a somersault at the troubled look on his face.

"Jack?"

"I didn't wear a condom."

Well, damn.

"I'm on birth control," I told him. "It's an implant in my arm."

He nodded but was no less unsettled.

An unpleasant thought hit me.

"I'm clean. I mean, I don't have—"

Jack's thumb glided over my cheek to my lips, and he silenced me.

His eyes roamed my face. Some of the unease in his expression faded, but the knot in my stomach was getting tighter.

"I've never not worn protection," he told me and frowned.

Was he mad . . . at *me*?

I turned my head, freeing my lips, and asked, "And that's my fault?"

Lightning quick, his hand went from my cheek to the back of my neck. He yanked me closer, while at the same time he dipped his head.

"It's my fault. I lost control. I was so caught up, wanted inside you so badly, I forgot."

Why did that make me giddy? It was totally irresponsible, yet I didn't care. The thought of little ol' me making big, bad, tough Jack Donovan lose control and forget a condom filled me with womanly pride.

"I see you like that," he noted.

I shrugged, fully coming back to my smart-ass self.

"We'll see how much you like it when I'm leaking out of you while you're kitted up, waiting for orders." Jack's lips twitched, and he finished with, "Though, I know *I'm* gonna like that part."

My eyes narrowed. However, I couldn't fully commit to the glare.

"Is that an alpha-male thing?"

"No, baby, it's a Jack thing."

I didn't have a comeback for that, so I remained quiet. So did Jack. His eyes no longer held any apprehension, nor were they glittery with lust. They now held something new, a warmth and tenderness I'd never seen—not from him, not from anyone in my life. Except maybe my mom and gran, though their warmth was different, a familial bond. Jack's was tinged with intimacy.

"I could get lost in you," he whispered. "You're so damn gorgeous, if I forget to brace, you steal my breath." He dropped his forehead to mine, and he quietly admitted, "It's been torture. Nine months of hell staying away from you."

My heart hammered in my chest as it swelled. The pain of watching him walk away from me in Vegas evaporated, the agony of losing him receding. Hope and happiness warred for the top spot.

Before I could respond, there was another knock on the door.

"Two-minute warning," Mason called out.

The moment shattered.

Jack lifted his head, stared down at me, eyes conflicted. "Let's get you cleaned up."

"I can—"

"You can, but I'm gonna do it."

All righty, then.

Jack stepped away, turned, and reached into the shower, giving me my first look at his bare ass. And good Lord, was it fine. I was still taking it in when he turned back around. I'd had the pleasure of feeling that thick, long dick, but seeing it made my mouth go dry. I licked my lips. Jack groaned. I continued to stare until I lost sight of his dick, and his chest filled my vision instead when he stepped back between my legs, reached to the side, and turned on the faucet.

Ass, dick, chest—his body was a wonderland of visual delights. I could spend hours perusing the ridges and valleys, the dips and hard plains of muscle.

The feel of a warm, wet cloth between my legs pulled me from my thoughts. I glanced up to find Jack watching himself gently cleaning the evidence of his orgasm from me. When he was done, he pressed the cloth over my pussy, cupping me there, and lifted his eyes to meet mine.

Watching him cleaning me was wildly erotic in a profound way—an intimacy that went beyond private and personal. In that moment, I knew whatever happened between me and Jack, I would never in my life share something so special with another man. This was Jack's, only his, and nothing could or would compare.

"Ready, baby?"

No. I never wanted to leave this cocoon of warmth he'd created. I didn't want anything to invade or threaten to take him away from me. And sadly, deep down, I knew once the real world came crashing back in, he'd remember I was who I was, and his frustration and anger would steal him from me.

"Yeah."

He leaned forward, pressed a sweet kiss on my lips that left me hoping it wasn't goodbye.

But I feared it was.

We were dressed and back downstairs.

Obviously, it had taken us more than two minutes.

Mason and Fallon were lounging in chairs, both wearing matching grins. The living room looked like battle central, with M4s and handguns laid out on the couch, vests and ammo stacked on the coffee table.

"Where's Pete?" Jack inquired.

"Went out to find little miss a vest to circumvent the argument he knew would ensue," Mason spoke up.

A vest was appreciated, preventing an argument much appreciated, however, Pete going out in search of one seemed to be a fool's errand.

"Where in the world is he going to find me a vest?"

"We don't question Pete's powers," Fallon informed me. "We just accept the fruit and don't ask which tree he shook down to provide it."

"Seriously? There's no way he's coming back with a vest."

"We'll see." Fallon lifted his shoulders and dropped them back down with a sigh.

"What's going on?" Jack circled to the real question.

"Shep called," Mason said, but not without flashing a knowing smirk.

I searched my feelings and wondered if I should be embarrassed he clearly knew what had been happening in the bedroom when he knocked. I didn't find a smidgeon of embarrassment or shame. So what if he knew? So what if he heard? So what if he dished out jibes? I was riding the high of Jack. Nothing was going to knock me off the wave of mellow.

"And? You going to enlighten us?"

"You sure you're back to firing on all cylinders after—"

"Don't," Jack gritted out, obviously not riding the same wave I was.

Mason's gaze flew to me, either to make sure I hadn't found offense in his would-have-been taunt, or to check if my brain had reengaged and I was ready for the rest of the brief.

I gave him a shoulder lift and a smile. He returned the gesture by busting out laughing.

"Yeah, I think you're a little bit of all right, Catarina Keys," he said as he chuckled.

I took that as a compliment.

Mason continued with his brief. "Word is there's an attack planned on the compound where Berta's holed up. They've been notified, and she's requested backup. We're her backup."

Jack's gaze shifted to me. I felt the weight of his stare. My Jack was gone. Angry, scorch-the-earth-if-you-put-yourself-in-danger Jack was back. "Did you know about the attack being planned?"

"No, Jack, if I knew my target was under attack I would've said something. I need her alive to deliver my intel."

"And that is?"

I blew out a breath, called up the imaginary patience I didn't have and never pretended to be in possession of, and then for good measure, counted to ten.

"She asked for information. The CIA found it for her but it took them longer than they thought it would. By the time they had it, she'd gone back underground. They sent me to give her what she'd asked for."

"I didn't ask for the mission brief. I asked what the intel was."

"And I gave you what I'm willing to give."

"I'm not sure I like that the CIA is involved," Fallon put in.

"I'm positive I don't," Mason volleyed. "Makes me twitchy and leaves me wondering how many ways they're gonna fuck our op."

"Why would they screw with your op?" I asked.

Mason morphed back into a seasoned warfighter, leaving the lady-killer smile in the dust and replacing it with a deep scowl.

"I mean no disrespect, but you asking that shows your inexperience with the Agency. Rule one: If they *can* fuck you, they will. Rule two: Always cover your ass, because they won't. Rule three is a mash-up of one and two: They'll let you swing to protect themselves. Whatever it is they want you to deliver to Berta is what's important to them at the moment, but that moment can shift second to second and something else can become more important. If they feel like we're in their way, they'll fuck us however they need to make sure what's important to *them* is what happens.

"We have one objective—get Berta the resources she needs to complete her mission. Once we have her and her convoy safe and secure, we're mission complete. The CIA catches wind, decides they don't want those bodies moved out of Honduras, they tip off the authorities, the authorities alert the gangs where we're headed and what routes we're using, we're screwed . . . as in dead."

A strange tightness coiled in my stomach. The fine hairs on the back of my neck stood on end. An instinct I'd spent my adult life honing and perfecting, one that had saved my life many times, alerted.

Something wasn't adding up.

And worse, I had a bad feeling I was being used as a pawn.

"Why wouldn't the CIA want Berta to escape the country with her convoy, whom I presume are women and children?"

Mason exchanged a look with Fallon before he refocused on me.

"What message are you delivering?" Mason shot back.

It wasn't annoyance I was feeling. It was panic when I begged, "Please, Mason, no games, no chess moves. Why wouldn't the CIA want her to leave?"

Mason's attention turned acute. "Berta's taking the president's wife, Maria Sanchez, and, at her request, their children, out of the country. If the CIA deemed it would be in their best interest, they could use this information to make nice with the president, and of course lord the good turn over his head for future use."

I needed to think.

The puzzle wasn't making sense.

Was I overreacting?

Jack's hand wrapped around my bicep and swung me to face him. "What's going on?"

"I need a minute."

"To do what?"

"To think. Something's not right. It never is, but pretense and duplicity are to be expected when dealing with the CIA. This isn't my first time working with them. So contrary to Mason's assessment, I'm well aware of all the ways the Agency can screw you over. Tom would likely sell his grandmother out, then claim it was for the greater good. However, that's not what's bothering me. It goes deeper than that, and now that I have more information, it's nagging at my gut. I feel it. I just can't figure out what *it* is."

Jack didn't let go, but he did tilt his head to the side to study me.

"Talk it out," he demanded.

"Jack—"

"No game. No intel-gathering expedition. Just talk through the problem."

I glanced around the room. Mason and Fallon were both alert, watching closely, but I didn't get the read from either of them they were playing me. This wasn't an elaborate setup to get me to tell them something I was closely guarding. I didn't have to look at Jack to know he wouldn't do something underhanded to get me to talk—get angry, yes. Yell at me, yes. Threaten wild and crazy warnings he had no intentions of inflicting, also yes. Play me dirty, no way.

"I have a subcutaneous tracking device in my hip," I announced.

"Motherfucker," Mason growled and got to his feet.

Jack gave me a little shake when my attention went to Mason. "Go on."

I sucked in a breath and braced for Jack's ire. "That's why I felt safe-*ish* offering myself up. That, and I researched the gangs in the area. I had a plan. I knew which territory I needed to be in when it happened. My location would be monitored. The CIA would get new intel on where the newer gangs were conducting business, and my location would be leaked in hopes Berta would be lured out of hiding. If not, an extraction team would be sent in to get me."

Jack's jaw was clenched tight, the muscle in his cheek jumping.

He wasn't pissed, he was murderous.

"Go on," he gritted through his fury.

"The urgency of the intel never made sense."

"Stop," Fallon said. "You're boxed in, focused on the intel, instead of looking at the whole picture. Start at the beginning. That's where the problem starts."

Damn. He was right.

But I needed to move to think.

I glanced back at Jack and asked, "Honey, can you let me go? I need to move to think."

My slip-up didn't compute until Jack's face went soft, his eyes gentled, and he gave my arm a soft squeeze before he let me go.

Damn, I wanted to kiss him. Or grab him and drag him back upstairs. Or maybe hug him.

"Cat?" Mason called.

"Right. Okay." I clawed my hands through my hair. "I left the Marshals Service after Vegas. I needed a change. I was approached by a woman named Jasmin Parker—"

"Nightstalker approached you?" Fallon asked, followed by a low whistle. "And you turned down working for Z Corps?"

I didn't bother asking Fallon how he knew Jasmin or Z Corps. I figured everyone in the private security sector knew who Zane Lewis was, and his teams. Further, I didn't need to ask how he knew I'd turned down the job; Zane's dislike of the CIA was legendary.

Instead, I told him, "Yes. I decided I didn't want to be tied down to a team. I wanted to be free to take the jobs I wanted to take and not ones assigned to me. I've spent my professional life on the receiving end of orders. I needed a change, but I have valuable skills I didn't want to go to waste. I hadn't yet decided exactly what I was going to do, when an old CIA contact from my Army days reached out and asked if I would be interested in a solo mission."

"How did this person know you were a free agent?" Mason interjected.

Good question.

"I've known Tom for years. He was the case officer on a terrorist threat in London I helped with. Over the years, I've consulted on other cases for him. I was never fully read into the situation, but given enough information to give my opinion. All of that to say, I know Tom, he takes spy games to the extreme, so when I asked how he knew I'd left the SOIB, and his answer was he had his ways, I didn't push because I knew it would get me nowhere. I actually assumed Jasmin's approach tipped Tom off."

I wasn't positive the CIA watched Z Corps that closely. It wasn't like Zane Lewis was a criminal, but he sure as hell had his hand in everything worth knowing. Surely they kept an eye.

Mason dipped his chin, so I went on.

"I met Tom at a strip mall in Virginia. Typical CIA off-site location. Nothing out of the ordinary. I already had all the proper clearances from the Marshals Service. I didn't need a higher level of clearance since my mission isn't a matter of national security, more a friendly gesture to an ally. That was how it was presented."

I turned on my heel and started pacing.

Where's the problem? Why isn't it coming to me?

"Berta had asked the CIA to find a man for her. She wanted his location. Well, they found him and have been trying to reach out to her for six months. Tom said it was urgent Berta get this man's location. But why? Why now, when it wasn't urgent six months ago? We've had months to send in an operations officer to get this intel to her." I stopped pacing, looked at Jack, and asked again, "Why now?"

"Without knowing who, I can't answer that. Maybe this man is now in danger. Maybe she gave them a time frame for this intel to be delivered and they're running out of time? There could be a plausible explanation."

"Derek Nicolson," I blurted out.

"Come again?" Mason grunted.

"I have Derek's location."

"No, you don't," Mason denied.

Something sinister crowded the room, and it was emanating from Mason. So dark and ominous, it had me taking a step away from him. That's when I noticed Pete was leaning against the archway leading to the kitchen. Even though his arms were crossed over his chest, his manner looked casual. However, upon further inspection, some of the menacing vibrations were also rolling off him.

I was missing something huge.

"Who's Derek Nicolson?"

"He was a piece-of-shit trafficker who favored *children*," Mason spat.

"Was? But isn't anymore?"

"Not unless he's doing that shit in hell. Though I'd like to believe not even the devil would find that shit acceptable and Nicolson is spending an eternity on the receiving end of the misery he inflicted."

My gaze flicked to Pete.

"Where'd they tell you he was?"

"Barcelona."

Pete shook his head. "Not even close."

"You took him out," I surmised.

"Yup, after Mase had his fun."

Well, that explained the dark and ominous.

"Now we work the problem," Fallon announced. "But first you need to get rid of that tracking device, and we need to move."

He wasn't wrong. It hadn't felt great going in, and I'd been given a local to prevent the pain. I was pretty sure the guys didn't carry around lidocaine, so coming out, it was probably going to hurt like a bitch.

"Will you do it?" I asked Jack.

"Fallon has more medical training than I do."

I didn't want Fallon taking it out. I wanted Jack.

With a sigh, Jack changed his mind. "Fallon, grab your kit and meet us upstairs."

"Sucker," Fallon mumbled under his breath.

Jack flipped him off, then turned his hand and offered it to me. "C'mere, Cat."

I went.

When I was within reaching distance, he tugged me the rest of the way. My hand came up and planted on his hard chest to break my fall. Once Jack had me where he wanted, his forehead gently hit mine.

"We'll figure this out."

I pinched my lips. Part of me embarrassed I'd been screwed over like an amateur, the other, bigger part pissed that someone I had trusted did the screwing.

Fifteen minutes later, I had tears in my eyes, the bloody tracker was in the sink, and Jack was cleaning the tiny incision he'd made.

"Took that like a champ," Fallon lied.

I'd actually bitten down on a belt, something I thought was an old-timer antidote. The nylon material only stifled my grunts, groans, and curses.

"Slap a BAND-AID on the scratch and let's roll," Mason said from the doorway of the bathroom.

Fallon looked over Jack's shoulder to check the incision. My jeans were around my ankles, a towel draped over my behind. I was turned in such a way Fallon couldn't see anything he shouldn't, and besides, I didn't think he was the kind of man who would look even if I was exposed.

"It's fine to glue," Fallon told Jack. "Sorry, Kitty, but the glue's gonna burn like a bitch. You might want the belt back."

Oh, I wanted the belt back. I wanted to keep it so when I found Tom, I could beat him with it.

"Just do it."

"Cat—"

"Do it, Jack."

There was a string of expletives, followed by a few grunts, but finally Jack got to work gluing.

Burn didn't cover the blistering pain.

"Goddamn motherfucking liar. My skin is melting," I groaned and closed my eyes. "Holy God. Fucking hell. Someone blow on it."

Jack leaned away from me.

"If you blow on that, you'll need to start over," Fallon warned.

"Oh my God, just blow, would you? I don't care about germs."

"Kinky," Mason muttered.

I blew out a breath trying to quell the pain.

"Breathe through it."

"I *am* breathing, Fallon," I spat. "I'm breathing fire."

"Baby," Jack cooed next to my face. "It's done. Just take a few deep breaths. It'll stop in a few seconds."

I did as Jack instructed. Slowly—so very slowly—the burn faded.

"The glue was worse than the cut," I said on an exhale.

"Sorry, baby." Jack pressed a kiss to my temple and pulled away from me. "Everyone out so she can get dressed."

"You've got a scary foul mouth when you're in pain, woman," Mason jibed.

"Fuck off."

"Yeah, you're gonna fit right in, Kitty Cat Keys."

"I'm gonna fit your balls in your throat if you ever call me that again."

"Spicy *and* kinky, you lucky son of a bitch."

I assumed Mason's parting shot was for Jack.

And for some reason, that made me smile.

Chapter Eight

We were running seriously late.

But still Pete delayed our departure.

"How's the hip?" he asked Cat.

"Better now that the tracker has been flushed."

He nodded. "Right, so that brings us to what happens now. The CIA knows it's offline. They'll either take that as someone found it and removed it or you've defected."

"They can think whatever they want and shove it up their asses."

Mason chuckled. Fallon smiled. But Pete wore the same serious expression I did. Catarina was playing fast and loose with an agency you wanted to tread cautious with. She was smarter than this, which meant she was hiding her real feelings behind bluster.

"Respect, Catarina, but you need to take this seriously. We gave Berta our word we'd help her. We have a plan in place and two of our teammates waiting for us in Belize. There are the lives of fifteen women and ten children who need this to go smoothly. Twenty-five souls who are counting on us to keep them alive. Before we walk out the door, I need to trust you've got your shit straight and you're on board. If you want out now, Shep's on standby for an extraction."

Catarina looked like she was preparing to give Pete a world-class tongue lashing. I braced for the fallout that never came when she relaxed her shoulders, blew out an exasperated breath, and calmed her temper.

"I have my shit straight and I'm on board."

Pete turned to me, pinned me with a look I knew was going to piss me off. Now I was bracing for a new reason.

"You know I don't pull rank. We're all equals on this team. But you know this is different, and I've gotta know where you are with this. If Cat's coming, I need to know you're not gonna go maverick."

Pete studied me. He might claim we're all equals, and we were to some extent. Pete ran the team like a collaboration. He valued our individual skills. He had a deep understanding of teamwork and knew when to step back when someone else's experience would better serve the mission. All things I appreciated about the man.

However, at one time, there was another woman on this team. It was his sister, not his woman, but he would've blown a mission to save her. Hell, he'd dissolved the company she was a part of just to get her to quit and settle down with my old teammate, Cole, who was now her husband. Pete would probably lose his mind if he knew the kind of ops Mia was currently working with Takeback. Or he knew and trusted that Cole would go rogue to save his wife.

Meaning, he'd pull rank when the situation suited him.

In other words, he didn't need to ask his question; he knew what my answer would be. Yet, I still answered.

"I'll do whatever I have to do to ensure Catarina's safety."

Pete looked harassed but not surprised.

"Jack—"

Fallon made a strangled sound and grunted. Cat turned her narrowed eyes in his direction. She stopped speaking to me to address *him*.

"I'm sorry, I don't speak caveman. Was that supposed to mean something to me?"

"Cat." Fallon wisely lifted his hands in surrender. "Let your man handle this."

Her mouth clamped shut, fury blazing in her eyes. She made a frustrated gurgling noise I was a hundred percent positive Fallon would pay for later. However, she waved a hand at Pete to continue.

Pete dropped his head forward, contemplated his boots, then motioned for the door.

"I'll let the two of you work it out," he declared. "But I leave you with this—you're a dumbass if you stand in her way of doing her job. If she's as good as you say she is, then she doesn't need you standing behind her with a pillow to cushion her fall. We all know the risks we take when we gear up." Pete pounded his tactical vest to make his point. "You take that risk, the same as the rest of us. And something tells me you'd be none too pleased if your woman didn't think *you* had the skills to take care of yourself."

Well, fuck.

With that successful dressing-down, I didn't say a word. Pete was correct on all fronts. I'd be pissed if she didn't think I was capable of doing my job.

And that's exactly what I'd done to her in the name of protection.

I'd belittled her—not her skill, her intelligence. I'd never stopped to consider what I'd seen as reckless endangerment of her life was actually Cat being smart enough to calculate the risks before she put herself in harm's way—something I myself did every day I strapped on a vest and holstered a weapon.

I wasn't overprotective; I was being an overbearing dick.

The issue was, I didn't know how to separate my feelings for her from those of just a teammate doing her job. The thought of her getting hurt set my chest on fire.

Mase's phone pinged. He glanced down, swiped the screen, and smiled.

"It's go time, boys . . . and girl," he announced.

Before I could stop myself, my eyes swept over Catarina's vest, making sure she had an extra magazine. I noticed my knife clipped into the webbing at her upper left chest.

"Thief."

"It's not stealing if I told you I was taking it."

Mason clapped his hands and rubbed them together. "I can already smell it in the air."

"Smell what?" Fallon asked.

"Those two." Mase jerked his head in my direction. "The sweet scent of their love is perfuming the air."

Catarina's nose crinkled, and she beat me to the comeback.

"Oh, I thought that was your ass gas. After all that chocolate, I thought it perfumed your flatulates."

I covered my laugh with a cough. The others did not. They let it rip through the room.

Catarina looked at me with a smile and winked.

How was it possible the woman was so damn hot even talking about ass gas?

I looked around the thick natural landscape through my thermal fusion night vision. Gone were the days of the green hue. The lush green countryside was lit up in yellows, oranges, blues, pinks, and purples. Berta's men patrolling the grounds glowed in yellow while the cooler environment blended out to purple. There was something to be said about the new technology, however, I still preferred the old-school white-phosphorous PVS-15s even with a shitty 40 percent field of view. What could I say? I didn't like change.

"I haven't pulled watch like this since I was five, playing Army commando in the backyard," Mason mumbled next to me.

"You had an M4 strapped to your chest at five? Who raised you, the Mafia?"

"I meant boring."

He wasn't wrong. The last three hours were mind-numbingly boring. But boring meant no one was shooting at us and Cat was safely tucked away inside Berta's compound guarding the women.

"Swear to God if you just jinxed—"

Automatic gunfire rang out.

"Bastard," I grumbled and pulled my M4 up to the ready.

"It's showtime."

"There's something wrong with you," I returned.

More gunfire pierced the night.

"There's a lot of *somethings* wrong with me. Probably stems from mommy issues. I wasn't loved enough as a child."

Under the teasing tone there was an underlying truth to that. In the months I'd been with the team, Mason had never opened up about anything personal. Out of all the men I worked with, Mason was the most closed off. He was also the first to crack a joke and lend a hand.

"Movement at eleven," he called out. "Engaging."

Mason's double-tap was thankfully muffled by my ear pro.

I continued to scan my sector. Other than two of Berta's men in the prone position, all was clear.

Mason popped off another round.

"You're having all the fun," I grumbled.

"Now who's got something wrong with them?" Mase chuckled.

My radio crackled to life with Pete's angry voice asking me, "Three, how are you looking over there?"

"Four has engaged," I radioed back. "I'm still clear."

"Four, your count?" Pete inquired.

"Two down," Mason answered. "Six incoming."

"Copy that. Two's moving to overwatch."

Fallon was Two, and he was on the move to the rooftop of a rickety old outbuilding. He'd held off due to the condition of the structure. It was a last resort and might not hold his weight for long. If Fallon was on the move, the north side of the compound was being flooded.

"Need help?" I asked.

"Not yet. Hold your position."

For a moment, I let my mind wander to Catarina. I had to remind myself she was trained, she knew what she was doing. We both had jobs to do, and mine was to make sure no one breached the house.

With that in mind, I stepped to the side, shifted to my eleven o'clock, and switched over from fusion mode to white hot. The world around me turned black and white, the jungle dotted with white heat signatures as the enemy combatants advanced.

There were more than six now—more like twenty. I popped off a round, a white figure dropped, and I moved to the next.

Sweat rolled down my neck.

The humidity was oppressive.

The mosquitoes were swarming en masse.

The quiet peacefulness of Berta's mountaintop hideaway was now spoiled by the devastating sounds of battle.

It was going to be a long fucking night.

Chapter Nine

I was listening over comms, but that was all I was doing.

Hiding away in the house, listening to the battle rage on outside.

My trigger finger itched to join the fight. To go out and help Jack and his team. But the whimpering of a little girl in her teenage sister's arms reminded me that I needed to stay with Berta and guard the women and children.

On the way to the compound, I'd learned the president's wife and children were to be picked up tomorrow morning after a scheduled visit to a hospital in Puerto Cortés. The timeline would be tight; the other women and children would already be aboard the boat that would take them across the Gulf of Honduras to Belize.

The other two members of the team, Aiden and Ryan, had already made contact with Berta's people in Hopeville, and the arrangements for new identities and safe passage were in place.

We just had to get through the night.

"Catarina, you should sit," Berta told me in her thickly accented English.

There was something melodic to her voice. It was soothing and calm, despite the sounds of rapid gunfire. I understood why these women responded to her so well, beyond the fact she was their savior—the Angel of Death. The woman who was not afraid of the gangs and had dedicated her life to avenging the women who had been brutalized or lost their lives to the senseless violence.

I glanced from the only entry point—a flight of stairs leading to the upper level of the house. We weren't in a traditional basement. The bunker had been built into the side of a hill with two exposed sides. Three layers of concrete-reinforced cinderblocks were the only things stopping the bullets from penetrating.

That meant we were trapped, with Berta's trusted soldiers patrolling the grounds and guarding the house. There were three men stationed on the level above—and me.

The last line of defense.

"Thank you, but I'm fine."

Berta patted my shoulder and smiled.

The strands of gray in the woman's dark hair, the wrinkles lining her forehead, and wary brown eyes told a thousand tales of death and vengeance. Yet, she was smiling. Standing as a pillar of righteousness and hope for the hopeless. I'd been to a lot of war-torn cities, I'd seen the devastation of corruption, the depravity, and the exploitation of people who just wanted to live in peace. I'd seen courage and optimism in the aftermath of war—the liberation that follows ruthless warlords being taken out.

But never had I seen strength like Berta's.

She was fighting a losing war, yet she refused to give up. In her lifetime, she'd never see the end of the corruption in her country, yet instead of fleeing and freeing herself of the nightmare, she stayed and freed her people.

That wasn't honor, bravery, or strength. There were no words to properly describe what that was.

"All will be well," she murmured. "The cowards always retreat at dawn. They attack under the cover of darkness. Without the shadows they are not brave enough to face me."

We had hours to go until dawn.

"Come, Catarina," she continued. "The little ones like it when you speak to them. They think you sound . . . funny."

I glanced back at the stairs, not wanting to give up my tactical position.

"You're making them nervous," she went on.

Damn it all to hell.

"Okay," I conceded, not wanting to make it more difficult on a roomful of already traumatized children.

I followed Berta across the small space and sat on the dirt floor next to a young mother with a baby in her arms and a toddler holding on to her back.

"Do you speak English?" I asked.

The woman nodded.

"How old are your children?"

It took her a moment to answer.

"Two. Three."

I took that to mean the baby was two months, the toddler girl was three years old.

The woman looked and sounded exhausted. I wondered, when was the last time she'd slept? When was the last time she'd had a decent meal, or spent even a few minutes not worrying about her babies? I didn't have food. I couldn't take away her fear. But maybe I could give her something.

"Do you want me to hold the baby while you get some rest?"

The woman stared at me with a blank expression. Berta quickly translated. The two of them had a rapid-fire conversation in Spanish I couldn't keep up with beyond the words *baby, sleep, good.*

Suddenly, she held the infant out to me. I took the baby, cuddled her to my chest, and hoped I gave the mother what she needed so she could get some rest and relax her arms.

Berta patted my head. "Gracias, querida."

"My pleasure."

I'd quickly found not even snuggling a cute little baby could calm my racing thoughts of Jack being in the middle of a firefight. Jack *and* the team. The only thing that eased my mind was when one of them called in over the radio. Of course, as luck would have it, Jack was the quietest, though I did catch snatches of his voice here and there.

I also found that cradling a baby made your arms tired, and I'd only been holding the tiny tot for a little more than an hour.

The gunfire outside had slowed to bursts with long lulls between. Some of the women had fallen asleep, including the baby mama and her toddler next to me. If what Berta had said was true and sunrise would send the men attacking the compound back into the trees, the guys only had to hold the bad guys off for a few more hours.

By some miracle, none of Berta's men had been injured—though I figured it was more because this was just their way of life. Every night was probably a battle. As experience went, Berta's men probably had more than anyone on Jack's team, and that was saying something, seeing as they were all former SEALs.

The baby started to squirm. Little baby lips puckered right before her lids opened and deep brown eyes appeared.

She was so darn cute, I wanted to blow raspberries on her chubby cheeks.

"Hey there, cutie," I cooed.

I didn't want to wake her mother, but I was pretty sure she needed a new diaper. I'd never in my life changed one, though I was fairly confident I could figure it out. I mean, I could drive an M1A2 Abrams—not that I'd been authorized to take the controls of the tank, but when you're in the sandbox, you find fun where you can.

"Five, post up, you have incoming."

It took my brain a moment to engage and remember I was Five.

I scrambled to my feet, doing my best not to jostle the baby or wake the mother. Berta's gaze came straight to me, going from relaxed to high alert in the space of a second.

"Here." I gently shoved the baby into her arms. "We have incoming."

In the blink of an eye, Berta's brown gaze turned lethal. She would fight and die to protect the people in this room.

"Go."

I turned the mic to my comms on and radioed back, "Good, copy."

I went straight to the stairs and took them two at a time, fastening the sides of my vest I'd released to get comfortable while sitting.

When I made it to the top, I grabbed my M4 by the barrel and pulled it over my shoulder. I let go, the sling caught, and I pulled the Rugger-Magpul RXM from my holster. I quickly pulled my hearing protection from the carabiner hooked at my side and slid the noise-canceling headset on over my earpiece. With my left hand, I slowly opened the door, keeping my RXM close to my chest.

Training day one: never lead with the barrel.

I didn't hear any sounds.

I pushed the door open just enough to slip through and silently closed it behind me. *Someone knows how to use WD-40.* As quietly as I could, I made my way down the short hallway that opened up to the main part of the house.

"I'm entering the house, east side," Pete called in. "Everyone else, hold positions."

Two "copy that" calls immediately came in—Fallon and Mason.

It took another few seconds before Jack's tight, rumbled "copy" came through.

In my mind's eye, I could see his angry frown.

The open living room, kitchen, and dining space came into view. One of Berta's men stood to the side of a window peering out, until he swung his rifle in my direction. I held my breath and waited for the man to recognize me. It was never fun being on the business end of a weapon—friendly force or not.

I heard the door to my right open. I pivoted and waited. Pete appeared and shoved his goggles up onto his helmet.

"Rough night?" I asked when he got close.

"Not for us," Pete told me. "Four tangos broke through. Fallon can't get a shot, and Mase and Jack are still on the other side of the building."

"You broke cover for four tangos?"

There were three of Berta's men in the house and me. Pete didn't need to come in.

"You've only got one man in the house. Two broke station and went outside."

I didn't get a chance to ask why the men had left the house.

The window to our far right shattered. Glass exploded into the room, followed by two men. I popped off a shot, hit my target in the shoulder, adjusted, pulled the trigger again, and he fell. Pete's target was down with one.

The window behind us broke. Pete went left for cover while I went right. Berta's man at the window went down, blood oozing from his forehead.

"One, you've got at least two more coming your way," Fallon announced.

The door swung open. I dropped to a hip, leaned out from behind a chair, and fired. The newcomer stumbled, his shot went wide, and I fired a second time.

Pete still hadn't answered the call, so I did.

"Copy that."

A second later, a barrage of bullets tore through the room, holes peppered the furniture, and pictures fell off the walls. I was pinned down but had a direct line of shot to the door and the now-shattered window opposite Pete, who was returning fire. The smell of gunpowder perfumed the air, reminding me I needed to slow my breathing. Let my body fall into my training, let muscle memory take over.

Easier said than done when your world's exploding around you.

After what seemed like forever, the gunfire slowed. I chanced a look in the direction Pete was shooting. Two assailants, one right after the other, tried to climb through what used to be a large picture window but now was nothing more than a battered frame. In rapid succession, Pete dropped the men.

The room went quiet. Eerily quiet. I used my wrist to wipe away the sweat rolling down my temple.

"I'm coming to you, Five."

Even though Pete wasn't more than twenty feet away from me, I heard his call through my earpiece.

I held my position, ignored the stock of the M4 digging into my side, and waited for Pete to make his move.

My eyes were alternating from the window to the door when I thought I heard what sounded like the snap of the changing handle of a rifle slamming closed. I slowed my breathing and strained to listen.

Nothing.

"Hold," Pete instructed. "Call positions."

Right, he heard it too.

"Overwatch," Fallon came back.

"Three and Four are still at the line," Mason returned.

The team was accounted for and not in the house. But one of Berta's men could've entered the house to help.

Shit.

The next minute felt like an eternity, and the house remained silent.

"Coming."

I held my breath, glided my finger down the trigger guard, and paused just shy of the pull that fired my weapon.

Two shots pierced the silence.

I rolled to my back, did an ab curl, and fired on the man advancing into the room. His shoulder jerked, then he disappeared back into the kitchen. There were three points of entry into the house; one was through the kitchen. The upstairs was basically one open room, but the cabinetry that jutted out to make the kitchen an *L* would provide cover and a place to hide.

I rolled back, peeked around the chair, and saw Pete lying face down on the floor.

Fucking shit.

I scrambled to my knees, tossed my rifle back over my shoulder, and crawled as fast as I could to Pete's prone body.

I heard the snap of the bullet breaking the sound barrier before I felt it whiz past my head.

I dropped to my belly, transferred my RXM to my left hand, and returned fire in the general direction. Then I went to Pete's feet, grabbed his ankle, and stood. I was pulling him back behind the couch he'd been using as cover when the shooter appeared with his rifle lifted.

I went into a crouch, saw he was fumbling to clear his jammed weapon, and used his bad luck as my opportunity to end the threat.

"Come on, Pete," I grunted, and pulled. His gear made it hard for me to slide him across the floor, or maybe it was the 1970s shag carpet that was inhibiting my movement.

We were almost there when an assailant ran into the house.

Fucking hell, where are they all coming from?

I let go of Pete and went to my knees. The angle was awkward, seeing as I was basically straddling his legs, but I couldn't leave him unprotected. I fired on the man, and my slide snapped back and stayed open. I dropped the out-of-ammo weapon and calculated the odds of getting my M4 back over my shoulder before the asshole got a shot off.

I didn't have to think. Berta appeared and unloaded on the man.

Unfortunately, his buddy didn't get the memo it wasn't safe to enter Berta Lanza's home and helped himself to the door behind me. Before Berta could stop him, his forearm went around my neck and he hauled me to my feet, using me as a shield. His other hand went to my hip as he pulled me back.

The idiot didn't have a weapon, or if he did, he wasn't holding it. I needed to get him off me before he commandeered my rifle.

Berta was yelling at the man in Spanish. The man was yelling back. He tightened his forearm across my throat. I turned my head into the crook of his arm to stop him from choking me out and reached up to my vest to find Jack's knife.

I snapped it open as the man jerked me up off my feet. My neck wrenched and pain exploded down my spine. I breathed through the pain. The asshole dropped me back to my feet, unhooked his arm, and in the process clocked me in the jaw. I immediately tasted blood. I freaking hated the taste of blood, despised it, just the thought of it made me want to gag.

It was an insane thing to think about while being manhandled by a man who meant you harm, but there you have it—the crazy shit one thinks about while in battle.

As soon as I got a handle on my gag reflex, I spun and plunged the knife into the side of the man's throat. He let me loose and I dove to the side, landing on top of Pete.

"Christ," he rumbled beneath me.

"Welcome back, boss."

I rolled off, clicked on my mic, and called in, "Need backup."

After that, I sat on my ass next to Pete with my M4 up and waited for the cavalry.

Chapter Ten

I had to keep reminding myself that Catarina and Pete were alive.

Cat was unharmed.

Pete's vest had saved him from a bullet hole in the chest, and Cat had done the rest.

But I couldn't stop seeing the blood on her hand and the bruise on her jaw.

"I'm fine," Cat groused when she caught me staring at her.

Daylight had come, and I found myself standing outside behind the house on what could be considered a back porch, if you used that term loosely and considered a porch mostly dirt.

It was almost a full-circle moment. Nine months ago, I'd walked away from Catarina after a night of mayhem and bloodshed. And here we stood again after surviving a night of mayhem and bloodshed of a different kind. Only, this time, she was in jeans and a tee and fully geared up instead of in a ripped-to-shreds party dress after being groped by a madman.

"I know you're fine," I told her.

"I could've helped with the bodies."

Only Catarina would bitch about not helping to move dead bodies out of the house. Berta didn't want the women down in the bunker to see what had happened. They'd heard enough; they didn't need to be stepping over the dead.

"You could've," I agreed. "But Berta needed you downstairs."

She nodded and looked off into the distance.

With the sounds of battle gone, I could hear the birds in the forest. There was nothing but beauty as far as the eye could see—as long as you didn't walk around to the side of the house.

I wanted to know what she was thinking about, but I knew better. It took time to process your actions on the battlefield. It took even longer for your mind to reconcile the lives taken over the lives saved. Some missions took longer than others. For me, the lives of the women in the bunker were worth taking out as many men as necessary to ensure their safety. I'd lose no sleep over last night's op.

"How hard was it for you to hold your position?"

That was not what I thought she'd been pondering. But it was an easy answer.

"More control than I knew I possessed."

Her head turned and her eyes landed on me—clear blue eyes I wanted to stare into for the rest of my life. Eyes I wanted to go to sleep to, wake up to, and one day look at my children and see those same blue crystals dance with happiness.

"Thank you."

Christ.

Arrow to my heart. I doubted she knew the blow she'd delivered but it landed, nonetheless.

"I was wrong," I admitted. "Pete was right. *You* were right." A cocky eyebrow winged up, and I took that as wanting me to continue with my apology. "I never should've doubted you. I have . . . control issues when it comes to you. In my defense, I've never loved anyone who was crazy brave and—"

"Wait. You love me?"

Well, fuck me running, I hadn't meant to go that far and admit the whole truth.

"C'mere, baby."

I held out my hand, and for once Catarina Keys didn't throw attitude as she happily walked her fine ass the handful of steps needed to get to my side. As soon as I had her hand, I pulled her against my chest and wrapped my arms around her.

Once I had her where I wanted her, I told her a story.

"I think I fell in love with the idea of you before I met you. It started when I read the dossier of this woman who was a high achiever, smart, physically tough. Her superiors raved about her work. Commands were clamoring to get their hands on this woman whose skill set was such that it made her invaluable. She was in high demand but went to work at the Marshals Service, using her supreme intellect to stop sex offenders.

"By the time I was done reading, I knew if I were ever to find a woman I wanted to spend the rest of my life with, she'd have to measure up to the woman in the report. That was the kind of woman I'd always wanted but couldn't find. Then in walked this blonde-haired, blue-eyed spitfire who was all attitude and sass, and it hit me—the woman who was meant to be mine was standing right in front of me. An hour later, I learned not only was she smart and gorgeous, but she was funny as hell. And I knew right then down to my soul, if I could somehow manage to win her, my life would be filled with nothing but beauty for the rest of it; until my dying breath, I'd have everything. Then I fucked up by being a twat. The end."

Catarina shook her head and whispered, "No, not the end."

Thank fuck.

"You willing to give me a second chance?"

"Let me tell *you* a story." She paused and adjusted her cheek on my chest and nuzzled closer. "There was a woman, and all her life she searched for a man who was big and tough and smart. He had to like to laugh and have fun and watch something other than sports . . ." Cat tilted her head back and looked up at me. "Do you watch a lot of sports?"

I felt my lips twitch, trying to stop myself from fully committing to the smile trying to break free, and shook my head.

Damn, the woman was fucking cute.

"*Phew.*" She readjusted her cheek and went on. "But see, a man like that, one who's strong enough to go head-to-head with this woman, he's hard to find. She's a lot to handle, and not a lot of strong, tough men are willing to put up with her attitude. And the men who are, are pushovers, and that's *totally* not her thing. She's looking for protective, and a little cocky—but not the bad kind—and bossy in the bedroom, but not overbearing, and he needs to have a little bad boy in him to keep up with her." She stopped again and glanced up. "Are you following?"

"Yeah, baby, I'm following."

I smiled down at her, and I swear to God the smile she gave me in return stole my breath. Uncaring she wasn't done with her story, I dropped my mouth to hers. My tongue glided over the seam of her lips. I felt the cut on her lip but pushed the knowledge of how she got that cut out of my head and got lost in the feel of her tongue sliding against mine. One hand skimmed up her back, under her hair, until I had a handful of silky brown locks. I had to admit, the dyed color was growing on me, but if I had my way, she'd go back to blonde. My other hand went to her ass.

Catarina moaned and pressed closer.

Alive.

In my arms where she belonged, with minimal damage.

Reluctantly, I broke the kiss, but only because I wanted to hear the conclusion of her story—which hopefully ended with the confirmation she was giving me a second chance.

"Damn," she whispered. "You're really good at that."

"Stop being cute and finish your story," I demanded.

With a sigh I knew she didn't mean, she kept her eyes on mine this time and went on. "So there she was in Sin City for work. Imagine her surprise when she walks into a hotel room and meets this really good-looking man. He's a little older, and has lots of gray in his hair . . ." She trailed off when she couldn't keep a straight face.

She was talking about my old boss.

"I'll make sure to tell Wilson you think he's a good-looking old man. He'll love that."

"You do that." She beamed a megawatt smile at me. "But then there's this other guy in the room . . . Now, he's the hottest man she's ever seen. Full-on pantie-drenching hot, and he's funny to boot. She takes one look at this man and she knows, down to the pit of her stomach, he could go toe-to-toe with her. Not only could he handle her attitude, but he'd love it. He'd be bossy and arrogant in all the right ways. And right then and there, she knew she'd never met the man who was perfect for her because she'd never met *that* man lounging back in a chair like he was the king of her world. And she fell in love. Then it took this man a long time to get his head out of his ass and figure out she was what he'd been waiting for his whole life."

Jesus fuck. My heart was ready to jump out my chest.

"Are you done?"

"No."

"Finish," I growled.

"The end."

My fist in her hair tightened. I gently pulled her head farther back so I could fully take in her pretty face.

"Yeah, baby, the end."

My lips hit hers. Story time never tasted so good.

Chapter Eleven

"Hey, Cat, wait up."

I stopped at Pete's callout and turned. He was jogging out of the house.

Two black vans had shown up a little bit ago. Berta wasted no time getting the women and children ready to be loaded in. We'd be ready to roll out any minute now. Pete, Mason, and Jack were going to the hospital to grab Maria and her three daughters. Fallon was coming with me to the port to guard the women and wait for the others.

"Everything okay?" I asked when he stopped in front of me.

"Just wanted to say thanks."

"For what?"

Pete tipped his head and took me in like this was the first time he'd ever laid eyes on me.

"I was out cold. You saved my life."

My eyes automatically went to his forehead. The guy had a big knot left of center. I was pretty sure he had a concussion, but Pete, being of the male variety, swore he was fine. I didn't say a word, seeing as I would've said the same after being knocked out on a mission while more work was to be done.

"Any of—"

"Wasn't anyone, it was you. So accept my gratitude, so we can move on."

"Right. You're welcome. But don't make a habit of thanking me for doing what teammates do. We have each other's back."

"Is that what we are, Catarina? Teammates?"

Damn, that was a slip.

"We are on this op."

He continued to stare at me. His gaze was so perceptive, I fought the urge to confess all of my past transgressions before he saw them for himself.

He was a saint, after all.

"Is your nickname because of Saint Peter?" I thought for a moment. "Isn't he the patron saint who holds the keys to heaven?"

"Yup."

He was lying.

"Why do I get the feeling you're lying?"

"Because I am."

"Are you going to tell me how you got your nickname?"

"Nope. That story's reserved for teammates. The kind who stay with the team and aren't a one and done."

Well, damn.

"Are you offering me a job?"

"No, I'm offering you a place on a team."

My stomach did a flip. I liked that I'd earned the respect of a man like Pete. But there was Jack to consider. I didn't want to be a distraction, and if he couldn't get over me being in the line of fire, I wouldn't risk his life or the lives of the other men on the team.

"Are you thinking about Jack?"

I normally wasn't so transparent. To make myself feel better, I chalked it up to Pete's superior situational awareness.

"How'd you know?" I tossed out the rhetorical question with a smile.

"He knows I want you on the team. We wouldn't be having this conversation if the team didn't agree you were a good fit."

Jack agreed.

He'd said he loved me, which still had me walking on air. And he'd admitted he'd been wrong. Not to mention, he hadn't ridden to the rescue until I'd called for backup. Though, he *had* been the first one to make it to the house, and Mason was huffing and puffing, bitching about Jack's 'my woman's in danger' superpower. But he'd waited. Then he'd come for me. He'd trusted I knew my limitations. He'd trusted me to take care of myself.

That was huge.

That was what I needed.

"What about Ryan and Aiden? They haven't met me."

"There's also Gavin. He's back in San Diego keeping an eye on the Dirty Plank. But you've won Mason," he weirdly stated.

"I'm not tracking."

Pete shifted uncomfortably and glanced around the forecourt. Berta and the rest of the team would be out soon.

"Mase doesn't trust easily. It took Jack about five months before Mase started to trust him, and that's not on Jack, that's on Mason. He's been my best friend for a long time, and sometimes I wonder if there will ever come a day when he lets *me* in. He's the best man to have your back in a firefight. He'll sit around the fire, have you busting a gut laughing, and he'll do it while drinking you under the table. But that's all you'll get from him. He'll trust you with his life, but not with his secrets or his scars."

I thought about Mason's devil-may-care smile, and my heart ached for him. I'd sensed the darkness in him, but it bothered me knowing how deep it ran.

"So what I'm saying is," Pete went on, "if Mason trusts you after forty-eight hours, they're all in."

It was good to know I had Mason's trust. I'd take it and keep it safe.

"Let me think about it. I just bought a nice condo in Prescott."

"San Diego's weather's better. And I think I got something you want that's more valuable than real estate."

"What's that?"

"Jack."

He wasn't wrong. I wanted Jack and Jack was in San Diego. And as cool as my condo was, I'd give it up in hot Arizona in a second to be with him.

"I don't know, those social media financial gurus say real estate's where the money's at."

"On second thought, Jack's place is a dump. You might wanna convince him to move in with you."

Oh no.

I didn't live in dumps. Not because I was some pretentious twit, but I'd bounced from filthy house to filthy house after my grandma died until a second cousin took me in and gave me a home. I made a promise to myself I'd never again live in filth and clutter.

Could I make an exception if it meant having Jack? Yes. Would I scrub his house from top to bottom like a woman on a mission to give her man a sparkling-clean house? Also yes.

"Damn, the look on your face is priceless." Pete chuckled. "I'm joking. He lives in a minimansion by the water."

It seemed like Jack and I had a lot to talk about—like how in the hell he could afford a minimansion in Southern California where the prices were insane. I'd seen houses for sale on the side of a busy highway for nearly a million dollars.

"I'm not money—"

"I know you're not." He stopped me from finishing. "I know you lost your parents, then your grandmother, and from there you moved from family member to family member, none of them keeping you long because they couldn't afford you. Until the last one you stayed with until you left for the Army."

That was a watered down, nice version of why they hadn't kept me. The truth was they didn't *want* me.

I wasn't embarrassed by how I grew up, so that wasn't what had my anger spiking. Neither was it a secret I was ashamed of. But I didn't like people knowing personal things about me that I hadn't shared with them directly. I hadn't even discussed with Jack how I'd grown up, and Pete knew.

"Did you share this with Jack?"

Pete's eyes narrowed. "I know you don't know me, so I take no offense. You'll come to learn that I don't share business that's not mine."

"But you'll snoop and find it for yourself."

Pete nodded, then verbally confirmed, "When it comes to my team, damn right. What I don't do is speak out of turn."

Some of my irritation waned. If I was in his position, I'd snoop too.

Yet, I wasn't ready to let it go.

"Did you find out anything else interesting?"

"Just that you have excellent credit and you need to pay off your car. The interest rate sucks. Better yet, sell it. Fords suck."

I was highly offended at this blasphemous statement. "I love my Mustang."

Pete shook his head. "You'll love a Camaro more."

I doubted that.

One of Berta's guards was coming out of the house with Jack. It was go time, but I had more to say.

"I can't work for a man who doesn't like Fords," I told him haughtily.

"Can you love a man who hates them?"

"No." I drew out the word and watched Jack as he made his way to us.

Jack did a slight head tilt when he saw me staring. His eyes flicked between me and Pete before they finally planted on Pete and narrowed.

"What's happening?" Jack asked me.

"You don't like Fords?"

"Hate them. I drive a Chevy."

My jaw dropped. This couldn't be.

"I've owned Fords my whole life," I told him.

"We're a Chevy family," he returned.

My hip hitched and my hand landed there. Unfortunately, the whole throwing-attitude thing was ruined when I winced. *Damn tracking device.*

"You didn't tear it open, did you?"

"No. I don't think so. Maybe. But we're discussing something important."

He took in my position. Any smart man would note the hand on the hip and wisely change his current standing on whatever the topic was, and change it before things deteriorated further.

But not Jack.

No. He doubled down.

"How often do you trade in your Fords?"

"Every four or five years."

"Right. Baby, one of my Chevys has over two hundred thousand miles on her and she still purrs."

More people were coming out of the house. It was really time to wrap up this conversation, but I was curious.

"How many Chevys do you have?"

"Four. Two pickups, a Camaro, and a nineteen-seventy-nine Nova."

Damn, he had me at Nova.

"You still got your 'Stang?" he asked.

"Yeah."

"You'll like the Camaro better."

Pete took this as his opportunity to rejoin the conversation. He did this by busting out laughing.

Jerk.

"I'll accept the job," I ungraciously spat.

"Thought you would."

I rolled my eyes, then turned to Jack. "You're sure you're okay with this?"

Jack didn't answer. Instead, he tagged me around the waist, hauled me close, then in front of Pete, kissed the hell out of me.

This was going to be the best job ever.

Jack broke the kiss, brushed his lips over my cheek, then kissed my temple.

"Be safe, baby. I'll see you in an hour."

With that, he strode away.

No way he'd flipped that fast.

"Is he leaving now so he's not tempted to yank me out of the van and cuff me to him?" I asked Pete.

"More than likely." Pete's smile died. "Give the man a minute to adjust. He's fighting against his instincts. He knows he can't hold you back, but everything in him is screaming not to let you face danger. But he's not stupid and doesn't want to lose you, so he'll figure it out."

Suddenly I wasn't so sure I wanted him to figure it out. That sounded like a whole lot of sacrifice on his part—fighting his nature without any compromise on my part.

"That doesn't sound like the makings of a strong relationship," I whispered.

Pete's lips pressed tight, his eyes went to the dirt, and when he sniffed, I didn't think he was going to comment. But then his gaze came back to mine, and a different Pete was standing before me. Not the commando, not the badass man, but a kind, brotherly type who was at the ready to impart wisdom and guidance.

"Sometimes it takes losing something important before you wake up and see what's actually *important*." He paused, so I nodded my understanding. "And if you're lucky enough to get it back, you work your ass off to keep it. But if you're smart, you understand what's really important, what you really want. What love really means is doing everything in your power to make sure the other person is happy and fulfilled and free to be who they are. Jack's lucky *and* smart. He's fighting now, but he'll win the battle because it's the only way to keep you, and for him to give you what you need."

I didn't need to think about what Pete said. He was right; my grandmother had taught me that love was putting others before yourself.

Which brought me back to my original thought—how much sacrifice was too much?

"Yeah, but what is it that Jack needs?" I asked before I could stop myself.

"For you to make it worth it." Pete stepped closer, clapped me on the shoulder, and added, "And before you ask, you giving him whatever it was when the two of you were out back, that's all he needs. Just that, Catarina. You be you, and he'll have everything he needs."

God, I hoped he was right. But I still wasn't entirely comfortable with Jack going against who he was just so I could be me.

Something to think about later.

"One more thing before we roll out." I blinked at Big Kind Brother Pete's abrupt change back to Work Pete. "Shep's looking into Tom and why the CIA sent you to deliver bogus intel. We haven't had time to talk about it, but tomorrow after the delivery's done, we need to find time. It's not sitting well with me."

It wasn't sitting well with me either. But with everything going on, I hadn't had time to give it much thought other than I was still pissed I'd been played.

"My phone's been off since the warehouse. Do you think I should call Tom?"

"Not until after the delivery's done."

Part of me wondered if Tom had sent out a recovery team to find me after my tracker went offline. The bigger part of me didn't think he did. I was probably expendable; the device was to find Berta, not to keep me safe.

"I think this is about the president's wife," I blurted out.

She was the only high-value target in the group of women. Unless they'd changed teams completely and wanted to stop Berta's efforts.

Pete nodded. "That's my thought too." Another clap on my shoulder. "Be safe. We'll see you in a few hours."

Pete sauntered away toward the van. My gaze followed him. I couldn't see Mason, but I could see Jack standing at the open door of the passenger's side.

The man of my dreams.

Tall and strong and perfectly made for me.

I drank him in, stopping at his clenched fist.

Yeah, I had to be me, but I also had to compromise.

There had to be something I could give him to even the scales.

My eyes went back to his. From this distance, they looked obsidian.

He jerked his head toward the other vehicles.

Bossy.

"*I love you,*" I mouthed.

His hands unclenched, and he smiled.

After that, I hightailed it to my ride.

Chapter Twelve

"Your woman doesn't like boats." Fallon mumbled his understatement.

Twenty minutes into the four-hour ride across the Gulf, my girl had turned sheet white. To be fair, it had been windy and choppy and the old forty-one-foot Carver was over capacity, and twenty people in the below cabin had made the air stifling.

"It's a good thing she decided on the Army," Mason put in. "She'd never make a Special Boat Crew."

"I wouldn't tell her that. She might enlist in the Navy just to prove you wrong," Pete joined in.

I leaned back in my chair and let that wash over me—the pride and respect in Pete's tone hit deep. It was the same way Wilson had spoken about Catarina during our op in Vegas. Wherever the woman went, she garnered the respect of the people around her.

And I almost lost her.

Movement out the window caught my attention. Aiden was strolling across the grass, coming back up from the small, private beach behind the villa. Berta's connections in Belize weren't your everyday, run-of-the-mill do-gooders. They were rich and powerful men who believed in her cause and bankrolled her rescues. That meant within minutes of pulling into a private dock, the women and children had been whisked away to start their new lives.

Mission complete.

We'd debrief with Berta tomorrow, then be on our way home.

My home was San Diego. Catarina's was Prescott. She'd accepted Pete's job offer, but she didn't need to live in California to spin up with us. She could stay in Arizona.

The thought of losing her again, even to distance, created a sharp pain. My hand lifted and rubbed the ache in my chest. I could move, rent my house out, go back to Arizona, a place I'd lived for a few years and swore when I left the heat I'd never go back.

But for Cat, I'd deal.

For her, I'd do anything as long as she was at my side.

On that thought, how long did a shower take?

Unreasonable fear licked up my back. She'd been gone too long. The house had been cleared. Ryan had walked the perimeter. Aiden was still outside patrolling the back for no reason other than he'd wanted fresh air. She was safe.

The bruise on her jaw came to mind. The way she'd stood over Pete, protecting him while he got his bearings. The fierce look on her face when I'd rushed into the house. No one was going to hurt Pete without getting through her first.

Danger.

She'd put herself in the line of fire—*again.*

That knot in my gut grew.

Before I realized what I was doing, I'd pushed back from the table.

Mason's hand grabbed my forearm, and, with force, he yanked me back down.

"Unless you're going up there for some sexy fun time, sit your ass down."

"It's been—"

"Not even five minutes," he interrupted. "I hear women take longer than that just to loofah. So, again, unless you're headed up there to offer to wash her back . . . *stay.*"

He said that last part like I was his dog and he was barking a command.

"What the hell is a loofah?" Ryan asked.

My gaze met Pete's. There was a lot the man was silently communicating, but the takeaway was that Mason was right, I needed to stay.

"No clue. Never showered with a woman," Mason casually threw out, like he hadn't just divulged something personal.

"Seriously?" Fallon quizzed.

Mason unwrapped a candy bar, his third since we'd been gathered around the kitchen table, and shook his head.

"Nope." Mason's tone made it clear that particular conversation was over.

"A loofah is used to cleanse and exfoliate the skin," Ryan explained with his head bent to his phone, obviously reading from the internet. "However, if not taken care of properly, they grow bacteria and can damage sensitive skin." Head lifted, his attention came to me, and he frowned. "Brother, I'd advise your woman to ditch the loofahs in favor of a good old-fashioned washcloth. If it ain't broken, no reason to court a bacterial infection in the . . . you know." He pointed in the general direction of his crotch.

"Who has a bacterial infection?" Cat asked as she walked into the kitchen.

I did a full body scan—hair wet and hanging loose around her shoulders, fresh jeans and tee, no shoes, no blood, all in one piece.

Safe.

She glanced around the table, made her decision, and walked directly to me. I adjusted my chair to get up so she'd have a place to sit, but the woman had other ideas when she plopped her ass in my lap.

That knot loosened, and my chest stopped aching.

"Do you loofah?" Fallon asked.

I had to hand it to the guy. He looked deadly serious for asking such an off-the-wall question.

"Do I loofah, as in, do I *use* a loofah?"

Fallon nodded. Cat answered, "No."

"Then you're bacteria-free."

I only had Cat in profile but still I saw her gaze go around the table.

"Should I be concerned five men are sitting around talking about shower sponges and vaginosis?"

"What's vaginosis?" Mason inquired.

Ryan already had his phone at the ready, thus he was quick to answer. "A common vaginal infection that happens when normal bacteria . . ." He trailed off, his lips turned down, and he silently read more before he put his phone on the table. "We weren't talking about *that*. I didn't know there was normal bacteria . . . *down there*. I could've gone my whole life and happily died not knowing."

Catarina shrugged. "The more you know . . ."

"The less likely you are to participate in your favorite pastime," Ryan finished with a lifted brow.

"That, or you're less likely to come away with a bad—"

I squeezed Cat around the middle. "Baby, please don't encourage them."

Catarina shifted to look down at me and smiled. "I'm trying to educate your friends on an important topic."

There was that smart-ass who had hooked me.

"I'm pretty sure Ryan's well educated on the topic."

Her smile widened and her gaze slid back to Ryan.

The guy was good looking. In the time since I'd been in California, I'd seen firsthand just how good looking the women who patronized the bar he co-owned with the rest of the team thought he was. If he didn't want to go home alone, he didn't.

"I can see it," she muttered.

"See what?" Fallon was staring at Ryan with a frown.

"How he'd be well educated on women."

Fallon relaxed back in his chair and crossed his arms. All he was missing was a beer in his hand and it would've been a sight I'd seen a lot over the months. It was his 'I'm settling in for a long shit-talk session' look.

Something he excelled at.

I glanced at Pete, Ryan, then landed on Mase. All of them were smiling at Cat. But Mase's lips were twitching. If I didn't shut this shit down, Mason would edge the conversation on for his own personal amusement.

"What about Ryan makes you think that? He had to *google* vaginosis."

"Actually, I use DuckDuckGo," Ryan corrected.

All eyes flew to him.

"What? I like the name. It makes me laugh."

"Fine," Fallon conceded. "But you still had to look it up."

"Don't be salty, ol' sailor. Just because she thinks I'm more educated than you doesn't mean she thinks you're completely *uneducated*. She just recognizes refined talent."

Mason's shoulders started shaking in silent laughter.

And here we go . . .

"You two are cute," Mase started, then waited until Fallon cut his gaze in his direction. "Fear not, brother, when we get to the topic of ropes and cuffs, it'll be your turn to shine."

I knew before she spoke Catarina was going to latch on to that like an octopus and wrap her tentacles around it until she'd squeezed every last bit of fodder she could gather.

"Really?" She giggled. "I didn't see that coming."

Mason sat back, damn proud of himself he'd given Cat something to chew on.

"Should I be offended?"

"I don't know, possibly," she told Fallon, then went in for the kill. "You're all big-guy cuddly like a teddy bear. If I had to guess, I'd say Pete . . . probably, Mason, definitely like tying up their women." She stopped for a moment, tilted her head, and stared at Fallon. "Wait, I can totally see it—you're one of those service Tops I've read about. You like the cuddly aftercare part."

The men around the table erupted into laughter. I buried my face in Cat's neck and shook with humor.

Aiden came into the room asking, "What'd I miss?"

"Cat here thinks Fallon's a cuddly service Top," Mason supplied through his laughter.

"That was quick," Aiden noted. "But it's good she's got him pegged—"

"No one's pegging me," Fallon groused. Then added under his breath, "I do the pegging."

Pete pushed back from the table, stood, and clapped Fallon on the shoulder, thankfully ending the conversation. Though he wouldn't be Pete without getting the last word in. "Just because you say it out loud doesn't make it the truth. Now, who's hungry?"

All eyes went to Catarina. Hers skidded to me.

"Are they looking at me because they think since I have a vagina, I should cook dinner?"

"Favor, baby. Don't talk about your vagina in front of the guys."

Her eyes sparked, and I knew what came out of her pretty mouth was going to be more sass. To stop this, and because I wanted to, I straightened and silenced her with a kiss.

It was closed-mouthed and too damn short, but it did the trick.

"I'm cooking," I announced.

"You can cook?" she breathed.

"Yup."

"Jackpot!" She threw her arms in the air and wiggled her fingers. "I knew you were a keeper."

I got up, helped Cat into the chair I'd vacated, and was walking to the fridge when I heard Fallon mumble, "What do you know about service Tops anyway?"

I paused to hear her answer.

"What can I say? I'm educated too."

The men all laughed again.

I didn't.

I was eager to hear more about this education . . . but that'd have to wait until after dinner and we didn't have an audience.

"I can't remember the last time I ate that much food," Cat said.

The bed dipped next to me, and I opened my eyes.

"Sorry, were you sleeping?"

"No, just resting my eyes." I adjusted my arm in a wordless invitation.

Cat accepted and cuddled into my side. With her head on my chest, her fingertips started making mindless patterns over my stomach. Every few seconds, she'd stop and press her fingertips into the muscle before she continued her exploration.

Exhaustion had set in. The last few hours after we finished dinner I was running on fumes. Still, if Cat's hand didn't stop inching lower, I'd manage to rally.

"You tired, baby?"

"I could sleep for a week," she yawned.

I tucked her closer. I'd never been the type of man who could sleep with a body draped over my chest—but that body being Catarina's, I'd sleep better than I had in years.

"We have a lot to talk about," she said into the darkness.

"Yep."

"But I'm too tired."

I gave her a squeeze and ordered, "Sleep."

"I just want to tell you one thing first."

"Okay."

"I'll move to California."

My arm twitched in an effort not to crush her to me.

She read my shudder wrong and quickly rushed out, "I mean if that's where we're going and you . . . um . . . want that."

"I want that."

"Me too," she whispered.

Her fingertips glided up my chest, stopping at my left pec, then her hand flattened and she left her palm there.

"Good night, Jack."

"Night, baby."

A few minutes later, I found I was right. In a tiny bed, in a villa on the beach, I slept better than I had for years, with Catarina Keys in my arms and the knowledge she was coming home.

Chapter Thirteen

I woke before Jack. I took the opportunity to study his features while he was still asleep and relaxed. He looked the same—all chiseled good looks and hot body—but his big-guy energy was shut down. I knew at the slightest sound he'd come alert and that vigor would spark to life.

But before that happened, I wanted to spark something else to life.

It was early. We had time, so I was going to explore.

My hand glided down his hard chest. A sprinkling of coarse hair tickled my palm, just enough to be sexy, not enough to need a tutorial on manscaping—in other words, absolutely perfect. I continued down over the ridges and valley of his upper abs and felt them jump under my palm. I pressed a kiss to his pec, decided my exploration should be multisensory, and added my lips and tongue to the study of the hard dips and crests that made up his ripped stomach.

"Catarina," Jack rumbled.

Mm, morning-grumbly Jack sounded delicious.

Since he was awake, I shifted my leg over his thighs, came up on my knees, and yanked the T-shirt I'd worn to bed over my head and tossed it to the side.

"Morning, Jack."

I meant for my greeting to come out sultry and seductive, but I was pretty sure I missed the mark and sounded like my lungs were starving for oxygen. Which they were. I could barely breathe when his dark eyes dipped to my chest and his body vibrated with a rumble. If I had any doubts about my bold move, or sitting astride Jack with my breasts bare and on display, that growl would've cured me.

But since I had no doubts—I mean, the guy had ripped my panties off and had not hidden he wanted me. If that didn't make a woman feel sexy, nothing did—what it did was embolden me.

I hooked the elastic of his boxer briefs and tugged them down. I walked back on my knees, pulling the boxers down his thighs, while at the same time praying I didn't get caught in the sheets and fall off the bed in the middle of my seduction attempt. Thankfully, I made it to the edge of the bed, shifted to my booty, and pulled the material free. I threw those too.

Only when the threat of taking a humiliating tumble off the bed was over did I allow myself to take him in—muscular thighs, long, thick cock topped with a thicker head nestled in closely trimmed hair, abs that were the thing dreams were made of, dime-sized dusty nipples, pecs that were fantasy inspiring, broad shoulders, corded neck. Then there were those navy-blue eyes that never failed to make me pause to take in their beauty. Now was no different.

"I think it was your eyes that I first noticed," I whispered, rolling onto my hands and knees.

Since I was staring directly into those beauties, I saw them fill with hunger. I crawled over his legs, halting when my hands got to his hips.

"I thought they were black. Then the light caught just right and I saw they were actually blue. I've never seen eyes so beautiful."

"Catarina."

I shivered.

"You're perfect, Jack Donovan. Top to toe, perfection. But it's more than that. You're more than this." I balanced on my left hand, lifted my right, and used it to motion to his frame. "You're everything I've been waiting for. Everything I've ever wanted. I don't know what I can give you that'll make fighting who you are so I can be me worth it. But I promise you, I'll spend every day trying to find ways to show you."

"Baby."

Low. Rough. Raw.

"This morning, we're gonna start with me blowing you, then later I'll try to think of something sweet to give you."

I glanced down at his erection resting on his stomach, felt my panties dampen, then bent forward and glided my tongue over it from root to tip.

"Fuck."

I smiled against his cock. Spent time toying with the tip with my tongue before I started my way back down, taking my time, getting his shaft nice and wet. This time on my way up, I reached between his legs and gently cupped his balls. Jack's thighs went stiff. His groan was low and hungry, so I tested the waters and gave them a firm roll in my palm.

"Catarina."

The desperate plea made my pussy spasm.

I stopped teasing him and sucked the head into my mouth. I slowly took him as far as I could, adding more suction on my upstroke. Over and over I bobbed up and down, keeping a leisurely pace. It was torture but I wanted him mindless. I wanted his control to snap. And the longer I worked his cock, the more his body vibrated, the hungrier his sounds became.

"Goddamn," he moaned.

I hummed my appreciation and, on a downstroke, took him deep and forced myself to take more, and only pulled back when I felt my gag reflex kick in.

His hands came off the bed, drove into my hair, holding my head at my temples.

"Again," he demanded.

I sucked in a breath and dropped my mouth down. His hips flexed up. The pads of his fingers dug into my scalp, I took him as deep as I could, and he only let me free when my noise turned desperate.

"Good fucking Christ." His growl slithered over me, down, and pulsed between my legs. "You swallow?"

His filthy question sent another wave of excitement through me.

With a mouth full of cock, I did the only thing I could do and nodded.

"Keep going, baby. I'm almost there."

I doubled my efforts and kept going. He didn't release my head as he bucked his hips, matching my strokes. I worked him with my mouth. My hand on his balls massaged and tugged until he shot off down my throat on a low, feral moan. That didn't wash over me—it burned over me.

"*Fuck,*" he grunted.

I swallowed.

Then before I knew what was happening, Jack's hands went under my pits and he was hauling me up his body.

"Face."

I couldn't process his demand or my new position, but to stop myself from falling forward, my palms landed on the headboard. Jack's hand landed on my ass with a slap.

"Scoot up, pussy on my face."

Um.

"Jack." His name came out wobbly because I wasn't so sure this was a good idea. I'd never done this before. I didn't know *how* to do this.

I didn't need to know how. Jack slid down, gripped my hip with one hand, used the other to yank the gusset of my panties to the side. I heard the fabric tear right before he pulled me down onto his awaiting mouth.

Then he ate. No, then he commenced devouring me. Jack didn't eat pussy—he overwhelmingly, spectacularly, with brilliant precision *ate pussy.* His tongue was magical. The stubble on his chin chafed in the best of ways. His thumb found my clit with aim that should've been impossible.

"Oh my God," I breathed.

I might not have known what to do, but my body sure did. All thoughts of smothering him or doing it wrong flew out the window. I rocked my hips and rode his face, reaching for a climax that was lingering just under the surface. My nipples pebbled. My belly got warm. My toes curled.

I was whimpering, so close, it was right *there* . . . then Jack's thumb was gone.

I whimpered again, this time unhappily. His tongue swiped up and circled my clit. His teeth grazed the sensitive spot. My whimpers turned into groans. He sucked my clit so hard, my back bowed, and I came on a chant of his name, or a call to God, or maybe it was a string of nonsensical words. I'd never know because I was flying apart. *Amazingly* flying apart, so high I was out of my body. I could do nothing but feel.

The only thing keeping me upright as pleasure tore through me was Jack's hands on my ass. He slowed his ministrations, gently kissing and licking me while my orgasm waned.

"Scoot down, baby."

Impossible.

"I would if I could get my legs to work."

I felt him chuckle against my pussy, sending aftershocks up to my clit, making it pulse.

Jack turned his head, kissed my thigh, then did all the work as he dragged me down while he sat up. I ended up sitting on his lap. His back was to the headboard, and we were face-to-face.

"That was . . . *amazing*," I told him.

He smiled.

"No, that was super-duper ah-maz-ing," I amended.

His smile broadened.

God, Jack. So handsome. I brought my hands to the sides of his neck, sat there in the morning quiet, and just stared.

I wanted this, or a version of this, to be how I woke up every morning. Jack next to me, smiling. I wanted to give this to him—happy, smiling mornings.

His hands on my thighs traveled up to my hips, farther up to my waist. His gaze dropped, and I saw his eyes following the path of his hands. Feather-light glides of his thumbs under the swells of my breasts. My nipples peaked, his thumbs grazed there too. Soft touches. Gentle caresses. It was sweet after the wild we'd shared.

Finally, his hands slid back down and settled on my hips and I got his beautiful eyes back.

"You just being you makes it worth it," he told me. "There's nothing you need to do. Nothing more you need to give me. What's inside me is mine. Don't take that on, baby. I don't think there will ever come a time when I don't worry about your safety."

There. He was giving me more when I was trying to balance the scales.

"You know I worry about your safety too."

"Then it's good you gave me a morning blow job to take the edge off, so I can concentrate on the mission instead of thinking of all the ways I wanna fuck you."

"Now who's the smart-ass?"

Jack's hands moved down and around to squeeze my booty.

"That's still all you. Great ass . . ." He leaned forward, pressed his lips to mine in a quick kiss, then finished with, "Smart mouth that luckily for me is better at giving head than it is with a comeback."

My lips twitched. "Aren't you all hearts and flowery compliments," I teased.

"How's this for hearts and flowers? You're gorgeous. You've got great tits. You give world-class head. Your cunt's so tight and wet, the second I got inside of you, I was ready to come. Never have I ever had to fight so hard not to blow. You've got the prettiest eyes I've ever seen, soft, silky hair that feels good in my hands and pooled in my lap. I just had your pussy on my mouth and I want to taste you again. But if there was none of that, and all I got was humor, your intelligence, your cute, and your attitude, I'd still be right here.

"But seeing as I'm lucky, I got your smarts, funny, sweet, and your pretty pussy, great tits, and—it's worth the repeat—your smart-ass mouth that gives the best head I've ever had. I'd say I'm coming out a winner."

"You're turning me on again," I warned.

"Then slide down and sit on my dick."

Was he serious?

Surely he needed more recovery time.

I didn't verbalize those thoughts but still Jack answered.

"You don't believe me?" His knees cocked up, one of his hands left my ass, the other gave it a slap, and he demanded, "Lift up."

I lifted.

I felt the head of his dick at my entrance and had my answer.

He *was* serious, and *no*, he didn't need more recovery time.

"Slide on."

I slid down.

Full of Jack, I groaned.

"Now ride."

I rode. Hard and fast, with my hands on his shoulders for leverage and my eyes locked on his. I loved he wasn't hiding his hunger. I loved that his gaze dropped to my chest and his eyes flared as he watched my breasts bounce. I lost his eyes when he tipped his head and pulled my nipple into his mouth. His tongue felt amazing, but his teeth felt better. He moved to the other side, tormented that nipple.

"Jack," I panted.

He lifted his head. My nails dug into his shoulders.

I couldn't believe I was going to say this already, but I was close.

"I'm gonna . . ." I trailed off.

I rocked harder, grinding my clit against the coarse hair at the base of his cock, that thick cock stretching me wide, so full of Jack I couldn't finish my thought.

"Fuck me, you feel good," he groaned.

"Jack."

I arched back. Jack's hands moved to my breasts. Gone were the gentle caresses. He pinched and pulled and rolled my nipples.

"Goddamn, I love your tits."

To punctuate his statement, he stopped pinching a nipple, lifted my breast to his mouth, and bit.

That act of savagery did it. My orgasm exploded. With my head tipped back, my neck straining, back bowed, my inner muscles clamped down so hard, I feared injury.

Unable to move through the pleasure, I lost my rhythm. Jack flipped us and took over. My body as well as the bed shook with his thrusts. Hard. Fast. Wild. Each drive prolonged my orgasm.

"More," I begged.

Over and over, Jack slammed into me. One orgasm slid into two. Either that or I'd experienced the world record for the longest orgasm ever.

"Gonna blow, baby."

Yes. I wanted that. I wanted him to join me in the bliss he was creating.

"Do it. I wanna feel you."

Jack's face went to my neck, his teeth sank in, and he groaned.

He took himself through his climax. I took his come, his teeth, his grunts, his cock twitching inside of me, and his big body on top of mine jerking with pleasure.

I knew his orgasm had slid away when he released his teeth.

"You can take a solid fucking, baby."

I heard the smile in his voice.

"I can take anything from you, Jack."

His tongue glided over where he'd bit me.

"I left a mark," he warned.

That filled me with an excitement I would have to contemplate at a later date, when I wasn't in a sex-induced fog. But even without the fog, I reckoned I'd happily wear his mark if it came with three orgasms.

No, I didn't need the orgasms. I just needed Jack.

"Do I get to mark you?" I asked.

"Baby, I'm yours. You can do whatever you want to do to me."

I didn't need to contemplate how *that* made me feel.

Giddy. Happy. Powerful. To name a few.

But mostly it made my heart pound in my chest and my belly fill with the warmth of acceptance.

Chapter Fourteen

With Berta and two of her guards taking up the chairs in the living room, Aiden and Ryan sitting on the smaller couch, and Mason, Fallon, and Cat taking the larger sofa, Pete was perched on the armrest next to Fallon and I was on the one closest to Cat.

And Berta was speaking.

"They're all safe and gone."

Meaning the women and children had already been separated into families and moved out of Belize.

"Maria wanted me to thank you again for the teddy bears. The girls enjoyed them."

Catarina tipped her head back and looked at me.

Surely she saw the girls holding the stuffed animals. Maybe she hadn't realized they'd come from us. The eldest, at ten, was a little old for a teddy bear, but we didn't want her to be left out. It was a small gesture, but even small, the girls had relaxed a little when we gave them the bears. We'd essentially kidnapped them, even if their mother had set it up to get herself and them away from an abusive home and give them a future they wouldn't have in a country that was deadly to their well-being. Anything to help ease the commotion and uncertainty while their mother explained what was happening.

"We're always happy to help," Pete told her. "Before we let you get on with your day, we need to ask you about Derek Nicolson and Tom Washington."

Berta's expression didn't change, nor did she prevaricate.

"Derek Nicolson is responsible for the torture and murder of an associate. Manuel was a good man, faithful to the cause. This Derek man came to La Esperanza to meet with Manuel. That night after they met, Manuel was killed in his home. Witnesses place Derek at Manuel's home."

The way Berta rapped out the information was testament to all she'd seen. There was no inflection, no sadness. Her tone was matter of fact—this was her life. Manuel wasn't the first of her friends to be murdered, nor would he be her last.

"How do you know I asked Mr. Washington for this information?"

I waited for Pete to field this question, but Catarina got there first.

"Tom sent me here to find you and give you Derek's location."

That garnered a response from Berta. She sat a little straighter, and her gaze turned sharp. "Where is he?"

"Dead," Pete supplied.

Berta's attention went to Pete. "Are you sure?"

"Positive. He's very dead and has been for some time."

The woman almost looked crestfallen that the man she was after would not feel her vengeance.

"There is a moral dilemma I carry with me," Berta softly began. "Spiritually with my Lencan ancestors, with the beliefs of my people. We are taught the value of our neighbors, the importance of these relationships. We hold reverence for the land, for the well-being and blessings we receive. To keep that balance we must live a life of morality, love purely. Without the ethical reciprocity, the land will die and the crops will fail. Our rivers will dry up. I fear in my quest to save my people, I am condemning them.

"My journey has always been the way of our warrior chief, Lempira. Only I don't wish to fend off the Spaniards, I wish to kill every man who dares to break the spirit of our women. Who thinks it is his right to touch, violate, and murder them. I can only hope Ilanguipuca will take mercy on our people, and she will not punish the land for my transgressions."

Berta paused a moment, jutted her chin in defiance, and finished. "I, however, will gladly accept my eternity in hell. Please send my sincerest gratitude to whomever sent Derek to his final resting place. One day, I will see him there. Until then, I have more work to do."

With that, she stood and motioned her men to do the same.

"As for Mr. Washington, he is helpful when it benefits him, but I do not trust him."

"Smart," Pete muttered.

The rest of us stood to say goodbye to a woman who had given her life to serve her people.

To guard her women.

To fight an unending war of cruelty and brutality.

"The villa is yours for as long as you wish to stay."

"Appreciate that, but we'll be heading out tonight," Pete informed her.

Berta made her way to Pete, reached up, and patted his cheek. "Until next time, Saint Young. Be well."

Before Pete could respond, the perimeter alarm sounded. I unholstered my sidearm, saw Catarina and the rest of the men do the same, with the exception of Ryan. He pulled his phone out of his pocket.

"Well, I'll be damned," Ryan drawled. "Tom Washington is at the gate."

"Alone?"

Ryan tapped his screen a few times to cycle through the different camera angles.

"Looks like it."

Pete transferred his Sig to his left hand and pulled his cell from his back pocket.

"Unknown number," he announced to the room before he answered. "Mr. Green, what a surprise."

He was making a point using a color as a name, something the spooks were known for.

There was a brief pause. "Sure, with the warning you tell your men to stay the fuck back, and, if you pull any shit, I'll shoot you if Catarina doesn't do it first." Another pause. "If you think I believe that, then you're dumber than I already think you are."

With that, Pete disconnected. "Ryan, open the gate. Tom would like a word." Pete's gaze went to Berta. "He knows you're here. If you'd like Ryan and Aiden to escort you off property so you can go about your day, we can do that."

"I'd like to stay."

Berta glanced at her two guards, reached behind her, and pulled a weapon I hadn't seen in years—a gold-plated .50 cal Desert Eagle AE. To make it even better, it was the Patriot version with **United States of America** engraved across the six-inch barrel and **We the People** scrolled behind the front sight. I knew there would be an image of George Washington's face etched into the top rail. The weapon was a pop-culture icon. How she sat with that beast in her waistband, I couldn't imagine.

"A gift from an American who thought Honduran women were for the taking," she explained.

A gift, my ass. More like a trophy from a dead man.

"I think I need one of those," Cat murmured.

Jesus.

"You may have this one. After our friend leaves," Berta offered.

"No, no, I couldn't."

"Every woman needs some bling, Catarina. As a thank-you. I have three more just like this one, though not gold. Men with small penises tend to like big guns."

She wasn't wrong.

"How are we playing this?" Fallon inquired.

"Tom talks. We listen. He leaves."

"And if we don't like what he says?" Mason asked.

"Lady's choice," Pete returned. "He played her, not us. We back Catarina's play."

I didn't think that was a good idea. Pete might think he knew Cat, but he did not. Shit could get out of hand quickly if she was left in charge.

"Messy," Mase rightly noted. "I like it."

"How about you don't knock the shit out of him until we completely hear him out," I suggested.

"Since when are you a stick-in-the-mud? I think I get at least one to the face for having to cut out a tracking device and one to the solar plexus for the burn of the glue."

I wasn't a stick-in-the-mud, I was a man attempting to control my temper. And if Tom was stupid enough to hit Cat back, I'd slice his throat.

"Suit yourself, baby. But warning—he swings back, he doesn't leave here breathing."

"Aw, that's the most romantic thing a man's ever said to me."

Smart-ass.

"You know me. All hearts and flowers."

I watched her cheeks tinge pink.

"I feel like we're missing something," Mason put in.

Thankfully Pete cleared his throat, reminding the team we had company.

"Aiden, you've got the back. Ryan, let Tom in and take the front. Fire only if fired upon," Pete ordered.

Both men immediately broke away to their positions.

Fallon moved to lean against the wall next to the back door that would give him clear line of sight to Aiden. Mason moved to the opposite side of the room, giving him a view of the front door. If someone slipped by Ryan, Mase would see them enter.

Berta and her men retook their chairs. However, Berta kept the Desert Eagle on her lap.

I heard footsteps on the tile floor right before an older man who looked near retirement, if the white of his hair didn't betray his age, entered the room. He was still fit but lacked the power of a younger man. Straight posture, chin high, strides confident like he thought himself important.

"Catarina," Tom greeted with a smile. "Glad to see you're well."

"I've been told I can't shoot you until I hear you out. But now that you're standing here, I'm remembering how supremely pissed I am at you. I trusted you, and you screwed me over. My suggestion—start talking before I forget I'm supposed to listen to what you have to say. But just so you know, before you leave, I'm punching you in the face."

Tom smiled like he was proud. "May I sit?"

"Will it make you hurry to the part where you tell me why you lied to me?" Cat returned.

"Always so impatient." Tom shook his head and moved around the furniture, sitting on the smaller couch. "I'm sorry, Catarina, but this is important, and I needed all of you in the same room."

"Why not just ask for a meeting like a normal person?"

Tom glanced over at Pete.

"It needed to be a private conversation," he amended. "You know, plausible deniability and all that."

"Right. Plausible deniability," Pete spat. "In other words, this isn't a *private* conversation, it's you wanting a fucked-up favor, and when shit goes sideways, you get to keep your hands clean."

"Yes, Saint. I have a favor, one I believe will benefit you as much as it will me. This conversation goes no further than this room. Actually, this conversation never happened."

I saw the tic in Pete's jaw. Plenty of people back in San Diego called him Saint. I found it interesting that all his employees at the Dirty Plank called him Saint and not Pete, even though all the guys called him Pete while at the bar. He hadn't minded when Berta called him by his given name. However, for some reason, he didn't like Tom using it.

"Get on with it," Pete sighed.

"Rafael Quintero."

The name meant nothing to me.

But as soon as the two words left Tom's mouth, the room went wired.

Fallon pushed off the wall. Mason was on high alert. Pete was fighting to keep his face neutral. And Berta was now very interested in what Tom had to say.

Shit. I had a feeling we weren't heading home tonight.

Chapter Fifteen

Saint 'Pete' Young

Pete breathed through the fire in his lungs.

Rafael Quintero was very dead.

His sister Mia was safe in Idaho with her husband, Cole.

The man couldn't hurt anyone anymore. But that didn't mean the unspeakable things Rafael had threatened to do to Mia had stopped waking Pete up in the middle of the night in a cold sweat.

Threats that Pete couldn't shake even after he'd ended the man making them.

Rafael was the reason Pete had pushed Mia out of the organization she'd helped build. The team still had safe houses around the world. There were still women and children occupying some of them. Women who had escaped domestic violence, who were still getting on their feet. Those houses would be available to them for as long as they needed.

But Mia going out on missions and helping the women and getting them safe—that had ended the day Rafael threatened to violate Mia in such graphic detail, Pete had thrown up after he'd slowly and meticulously carved out Rafael's insides. And it wasn't the disembowelment that had made him queasy.

Pete had also lied to his sister and Cole and told them he and Mason, Fallon, Aiden, Ryan, and Gavin were officially retiring and concentrating on the Dirty Plank, the bar they owned together. Not that he was under any illusion she actually believed him, it was just she was so loved up with her husband, she hadn't called him out on it.

Pete looked across the room, caught his best friend's gaze, and saw the same revulsion in Mason's eyes.

Mason was the only person Pete had told what really happened in Mexico. The rest of the team knew Mia had needed an extraction when she'd caught the attention of the wrong people. They knew she'd reported Rafael had possession of a seven-year-old little girl. And they knew what that meant, and why Pete had used himself as bait to be captured. Further, they knew Pete had taken out the warlord, but they did not know how or about the threats.

"What about him?" Mason casually asked.

That calm, cool tone was deceiving. Mason adored Mia like a sister. If it hadn't been Pete in Juárez, Mason would've hung the warlord by his balls and taken his time torturing him.

Tom's gaze found Pete's. With a lift of his brow, the man nonverbally asked a question.

"My team knows I took him out. He's dead. Why are you bringing him up?"

"Do you know what happened to his crew after you left?"

"You mean after I rescued his prostitutes, most of whom were children?"

Tom held up his hand in surrender and, for the first time since he'd entered the room, showed emotion.

That being extreme disgust.

Maybe he wasn't a total prick after all.

"I'm not condemning your actions. I'm asking you a question."

"Other than checking on the safe house we have in El Paso, I haven't been near Juárez since I left. Why?"

Tom shifted his gaze to Berta and gave her a small nod of respect.

"Rafael's cousin, Carlos, has taken over. He knows you took out Rafael. He knows Mia was in Juárez, and why . . ." He let that hang. Undoubtedly for dramatic flair. The prick wanted a favor and bringing up Pete's sister was a surefire way to get his attention. "Carlos has put out feelers as to her whereabouts."

Goddamnit.

That was going to be a problem, and not just because Mia could be in danger. Stopping Cole from going out on the hunt to put Carlos down was going to take no small amount of effort. But if Pete couldn't talk *Mason* down, shit would turn catastrophic. There was taking out a threat, then there was Mason off his leash. No one threatened to harm the people Mason loved without swift retribution that assuredly would turn messy. On the contrary, Pete's reckoning would be carefully planned and executed in a calculated manner.

Before Pete could question how Tom had come to this intel or why he hadn't shared it earlier, the man went on, "Carlos did away with the loans, kept the gambling, but only because he can get payoff in trade."

That was not shocking nor surprising. Taking out warlords was like a game of Whac-A-Mole. One goes down, and two others pop up.

"And he's expanded his stable," Tom finished.

Pete didn't have to ask if Carlos's stable of prostitutes included children. He knew it did. The disgusting truth was there was a market for fresh young girls, and he'd learned a long time ago that the only way to survive in his line of work was to remember the people he saved, and not all of the ones he couldn't. It was the only way to keep a sliver of sanity.

"Explain why you sent Catarina to Honduras to find Berta and give her bogus intel," Jack demanded.

"Because I need her expertise to find a woman for me, and she needs access to Berta's network."

From across the room Jack made a strangled noise, clearly not pleased with Tom's request.

"Cut the shit, Tom. You said you needed all of us in the room for this conversation. Not just me and Berta. And if that was the case, you could've told me that in Virginia. This isn't about me *or* Berta. It's about Pete and his men. Spit it out already."

Pete stopped his lips from twitching, but just barely. Catarina Keys was something else. She reminded him of his sister, but more ballsy. Jack was a lucky man.

"I need Saint and his team to go back to Juárez with you."

"Who is this woman?" Mason asked.

"Calista Ventura."

"Dios mío."

Everyone's attention went to Berta. The woman looked ravaged.

"How long, Tom?" Berta seethed.

"Three weeks."

"And you did not call me. Instead you . . ." One of Berta's hands came up and swept the room. "Set this up."

"I can't have any involvement in this, Berta. None. If the CIA knows I've breathed a word of this, I'll be prosecuted for treason."

Treason?

"Why doesn't the CIA want this woman to be saved?"

Tom looked uncomfortable for a moment before he said, "Because she's an enemy of the state."

Well, that didn't mean shit to Pete. If the government knew what he and the team did, they'd consider them felons. There was this gray area where the real world happened. The place where good people did bad things for the right reasons.

"What's she accused of?" Fallon joined in.

"Murder."

Again, that meant nothing; murder was up for interpretation. The deceased was not always the victim.

"Who did she murder?" Pete took over the questioning again.

"A senator's aide." Tom paused, then under his breath mumbled, "And two other men."

Well, shit on a shingle.

"If she's wanted for the murder of three men, why are you helping her?"

Tom seemed to be considering his options.

Berta had obviously grown impatient. "Calista is a brave woman. Young, still learning how to be patient and when it's time to strike. Many years ago, her older sister was taken. Her family searched and searched. Years passed but she never gave up hope. Then her sister was found overdosed in Berlin."

"She was trafficked," Catarina noted.

"Yes. Calista has made it her mission to bring awareness but also to rescue and return victims home. Much like what Saint here does. These women need a champion, a savior, and she has a beautiful soul, so she's decided that savior will be her. She reminds me of you, Catarina. Mia too. Brave. Strong. But not as smart. She wants to save the world, not just those she can.

"I have counseled her and warned her; if she continues on her path, she will drive herself mad. But for her, they are all her sister, someone's sister, possibly someone's mother, and she cannot see past it. I also warned her to be careful in Juárez. She wasn't ready for the danger that lurks there, the evil. They are devils preying on the weak."

Pete didn't have to look at Catarina to know she was all in to rescue this woman. The same as he didn't need to look at Jack to know the man was in danger of a stroke.

Berta made her position known. "You may use any and all of my resources to find her." She stopped and scooted to the edge of her chair. "But hear me, Mr. Washington, this is your only warning. Don't ever play games with me again. And don't ever set a young woman in harm's way to get my attention. Yes, I got word there was a brown-haired, doe-eyed American who was ripe. Yes, I had my people in Tegucigalpa trying to find her before she got hurt. But anything can happen, and she *could've* gotten hurt. There are other ways to get what you want. Never again, or our arrangement is over."

Tom looked properly chastised but not sorry.

"Why is Calista so important to you you'd risk your freedom, Catarina's life, and Berta's censure? Not to mention, drag me and my team into this?"

"Her father saved my life."

Pete studied the man. That might've been true, but there was more to it.

"We can sit here all day and play this game; it's not someone I care about in the hands of a madman," Pete said. "Or you can stop wasting my fucking time and tell the truth."

"That's the truth," Tom lied.

When no one spoke, Tom looked at Catarina.

"After you left the Marshals Service and became a free agent, I looked into you and your last op. I knew about Las Vegas. I knew you had a connection to Jack, and I knew Jack worked with Pete. I knew what happened in Juárez, and that Mason would be all in to take Rafael's cousin down once he learned of Carlos's interest in Mia. If Mason's in, Pete will have his back, and I'd have an off-the-books team to rescue a woman I care a great deal about. I used you to get to them and Berta. I'd apologize for that but I'm not sorry. I'd do anything, including betraying my oath, to save Calista."

"You're a fucking dick," Jack growled.

"I'm more than that, Jack. But right now, I'm a man desperate to save a woman."

Goddamnit.

Pete knew what was coming before it happened.

"I'm in," Mason readily agreed.

Tom had been right; Mason was all in. If he couldn't get his hands on Rafael, the cousin of the man who'd threatened the violation and murder of Mia would do.

Pete had come to understand his own demons and how to tame them.

Mason had no interest in taming the beast within.

This was going to get messy.

Chapter Sixteen

The beast had been unleashed.

And it wasn't my Jack who looked murderous; it was Mason.

The sight was frightening.

The vibe in the room was inching toward nuclear, and I wasn't sure how to cool it off before it blew.

"Do you know where she's being held?" Pete asked.

He was off too. There was an edge to him that ratcheted up his intensity tenfold. And whoever this Rafael Quintero was, he seriously tweaked Pete and Mason both. Pete had said he was dead, but clearly his ghost still haunted both men.

"Why'd you wait three weeks?" Fallon inquired.

Tom blew out a breath and almost looked human, and not like the conniving, manipulating bastard he was.

"As Berta explained, she's on a mission to save the world. Sometimes I don't hear from her for months. And before you ask why I haven't stopped this insanity, there's no stopping Calista when she sets her mind to something. Before her father died, he tried. Her mother worries, but after they lost Liliya, she became emotionally unavailable."

"Is that a nice way of saying the mother's checked out?" Fallon stopped Tom to ask.

"Completely and totally," Tom clarified.

"If you don't hear from her often, how do you know she's been taken?" Pete asked.

"I have a source in Juárez. He's not always reliable. But he tells me there's an auction, and among the women there's a Russian."

"She's Russian," Fallon spat, like the word tasted bad. No, scratch that, Fallon was staring at Mason with a brow lifted. Maybe it wasn't dislike; maybe it was something else that had Fallon forcefully saying the word.

"By blood. Her father's Irish American, her mother is Russian. But you could say the Russian in her overpowers the Irish or the American genes her father gave her."

"That explains a lot," Jack muttered, and my eyes shifted to him. "You ever get on a Russian's bad side?"

I shook my head. "I don't think so."

"Then you haven't. You wouldn't have to think, you'd know. I knew this Russian kid in school. We were in like seventh grade. Some assholes picked on him, mostly trash talk, but one of them tagged up his locker. This kid said nothing. Did nothing. Years later, we're seniors, the kid's now six foot, and I swear he worked out every day since the locker incident. He was huge. He waited, found his time, then beat the hell out of the boy who messed with his stuff. Right before he knocked him out, the kid said something about his locker being vandalized. Four years he held that grudge. If you can avoid it, never piss off a Russian."

"Truth," Fallon chimed in.

"So this auction." Pete brought the conversation back around. "When and where is it taking place?"

"According to my source, a week. Again, he can be unreliable. As to the where, Juárez. He doesn't have a location."

"Anything on the buyers?" Berta asked.

"Just murmurs the final destination is Dubai."

Berta made a disgruntled humming sound.

Dubai was a hotspot for prostitution. More, it was a hotbed for trafficking—buying and selling of women to rich and powerful men from around the world.

"Is she pretty?"

Mason's question had Berta's shoulders snapping back. "Why does that matter?"

Mason softened his features and injected a healthy dose of respect when he answered Berta.

"Because a beautiful Russian woman would attract a certain type of buyer, especially if they're going to Dubai. Anyone in the trade would know this. There are those who want to buy women for their stables to rent, and there are those who want to own a harem of beautiful women. Two different types of animal."

"Calista's mother was a model in Russia. She's a very beautiful woman, and Calista and her sister inherited those looks. Calista resembles the model Kate Grigorieva, or so her father used to say."

I didn't know who Kate Grigorieva was. I looked around the room, hoping someone would offer some insight. No one did, at least not verbally, but Fallon was staring at Mason again.

"Then she won't make it to auction," Mason announced. "Her pictures would've been sent out. A private buyer will come inspect her and buy her before the rest of the girls get sold."

"Mason's right," Pete concluded. "We need to get home and prepare an extraction before she's moved—if she hasn't been already. And we need to make arrangements to get the other women out and someplace safe."

"El Paso's full," Mason returned.

"I have an idea," Pete said, then turned to Tom. "You owe me a marker. You also owe Catarina one. Or you can owe me two, and I'll talk her man outta kicking your ass the next time he sees you. And I want .223, .308. and 9mil ammo delivered to my place in Jamul. Enough for six shooters."

"Done," Tom quickly answered while staring at Jack. "One day you'll understand why I did this. You should also know Catarina was never in any danger. She had a man on her at all times until she met up with you. Then I knew she was covered and pulled him back."

"Don't hold your breath," Jack muttered.

Something hit me.

"I cut the tracking device out of my hip. How'd you find us?"

"Your burners. There are trackers in those too."

Son of a bitch.

I had three burner phones in my backpack.

I glanced at Pete. "Oops?" I offered.

Total rookie mistake. I'd led Tom directly to us.

"Yeah, Catarina, oops," he returned dryly.

Tom stood, looked around the room, didn't offer handshakes or any gesture of the kind, but he did pause on Berta with a thoughtful gaze.

"Everyone is safe?"

"Indeed," Berta returned.

Tom declined his chin. "Thank you."

Why in the world was Tom thanking Berta?

I didn't get a chance to question Tom before he swiftly made his exit.

Then it was Berta and her men who were on their feet, looking impatient to leave.

"Here, lovely." Berta held out her Desert Eagle to me.

"Berta, I can't accept that. It's too much."

"My gratitude for your help."

Well, shit. I couldn't say no to that without being rude.

"I'll take good care of her," I promised.

Berta leaned in close and quietly told me, "You don't take care of her. She will take care of you. Use her wisely with the purest of intentions and think of me every time you pull the trigger."

This woman was something else. The Angel of Death with a kind spirit and heart.

"I'll never forget you."

"We'll see each other again, Catarina."

I hoped she was right.

Berta and her men left. Ryan and Aiden came back into the house and were briefed.

Pete was no less on edge when he mentioned Rafael's name. Fallon and Jack had also picked up on it, but it was Fallon who questioned it.

"What really happened in Juárez?"

"That's not for now." Pete brushed him off.

"Brother—"

"I didn't say I wouldn't discuss it. I said not for *now*."

I'd never heard Pete use such a harsh tone. Whatever it was, he seriously wasn't ready to discuss it.

"Okay." Fallon gave in. "Should I call Shep and get us an earlier flight?"

Pete sighed and came back to the man I was getting to know. "I was a dick. That wasn't right. My apologies. I just . . . just give me until we're home. I need to be on the mountain when I tell everyone. And Gavin needs to be there."

Yes, Gavin. The last man on the team I hadn't met.

Pete had explained that the men rotate out for missions so someone is always in San Diego to watch over the Dirty Plank. I wondered if Jack and I would rotate out—even though neither of us had anything to do with the bar.

"No worries." Fallon quickly accepted Pete's apology. "We'll talk when we get home."

Mason had been unusually quiet.

"What's going on?" I knocked his knee with mine.

"Nothing. The last two days are just catching up with me."

I didn't think that was the truth. Mason seemed to be the type who could keep going until the job was done. But I wasn't going to push.

Jack came up next to me and held out a bottle of water.

"Thanks."

I cracked the top and had the bottle to my lips when Mason mumbled, "That's it?"

Without lowering the bottle, I asked, "What?"

"I just gave you a bullshit blow-off."

"I know."

I chugged half the water and was recapping the bottle when Mason continued, "And that's it? No wheedling, no snit because I don't want to talk, no calling bullshit?"

Wordlessly, Jack moved away from me and Mason.

"Is that what you need?"

"Need?"

"To open up, say what you really mean," I explained. "Do you need me to wheedle and nag until you tell me what's on your mind? Or do you need me to give you space and time to learn to trust me, then when you're ready, you'll feel like you can tell me the truth instead of giving me some lame, bitch-ass 'I'm tired' when I know that if bullets started flying, you'd be wide awake and on your A game?"

When I was done, Mason was staring at me like I was a new breed of alien that had never been discovered and had been beamed down to Earth for him and him alone to discover. Either that, or he was staring at me like I was a pain in the ass who talked too much.

I wasn't sure, because Mason's expression didn't give away much.

"I trust you."

He didn't.

I raised an eyebrow.

"I trust you enough," he repeated with a variation.

"Enough to have your back in a gunfight but not enough to tell me why you're sitting here brooding."

"Pete is broody. I plot."

"Okay. So not enough to tell me what you're plotting."

He was quiet for a second, his gaze firmly on Pete's back across the room.

"One day Pete's going to tell you about Mexico . . . and what happened after I got there. After you hear the story, maybe you'll understand, maybe you won't, and you'll see me for the monster that I am."

I didn't like how Mason was starting this justification of his plot. Not because I was worried what he might say, but because I didn't like that he thought of himself as a monster.

"I'm going to kill every single one of those men who're there to sell those girls."

"That's the plan, Mase. We're going in to rescue the girls."

"No, Kitty, that's *your* plan . . . rescue the girls. Mine is to make sure that none of those animals are left breathing."

I didn't know what Mason was expecting me to say, so I said nothing.

"You don't look disgusted."

"You think I should be disgusted because you feel no guilt taking the lives of men who rape and sell women? Do you think I should feel guilt over the lives lost last night, while I was in that house protecting those women in the bunker? One second I was cuddling a baby, the next I've got my weapon in my hand, then three minutes later, I'm killing bad guys. Are you disgusted that I slept last night? Didn't miss a wink, all warm and comfy. No thoughts of the bodies we left piled up."

Mason's lips curved up into a smile. "So that's why you were up bright and early having a dance party in your room."

I felt heat hit my cheeks. Mason heard—damn. I searched my feelings and found I didn't care, and shrugged.

After a moment of silence, he bumped my knee with his.

"Thanks, girl."

I couldn't contain my snort. "Anytime, *boy*."

Mason shut down his brooding—I didn't care what he'd said, he was totally brooding—and switched back into his cocky, playful mask.

"You know, there's a difference between men and women."

"I'd say there are many differences—plural—not just a difference."

"Right. Well, one of them is a man will call a woman *girl* as an endearment," he educated. "But when a woman calls a man *boy* and does it all snarky, there's something inside him that clicks and makes him want to prove his manhood."

"In other words, women are smarter than men and don't feel the need to pound our chests and drag our knuckles on the ground to prove we're the dominant species."

"No, Kitty. Women do that by batting their eyelashes, giving a man soft looks, and showing him what she thinks he wants to lure him in. Men like to think we're the masters of our destinies, but the truth is, women have the power—they either feed the soul or they suck it dry. One of those gives a man what he needs, the other crushes his will to live."

He wasn't wrong. But I didn't think he was speaking in generalizations. He was speaking from experience. Some woman had crushed his will to live. I wanted to know the story, but I knew he'd never tell me.

"Well, whoever she was, she was a fool." With that, I patted his knee again and stood. "I'm gonna go pack up and ditch the phones Tom gave me."

"Cat?"

I turned to look at Mason. He didn't say anything right away, but something was working behind his eyes.

"Not all women are like you."

"No, they're not."

"He's lucky."

I took that as the compliment it was meant to be.

"*We're* lucky."

"Glad to have you on the team, Catarina."

I took that compliment and locked it deep.

"Good to be on the team."

That meant when I walked away from Mason, I did it smiling.

Chapter Seventeen

Catarina stood with her backpack over her shoulder, arms crossed over her chest, eyes on my truck, frown firmly in place.

"If I'd seen this first, I would've been worried," she strangely said.

I beeped the locks and reached for the door handle. "What?"

"It's jacked up," she rightly noted.

"Yeah."

"Chevy Silverado HD, all blacked out and jacked up. That gives a woman pause, Jack. You know what they say about men with big trucks . . . they're overcompensating for the small penises."

I opened the passenger door and held out my hand. "Then it's good you've seen my dick and know that's not the case."

Cat swung her pack off her shoulder and handed it over.

"See you tomorrow," Mason yelled from across the parking lot as he pulled himself up into his truck.

Cat looked in his direction and waved. "Guess he's not part of the Chevy family."

Mason wasn't part of any family except maybe Pete's, but that didn't extend to truck manufacturers.

"Mason is his own man."

"His has a lift too."

We'd just gotten off a six-hour flight from Belize. This after two hours in the car to get to the airport. It wasn't late but it was well after dinner, and I was exhausted and hungry. Still, I'd stand in the parking lot of Brown Field having a ridiculous conversation about nothing if that conversation was with Catarina.

"I can't say for certain," I started. "I don't have personal knowledge and don't want it. But if the rumor is true, that lift on his truck says not one thing about what he's packing."

Mason's Ram roared to life.

"What about the exhaust? Does that say something about what he's packing?"

Mason gunned the engine, showing off for Catarina, and fishtailed out of the parking lot.

"Not sure what that says, baby. Hop up."

Her foot went to the running board, and she heaved herself up. Before I could close the door, she asked, "So what's the rumor?"

I should've known she wouldn't let that go.

"That he's hung like a horse."

Her eyebrows shot up to her hairline. "Damn, that must suck for him."

That wasn't the reaction I was expecting. Out of sheer morbid curiosity, I asked, "Why does that suck for him?"

"Because, Jack, size matters," she solemnly informed me. "There's too small, too big, just enough, and holy wow. Women like just enough and holy wow if they find it. But too big is just that—too big. A woman will see that, consider her vagina's future, and not want the repercussions of too big. Hung like a horse is way too big. Then there's running; who wants a horse cock between their legs when they're out for a jog? I mean what does he do, tape that bad boy up so he doesn't bruise his thighs? And just in case you were wondering, you fall into the holy-wow category."

Fucking hell, she was funny.

"Good to know."

"So? Do you think he has a shaft sling that contains it or does he tape?"

A shaft sling . . . good Christ.

As funny as she was, I was done talking about Mason's dick.

I leaned in, hooked her around the neck, and took her mouth. Then I got her tongue and didn't let her go until she groaned down my throat, and *my* dick twitched in warning it was time to get my woman home before I committed a felony and fucked her in my truck in a semipublic parking lot.

On a smile, she said, "I take it you're done discussing Mason's package."

Yeah, I needed to get my woman fed and home.

To conclude the conversation, I closed the door, made my way around the hood, opened the back door, tossed her bag and mine into the back seat, and hauled my ass in.

She was still smiling when I hit the ignition and the dash lit up.

"It pains me to say this, but it's a sweet ride."

"I needed something to take up to the mountains when we train."

"You said you had two trucks."

I pulled out of the parking spot much slower than Mase and answered, "She's an old nineteen-seventy-seven square body. The C10's lowered, wouldn't make it up the mountain, and I wouldn't risk her getting dinged up."

I was pulling out of the lot and rolling to a stop at the red light, waiting to make a right, when Catarina asked, "How far do you live from here?"

I wanted to correct that question to "How far do *we* live from here?" but I refrained.

"This time of night with no traffic, fifteen minutes. My house is out on the strand."

"I haven't been down to San Diego in a while," she told me. "Is the Gaslamp district still the place to hang?"

"Can't say I've been in that area since I've been back. If I go to a bar, I go to the Dirty Plank, and that's in Imperial Beach."

"Tell me about the Dirty Plank."

"Can't. You have to experience it for yourself. We'll swing around for lunch before we head up to the mountains."

Catarina fell silent, but I could feel her eyes on me instead of the sights. Not that there was much to see in this part of town, just a bunch of condos, houses, and palm trees. The beach was too far away, and the mountains were to our southeast.

"Tell me about your family," she said.

I glanced over at her. She had her body turned facing me, elbow on the center console, chin resting on her palm, fingertips resting on her cheek. In the dim light of the dash, she looked younger than she was—not innocent, but the hard edges had softened. There was no danger lurking, no bad guys to engage, no reason for her to be on alert, so that part of her had shut down. This was a side of her I'd never seen.

From Vegas to Honduras to Belize, there had been moments when I'd seen her relax, but never completely powered down.

"I have an older sister, Anna. She was a biochemical engineer."

"Was?"

I didn't miss the uncertainty in Cat's question.

"Was," I confirmed. Then to put her mind at ease, I quickly added, "Now she lives in Alaska. She worked for a big pharmaceutical company in Durham. She fell in love with a pilot. After they got married and she got pregnant, they decided to move to Thorne Bay, where Craig grew up. Now she's got four kids and twenty acres, and every time I talk to her, she's got a kid screaming in the background, and she's never been happier. Her husband still flies, but he does medevacs, wilderness flights, things like that. My mom passed away five years ago. Somehow, my sister convinced my dad to move up there. After all the years he bitched about the snow when I was a kid, I thought he'd pick a beach for his retirement."

"I'm sorry about your mom," she whispered.

"So am I. She was a good mom, the best." I had to stop and breathe through the pain that five years later had not lessened. "I miss her."

I felt Catarina's hand on my shoulder before it slid down my arm and wrapped around my wrist. Then I gave her the rest.

"My dad retired a year after my mom's heart attack, and Anna went to work on Dad. It took her another year and another grandchild for him to sell the house in Minneapolis. Now he lives about fifteen minutes from my sister and sees his grandchildren pretty much every day."

"What about you? Do you go to Alaska to see them?"

"I went up for a visit before I moved down here. If Craig's not available to fly you up from Ketchikan, it's a pain in the ass to get there. A ferry ride from the airport over to the mainland, then another four-hour ferry over to Hollis, then you've got another hour and a half up to Thorne Bay. Last time I went up, he was out flying. It took me almost six hours to get to my sister's place *after* I landed in Alaska. I swore I'd never go back unless Craig came down in his seaplane to pick me up."

"I don't believe that."

I loved my sister, my dad, and my nieces and nephews, so she wasn't wrong. I also liked my sister's husband, and the fishing wasn't bad. Though I didn't like it enough to move there, which was my sister's constant refrain.

"What about you? Where's your family?"

I felt her hand on my wrist spasm and chanced a look over at her. She was staring out the windshield, her expression completely devoid of emotion. I twisted my wrist free, reached for her hand, laced our fingers, and rested our hands on my thigh.

"I'm an only child. My parents died when I was four. Snowmobile accident. They went away for the weekend for their anniversary. I was with my grandmother. After they died, I stayed with her."

"Damn, baby, I'm sorry."

I couldn't imagine losing both parents at such a young age. Losing my mom in my thirties had been torture on me and my sister.

"I don't remember them," she softly confessed. "I remember the stories my gran told me. I have pictures of them. But I don't have any real memories."

Christ, that was rough. I had a memory bank full of good times.

"Growing up, I knew I was missing out, but I didn't feel like I was. That probably doesn't make sense, but I didn't. I didn't have my parents, but I had my grandmother. She did everything she could to make sure I knew how much she loved me. I can't really remember losing my parents. I can't remember if I cried for them, though I'm sure I did. But I was four. All my childhood memories are with my grandmother. Now, when *she* died, that hurt. I didn't think I'd ever stop crying."

"How old were you?"

"Fourteen. She had type one diabetes. She'd had it her whole life. She took care of her health the best she could—stayed active, was vigilant with her diet and insulin. She went to sleep one night and never woke up."

Holy fuck.

"Baby."

"I looked it up—nocturnal hypoglycemia—it's called the dead-in-bed syndrome. Her blood sugar dropped in her sleep. Almost half of severe diabetic shock episodes happen at night while sleeping. If I had known, I would've slept next to her. I would've watched over her the way she looked out for me. But I didn't know, and she died in the room next to mine while I was asleep."

"Catarina." I squeezed her hand.

My attempt at support was lame. But I knew firsthand no well-meaning words could take away the pain of losing someone you loved.

"After she died, I went to live with my uncle and his family. That's my mom's brother. By this time, my parents' life insurance had run out. My uncle tolerated me being in his house, having another mouth to feed, but his daughters and wife did not. Especially his oldest daughter, who now had to share a room. I lasted there about a year. Then I moved in with my aunt—my dad's sister and her husband. They didn't have children. That was by choice, and neither were happy to have a fifteen-year-old with a chip on her shoulder and an attitude problem."

What the fuck?

My hand on the steering wheel tightened.

"They said that shit to you?"

"Every chance they got. Though it was more her than him. My aunt thought my dad had a stick up his ass while they were growing up, and she said I'd inherited it from him. I might not've had memories of my parents, but I didn't like her talking badly about them. One night there was this huge blowup. She called CPS and had me removed from her house."

"I don't know what to say." Well, I did, but none of it was good. "Actually, I do. Your aunt's a world-class bitch."

"Yup. Thankfully my mom's cousin, Lina, took me in. She was divorced, had two sons, lived in a not-so-great trailer in a not-so-great trailer park. She was a waitress at a truck stop. One of her sons was a little older than me. Her other son was twenty and still living there. He actually moved in with his girlfriend so I could take his room.

"You know, my uncle and his family didn't live in all that great of a neighborhood and didn't have a lot of money. The house was old, cluttered, and messy. My aunt's house was a wreck. Her and her husband drank their paychecks away. They were at the bar more than they were home. I can't be a hundred percent sure—living with them was a nightmare—but I don't remember either of them cooking.

"But Lina's trailer was spotless. Her boys had no father. They were big boys, rough looking, but they had good manners. Lina made sure of it. She was kind to me. She cooked dinner before she went to work. She asked me about school and how my grades were. The son who moved out, Lars, came around a lot to check on his mother and little brother, but also on me. Steven, the one who lived there with us, acted like my big brother."

Thank fuck she'd ended up with a family that showed her love and kindness after she'd lost that from her grandmother.

"I joined the Army because of Steven."

"Really?"

"When I was a senior, Steven was working at an auto parts store. His job sucked. There wasn't much opportunity in Fredericksburg. San Antonio's an hour drive each way. He decided to go into the military. I went with him to the recruiter and listened to the First Sergeant talk about all the opportunities available. I knew then I was going to join. But after Steven came back to visit after he went through basic and AIT and I saw the change in him, I knew that was what I needed.

"I graduated high school, got a job as a waitress, worked my ass off making as much money as I could. Right before my nineteenth birthday, I went back to the recruiter and enlisted. Six months later I shipped out, and when I did, I handed Lina the keys to a fifteen-thousand-dollar car I'd bought her. It wasn't enough, but it was the only way I could thank her. Out of all the people in my life after my grandmother died, Lina was the only one who showed me kindness, and she was the one who had struggled the most financially. Yet she never made me or her boys feel like a burden. She taught me that kindness was free, and if you didn't show others compassion and consideration, that made you a plain asshole."

I wasn't surprised to find that under Cat's tough exterior there was a heart of gold. What I was surprised to learn was there was no bitterness, no anger toward those who had treated her like shit.

"Hey!" she shouted. "There's an In-N-Out. Can we stop? I could murder a Double-Double with grilled onions and extra sauce."

I ignored the emotional whiplash while I signaled, changed lanes, and narrowly made the exit.

"I gotta ask, baby, are you using food as a way to change the subject?"

"What? No. Why?"

"That was an abrupt outburst."

I heard her chuckle but didn't take my eyes off the road.

"No, I really am starving, and I love In-N-Out. I'm not changing the subject, though there's not much more to say."

"Do you talk to Lina? Steven? Lars?"

"Oh yeah. All the time. Well, not Steven so much. He's still active duty, stationed in Korea. Lars is married, not to the same girl from when I moved in. Thank God, that chick was a pill. He met this girl online and moved to Houston to be with her, and talked Lina into moving down there with him. I haven't visited in about a year. But they're doing well. Lars has two little girls—Irish twins. They're absolute terrors. I mean that in the sense I think they'll grow up to be criminals. I wouldn't be surprised if at six, they're planning their first bank heist."

I didn't bother hiding my amusement and laughed.

"No, really, I'm serious. Lars made them this nook under the stairs as a little playhouse. I think they go in there and plot and plan. Lars thinks they're little princesses and spoils them. Lina says it's because he didn't have a dad growing up and he's determined to be a good one. His wife, the heathens' mother, does her best to rein them in, but I think she's realized it's a lost cause and is saving for bail money instead of college."

"Can't say I won't spoil my girls," I told her. "I have a good dad. He was tough but fair. But he did his fair share of spoiling Anna—one of those ways is him selling the home he bought with his wife and raised his family in to give her what she wanted."

"And your mom? Did she spoil you two?"

I waited until I found a parking spot and rolled to a stop so I could give her my full attention.

"My mother spoiled the hell out of me," I told her. "Make no mistake, she loved Anna. But she thought the sun rose and set with me. Anna's my dad's. He loves me and taught me how to be a good and decent man. Lots of lessons while I was growing up, but the most important one was how he loved the women in his life. My sister is Dad's favorite, his princess. My mother was the queen of his world. He taught me by example how to love to an extreme. But my mom was all about me. Her and Anna were close, very close, especially when Anna got older and in high school. Mom was always doing stuff with her.

"Don't take this the wrong way; I'm not looking for a mommy, I don't need a woman to take care of me, but my mom taught me how I should expect a woman to love me. And that has nothing to do with her spoiling me. She openly adored my dad, loved the family they created. But if I had to guess, what she loved the most was the way her husband loved his daughter. I want to give that to my family. I want to give to my wife what my father gave to my mother, so my wife can give to my children what my mom gave me."

Cat untwined our fingers, lifted her hand, and traced the line of my jaw.

"I love the way she loved you," she whispered.

"I do too."

That was an understatement.

"I love the way you love her."

I remained quiet. Cat continued tracing my jaw up to my temple and back down, her eyes following her finger. A soft, sweet touch.

"What's your mom's name?" she asked.

"Nora."

Her eyes dashed to mine and flared.

"Nora? Really?"

I nodded, not understanding the sudden change.

"That's my gran's name. Nora Mae. My mom's name is Faye Nora, after her mother."

My hand shot out and tagged her around the back of her neck. I tugged her closer until our foreheads touched. My sinuses clogged, and I felt my eyes itch.

"My sister tried to name her first daughter Nora," I told Cat. "My dad explained the DEFCON-level war she'd start if she took that name from me. Anna chose another name."

"Then it's decided," Catarina whispered.

"It's decided," I confirmed.

"I have Lina, Steven, Lars, Lauren, and the heathen twins, and that's all I have."

I didn't understand where she was going, so I remained quiet and waited for her to continue.

"I'm not ready yet. I need a few more years of doing what I'm doing. I still have the fire in my belly. But when the time's right, I want a big family, and I want to be home with that family. I don't want my babies losing me like I lost my mom. I want them to have what you had. I want to spoil my boys and give my Nora a daddy who thinks she's a princess and will love her and tell her the sun rises and sets with her."

Give my Nora a daddy who thinks she's a princess.

Goddamn, I wanted that with Catarina more than I'd ever wanted anything other than my mother to still be alive.

I had to sniff and clear my throat before I could tell her, "When you're ready, I'll give you everything you want."

"A few years, but no more than four. If I see the words *geriatric pregnancy* on a single form, I will lose my shit, and it might get messy. Lauren might have to dip into the heathens' bail account to get me out of jail."

And my smart-ass Catarina was back.

"I'll make sure to fill out all the medical paperwork. We can't have my baby mama in lockup."

"That might be a good idea. Or we can have an at-home birth."

I held my breath waiting for her to tell me she was kidding. That wait was in vain. And with that, an irrational fear about something that had not happened and would not happen for years to come started pooling in my gut.

"Baby, you are not giving birth to our children at home. You'll be in a hospital with medical professionals."

"Women have babies at home every day."

The insanity of that stunned me into silence.

"Nothing to say to that?" she hedged.

"I reserve the right to circle back to this conversation at such time an appropriate comeback pops into my head."

"Nope. Gotta be quick, Jack. No comeback, you lose."

Seeing as we were discussing our future children, there was no losing when it came to this conversation.

Future children with Catarina.

"You realize we're planning where you'll give birth to our children in the parking lot of the In-N-Out off Coronado Avenue."

Cat tipped her chin, pulled her forehead off mine, and pressed a kiss to my mouth.

"The *where* is never important. The *who* is."

"Remember this morning when I was being all sweet, hearts, and flowers?" I asked.

"Feel like that was five hundred years ago, but yes, I remember you telling me how bodacious my breasts are."

I couldn't stop my laugh from spilling out.

"I was going to say, I forgot to include wise in the list of things that are perfect about you. But since you used the word *bodacious*, I'm retracting my amendment."

Catarina pressed her lips against mine again. This time, she didn't pull away far when she mumbled, "Admit it, you love me."

Like gasoline to fire, my heart lit.

"No, baby, I love the fuck out of you."

I felt her smile against my lips.

"I love the fuck out of you too."

She was right, it was the *who* you were with that was important.

But right then, as those words settled deep in my soul—the *where* was important too. Where we were going together. The future we'd have. The mistakes we would make. The forgiveness we would need. The love we'd give each other. The family we would make.

Chapter Eighteen

Pete had not exaggerated.

But what he'd left out was that Jack's house was staged—as in, it was a show house.

"This is freaking me out," I told him.

He'd given me a mini tour of the downstairs, with the promise he'd show me the rest tomorrow. I didn't quibble. My belly was full of the best hamburgers on the planet, I'd slurped down a milkshake, and now all I wanted was to brush my teeth and fall into bed.

But seriously, his house was giving me a complex. I wasn't sure if I could live in a house that looked staged and ready to sell. Hell, I didn't think *he* should live in this house. Not because he didn't deserve nice things, but no part of this house that I'd seen was relaxing and inviting. None of the couches—yes, he had more than one; he had four—said "Sit and chill while catching up on Netflix and eating Doritos."

Jack remained silent and directed me into the master bedroom—his huge bedroom. And decorating this room was furniture that looked heavy and expensive. But what caught my attention besides the four-poster bed were the double doors that led out to a balcony. I only had a few seconds to take in his room before we stepped into his bathroom.

"Okay, I've changed my mind," I breathed, taking in the splendor of the en suite. "I could live in here."

"I bought this house as an investment," he told me. "I also bought it fully furnished. It's too much house for me. It was also more than I wanted to spend. But this bathroom and the deck off the back, which you'll see tomorrow, is why I bought this place. The balcony off the bedroom isn't bad, but the deck is peaceful with a great view of the ocean. The sunsets can't be beat. I'm rarely here, so I don't use the furniture—which I don't like, but it'll help sell the house. Even though I spent more than I wanted, I still got this house for a steal. It had fallen out of escrow twice. The sellers had already bought a new house in Montana and moved. They needed to dump this place. Pete knows the agent who was listing it. I came in with a cash offer, they knocked down the price, and I bought it. You wanna sell the furniture and replace it with yours or buy new, we can do that. But I have more than a year left before I can sell so I don't get nailed with capital gains tax."

Shit. He thought I didn't like his house.

"I didn't mean . . . I was joking. Your house is beautiful. It's a showplace."

"What I'm trying to tell you is, I'm not married to this house. I never planned on staying in this house. You're right; it's a showplace, not a family home. It has no yard. And floor-to-ceiling windows that would give me a heart attack to have a toddler bang on. But until we can sell and move, I want you to be comfortable."

At that moment, Jack surely didn't look comfortable; he looked the extreme opposite of that.

He kept saying "we" in regard to the house. Obviously, he hadn't changed his mind about me moving to California.

"Okay, Jack, I'm just going to come right out and ask. What's going on?"

Both his hands came up and he pawed through his hair. Now I was freaking out, and not in the kidding way.

"Jack?"

"I want you to move in here with me. You said you were moving to San Diego, but you didn't specify where. I want you here."

If it was possible for a heart to pound so hard it broke ribs, mine would've.

"And you're afraid I won't like your mansion on the water with staging furniture, and I'll opt for an apartment to move into instead."

"Something like that," he grunted.

I'd never seen Jack unsure of himself. I'd call it cute, but it wasn't, not when what he was unsure about was me.

"Jack, honey, I don't care where I live as long as it's with you. This place is off-the-charts gorgeous. If you want to sell it in a few years, sell it. If you want to stay and raise fifteen kids here, then that's what we'll do. If you want to move to Alaska to be next to your family, then that's where we go."

"Cat—"

I reached up and pressed my fingers against his lips to silence him.

"I've been worried. I see what you're doing, how you're fighting who you are to give me what I need right now. I was scared that you were giving up more than I was. That the scales were tipped so far in my direction that I'd be unable to even it out. But I was looking at it all wrong. I was thinking about it in the short term when we're playing the long game. We'll work it out, Jack. The only thing that needs to be decided has been decided—the rest, the details, those don't matter."

With my fingers still on his lips he asked, "Fifteen kids?"

I shrugged. "I'm an only child. I grew up with my gran but no other family around. Are you not up for the challenge?"

I felt Jack's lips twitch under my fingertips. "Up to the challenge of making fifteen babies, fuck yeah. Raising all those little fuckers, no. And I'm man enough to admit when I'm visiting my sister and her four are running around, that's about my limit. We have four boys, we'll have a fifth in hopes it's a girl. We have four girls, we're stopping."

"Um, no. If we have four girls, we're having a fifth so I get my boy."

Jack's eyes went soft. In the dim light of the bathroom, they were black. I hoped my future boys got their daddy's eyes.

"Decided."

"See? We're already rockin' the hell out of this relationship gig."

One minute Jack was standing in front of me, laughing at my stupidity, the next his arms were around me and his tongue was in my mouth. I had yet to decide which I liked more, making him laugh or him kissing me, when he broke the kiss.

"You wanna shower before bed?"

I glanced over at his magnificent walk-in shower and suddenly wanted to wash off my day.

"Yeah."

"I'm gonna go lock up and set the alarm. I'll be back up in a few minutes to join you."

"'Kay."

I didn't know how long it had taken Jack to come back. It could've been the few minutes he said it would be or it could've been an hour. Once I was under his rainfall showerhead and the hot water was rinsing my long day down the drain, I lost track of time. I was in a daze of magical shower euphoria, but not enough of one that I missed Jack's big, naked body against my back.

"I like your shower."

"*Our* shower," he corrected.

"I was thinking on the plane, I'll keep my place in Arizona. We can Airbnb it for now. If it turns into a pain in the ass, we'll sell."

"Whatever you want."

Jack. That was all I wanted.

That was easy.

I turned in his arms and looked up at him. "I feel small next to you."

He frowned immediately. "I don't ever want you to feel small."

Good Lord, could I love this man any more?

A few seconds later, when he reached behind me and grabbed a bottle of shampoo, I learned I could.

"Turn back around."

I turned.

Jack commenced washing my hair. Strong hands massaged my scalp around my temples before lathering the strands.

"That feels amazing," I groaned.

"Are you gonna leave your hair this color?"

It took me a moment to realize what he'd asked. "You don't like me with brown hair?"

"Honestly, when I first saw the color, I was pissed. I fell in love with you as a blonde; that's how you came to me in my dreams. Seeing that gone was like a punch to the gut. But now I'm used to it. You're gorgeous either way."

That's how you came to me in my dreams.

I spun to face him, tilted my head up, and forgot I had shampoo in my hair until I had suds in my eyes.

"Ouch." I closed my eyes and muscled my way under the spray to wash off my face.

I felt Jack's hand swipe my forehead. "Jesus, baby, what the fuck?"

My hands bumped into his as I tried to get the soap out of my eyes.

I chanced reopening my eyes. I gave it a second. When I didn't feel the burn, I asked, "You dreamed of me?"

He moved me back under the spray. "Close your eyes and tip your head back."

I did as he asked. He went to work rinsing the shampoo out.

"I dreamed of us in Las Vegas, just the two of us there, having fun. I dreamed of waking up next to you in my bed in my Idaho house. I dreamed of us horseback riding—and baby, I gotta admit, that one threw me. My ass has never been on the back of a horse, and I have no interest in ever riding."

My body started shaking with laughter. "Well, I moved to Texas after Gran died, so I have been on the back of a horse, and I'm not a fan."

"I dreamed of me kissing you, us making love. I dreamed about eating your pussy, you giving me head."

I felt myself smile. "Was it good?"

"Hell yeah. Woke up hard, jerked off to my dream Cat."

His hands went to my shoulders, and he turned me. I took that as I was clear to open my eyes.

"I missed you when you were gone. So many times I had your number pulled up on my phone, but I couldn't get myself to call. I was afraid to hear your voice. I'd convinced myself that if I really loved you, I had to stay away from you. I had to let you go so I didn't suffocate you. In my stupidity, it never occurred to me that I was the problem. That to have you, all I had to do was trust you. It was my fuckup. And I hope you know how sorry I am."

And there he did it again, made me love him even more.

"You're talented, Jack Donovan. I think you're the only man on the planet who can turn me on one second and make me feel warm and melty the next."

"I'm good like that, baby."

I stopped teasing and got serious.

"I missed you too. And I had your number. I should've called you, but the way things ended, I was afraid I'd messed everything up and you hated me."

Watching Jack walk away had been the worst. Worse than the worst. I had felt my heart break and hadn't thought it'd ever be whole again.

"I could never hate you, Catarina."

Jack leaned forward, his mouth aiming for mine, so I rolled up on my toes and met him halfway.

And just because he was Jack—not only talented but an overachiever—he had me turned on and panting into his mouth while that warm and melty feeling was still coursing through me.

Chapter Nineteen

"Jack."

Catarina's neck arched with her moan.

My hips pumped faster. Her sleek, tight wet clutched my cock.

"Jack."

Her pussy clenched tight.

There it was, my name falling from her lips while she went over the edge.

My mouth slammed over Catarina's to capture her groan, and I powered in harder. I fucked her through her orgasm. Pulses turned into flutters. I broke the kiss and pulled out.

"Knees."

It took Catarina a moment to focus on my command, but then she scrambled to do my bidding.

"Cheek to the bed."

She did that too.

My hands went to her hips, my eyes fell to her perfect ass perched high. On their own accord, my palms slid down over her ass.

"Time for your spanking, baby."

I saw her cheeks clench, followed by a shiver.

"Whatever you want, Jack."

The dichotomy of emotions hit me. The need to possess and mark her mixed with overwhelming love and affection. The need to fuck her so hard she'd feel my possession, and the need to slowly caress and make love to her.

"Right now, I want to turn your ass red." My hands slowly drifted over smooth skin. "I want to see my handprint on your ass while I'm taking you. I want to hear you mindless. I want you to feel me so deep you never forget who you belong to."

"Then do it."

My cock jerked, straining to get back inside. I dipped down, found her slick opening, and slammed home. Tight heat welcomed my intrusion.

My hips pulled back. On an inward glide, my palm came down with a smack. Cat's pussy rippled. Oh yeah, my girl was going to take her spanking and love it. Two more thrusts followed by cracks to her ass had color blooming.

"More?"

"Yes."

Her groan drowned out the sound of my palm landing on her ass. I rubbed away the sting and drove my hips forward.

"You gonna come for me again, Catarina?"

"You gonna make me?"

Christ, I loved her smart-ass mouth.

I bent over her, brushing her tangled mess of hair off her back and face as I went. With my chest flush to her back, my cock buried as deep as I could get, I gently kissed her temple.

"Baby, I'm gonna make you see stars."

Then I set about doing just that. This was not fucking. It wasn't lovemaking. It was primal instinct. There was no rhythm to my thrusts as I drove into her. Pure madness. Raw, savage need to rut. To make her feel the pleasure she was giving me. To pull the sweet mews from her lips. I didn't want to claim, I wanted her to surrender—to relinquish herself to me.

"Do you love me?"

"Yes."

"Tell me," I demanded.

"I love you, Jack."

I unfolded, came up on my knees, grabbed her hip with one hand while the other one snaked around her belly, down, and found her clit.

"Again."

"Oh my God," she moaned and bucked her hips.

"Tell. Me," I commanded.

Her pussy quivered and clutched, bringing me closer to blowing. My finger on her clit pressed harder. Relentless in my pursuit to get what I wanted.

"Now, Catarina. Tell me."

"I love you."

On a long groan she flew apart, bucking so hard my hand slid from her hip to her back to hold her down.

"Yeah, baby, you love me. Don't ever forget it."

"I . . . God . . . I won't, Jack."

My gaze fell to her red ass. *All mine.* It dropped lower. I watched our connection, my cock tunneling into her, coming out wet with her excitement, driving back in until it became too much, and I exploded with a violent shudder.

I slammed in, stayed planted, and let her pussy drain me dry.

"I love you so much it scares me, baby," I groaned through my climax.

The tension waned, my muscles relaxed, and I slowly glided in and out, watching myself take her gentle after I'd fucked her rough.

My hand slid over the pink mark on her ass. "This okay?"

"Oh yeah."

"You sure I didn't hurt you?"

"Only in the best of ways. That was . . ." She trailed off.

When she didn't finish, I glanced up at her face. Her pretty face flushed with sex, her eyes clear and soft.

"Animalistic," she finished.

She wasn't wrong. The woman turned me into a straight-up animal.

I pulled out. Kissed the mark on her ass, rolled to my side, pulled her with me, and fitted my chest to her back. Catarina snuggled back and tangled our legs together.

"Do we have time to snooze?" she said as she yawned.

"Yeah, baby. We're not meeting the team for another few hours."

It didn't take long for Cat's breaths to even out and her body to go lax.

I wasn't the type to lie in bed and cuddle. When I was awake, I was up. I had better things to do than laze around. But I couldn't get myself to let her go.

This was not the first morning I'd woken up to Catarina wrapped around me. But it was the first we'd woken up together in our bed, with no bad guys lurking. No immediate threat of danger.

Yet, there would be soon.

We'd be leaving for Mexico, on a favor for a shady CIA officer who I didn't trust. Catarina would be back in the field, in the line of fire.

That scared the fuck out of me.

I thought back to our conversation on the drive home from the airport. We were talking about having babies. Then I went to the conversation in the bathroom before our shower—long term, our future. I wanted that—all of it. Marriage, children, the whole thing. I just needed her to be with me to have it.

I blew out a breath.

Catarina was well trained, skilled, smart. But that didn't mean that reckless streak had dissolved.

Fuck.

I kissed the back of Cat's head and rolled out of bed.

I needed a workout and to make a call, not in that order. I grabbed a clean pair of sweats out of my dresser, went into the bathroom, cleaned up, tagged my phone off the nightstand, and made my way downstairs, scrolling through my contacts until I found the one I needed.

"It's early," Lincoln Parker answered.

I couldn't call the man a close friend, but he was a friend. He also had married a woman who was arguably more badass than Catarina, and that argument would be flimsy. Both women were insanely tough.

"If you're not busy, I need some advice."

"Whatcha got."

"It's personal," I warned.

I heard him chuckle.

"A woman's got you tied in knots," he rightly surmised.

"Catarina Keys."

Linc whistled before he said, "Damn, brother. Jasmin met with her a few months back, tried to get her to come work with us at Z Corps. Cat turned my wife down. To say she was bummed would be an understatement. She's wanted Catarina Keys on our team for a long time. Jasmin's of the mind they're twins born a few years apart by different mothers."

I knew Jasmin had approached Cat after our mission in Las Vegas. It had been an excruciating debriefing with Wilson McCray as we wrapped up our final report on the mission. At the time, I was doing everything I could to stop myself from calling Cat. Unfortunately, it was a battle I'd won, and I lost time with her.

"How do you do it?" I cut to it.

"Do what?"

"Not lose your mind every time Jasmin goes out on a mission?"

"Who the hell says I don't? Brother, you think watching her strap a vest on is easy? That I haven't had to stop myself from ripping the damn thing off her body and cuffing her to the desk to keep her ass in the office? Every. Damn. Time."

They'd been together years, had twin boys, and by the sound of it, he still struggled.

"So you're telling me it doesn't get any better?"

"Oh, it gets better. As the months slip into years and I get to wake up every morning with my wife at my side and my boys causing mayhem and chaos, it *keeps* getting better. But does seeing my wife put herself in danger get easier? Fuck no."

I opened the cupboard to pull out the coffee canister and noted, "This isn't making me feel any better."

"Well, shit, Jack, I didn't know you wanted me to lie."

I stared at the counter, feeling the burn in my chest getting hotter.

"I can't fuck this up," I mumbled.

"Then don't."

Easier said than done when I had an anvil sitting in my gut and we were close to going back out.

"It goes against the grain," he started. "We're the protectors. We provide the shield. It's hard for men like us to fathom it any other way. But, Jack, you hooked up with a woman who is exactly like you. *She's* the protector. *She's* the shield. Now ask yourself: The man you are, would you have it any other way?"

I didn't need to search my feelings. I didn't need to think about my response. Unreservedly, the answer was no. I'd always known I'd need a strong woman at my side. I'd need someone to push back and keep me in check. I needed a partner.

"It's a double-edged sword, Jack," he went on. "Both edges slice—yours and hers. Dulling her side doesn't make yours sharper, it weakens the sword. She will be your greatest asset and your greatest weakness in battle. It doesn't get easier, but none of it is. The things we see, the things we do, none of that is easy."

He wasn't wrong. Nothing about the jobs we did was easy. Each time we went out, we came home with new marks on our souls.

"But I can tell you this, watching my woman do her thing—kick ass, be that shield, rescue hostages, protect those who need her protection, whatever the mission calls for—the one thing I always feel is pride. Here's this badass, tough warrior princess, and she chose me. She doesn't need me to keep her safe. She's saved my ass many times, she's been *my* shield more times than I can count.

"Here's the trick, Jack. What you need to remember is, you're strong with her at your back. Together, you make the sword. Two shields cover front *and* back. Learn to use her strength in battle and the two of you become unstoppable."

Fuck.

There it was.

What I needed.

"Thanks, brother."

"You get what you needed?"

I leaned my hip against the counter and looked out the window. The morning sun shone over the ocean. And not for the first time, it hit me. I indeed had everything I needed, only now I was armed with Lincoln's wisdom.

"Yeah, brother, I appreciate you taking the time to give that to me."

"Anytime."

The topic changed to his boys and their antics, what was going on in Maryland, and the new case they were working on. Linc's brother Zane wasn't fond of the CIA; he worked with them when it suited him and benefited his company. But if the juice wasn't worth the squeeze, he told them to kick rocks.

"You ever heard of CIA Officer Tom Washington?"

"No, but I can ask around about him."

"We've got Shep on it, but if you wouldn't mind asking your team, it wouldn't go unappreciated."

"Something in particular you're after?"

I filled him in on our last mission—Catarina being tagged and her phones being tracked—and Tom's excuse for plausible deniability and Calista being wanted for murder.

"I have heard about Calista Ventura," he informed me. "She's wanted for questioning in the deaths of three men. One of them is Victor Stone."

"Do you know anything about that?"

"Victor was a congressional aide. The other two were lawyers, lived in Virginia, worked in DC, and they were found dead in the home of a White House staffer. Haven't heard anything on motive. Though Stone's got a reputation of being a monumental asshole."

"What kind of asshole?"

"The kind who thinks buying a woman dinner means he's owed something in return. No formal complaints had been filed, but word was he didn't like being denied what he thought he paid for."

Monumental asshole didn't begin to cover the special kind of fuckwad Stone was.

Hopefully, Shep would have more for us by the time we got up the mountain.

"Something feels off," I told Linc.

"Something's always off with the CIA."

No truer words.

"Part of me gets why Tom would want to meet off US soil. I also get why he'd tag and track his asset. But the timing of it with the president's wife and kids being part of the target package is the coincidence I'm struggling with."

"You said Tom's helped Berta in the past; could be that he really did want the use of her network to help Calista? Though, it'd be a win-win for him to have the whereabouts of the president's family in his back pocket, should he need it in the future. But if Berta's smart, and I know her reputation so I know she is, the wife and kids will be shuffled around until they're lost, never to be found."

I hoped that was the case.

"But," Linc continued, "I've been dealing with the CIA for a long time, and I've never known one who wasn't an opportunist, and that includes the former case officers who work for us." There was humor in his tone. "Thankfully, they're now on our side, and we get the benefit of their manipulation."

"Good to know those skills didn't go to waste."

I heard footfalls padding through the living room.

I turned, and my breath arrested.

She'd pulled on the T-shirt I'd tossed on the floor last night when I got home.

"Cat's up, gotta go."

"I bet you do."

I watched her walk into the dining area and stop by the floor-to-ceiling windows.

"Thanks again."

"Anytime. I'll hit you back when I know something."

Linc disconnected. I tossed my phone on the counter and made my way to Cat.

"You were right about this deck. The view is amazing."

She wasn't wrong about the view, but I wasn't looking at the beach.

Pride hit fast and furious.

Catarina had chosen me.

I could lie to myself and say I claimed her, but the truth was, Catarina did the claiming. She was a high-value woman, and there was no way she'd settle for anything less than what she thought was the best. She'd claim *her* mate, the strongest of the pack, *her* partner.

Lincoln Parker was one smart son of a bitch.

Chapter Twenty

I glanced around the Dirty Plank, leaned closer to Jack, and whispered, "Don't tell the guys, but In-N-Out is better."

He busted out laughing.

It was lunchtime. The place was hopping. Jack hadn't told me anything about the place so I hadn't known what to expect, but even if he had, I still wouldn't have envisioned an upscale tiki bar right on Seacoast Drive. There was outside seating with a view of the Portwood Pier Plaza and the Imperial Beach Pier. Rent on this place had to be wack. Though with all the tables full and every stool taken at the bar, I'd bet they turned a mighty profit.

"My lips are sealed."

God, I hoped not; he made magic with those lips and tongue.

"Can I get you two anything else?" our server, Chloe, asked.

I shook my head.

"No thanks, Chloe."

"I'll put it on your tab. Have a good day."

I glanced from the very beautiful woman to Jack. "Tab?"

"What she means is trash," Jack explained. "When I first started coming here, I tried paying. None of the guys would let me. I got sick of arguing so I just leave a big tip. The guys don't say shit about that because they like their people being taken care of."

That was cool of the guys.

"Pete said someone always rotates out and stays back at the bar. Does that include you?"

"Yeah. A month after I got here, the guys went out for a few days. I stayed behind. They'll probably ask you to pitch in too."

I took another look around the room. There were no cheesy palm thatch decorations like in a traditional tiki bar. Instead, it was a mix of surfer and Team Guy. The guys had played off the old Navy tradition of original crew members being Plank Owners. There was a huge slice of live-edge wood hanging behind the bar. A Trident was burned into the far right side; on the left, Big Navy's anchor insignia. Between the symbols, a rusty rectangle of metal was screwed into the wood with the words **HERE I AM. SEND ME.** engraved on it.

Isaiah 6:8.

The monstrosity was out of place, yet it fit perfectly.

Those five words embodied the men who owned the bar. Rotating out, leaving one behind, but all of them wanting to be the one to charge into battle.

The walls were cluttered with surfboards, wood skimboards, beer brand plaques, stickers of all kinds. There were a few framed black-and-white pictures of the guys together in various places around the room, all in uniform. It was cool and hip.

Right now the patrons were fifty-fifty male, female. Couples, women having lunch together, men sitting at the bar. The vibe was chill and relaxed. I'd guess the evening crowd would be the same ratio of men and women, but no doubt the vibe would be different. Women would be on the prowl.

"How rowdy does this place get at night?" I asked.

Jack's lips twitched, and his brow raised.

"Frog Hog heaven?" I guessed.

"Nailed it," he told me.

I got it, men in uniform were hot. In the Army, there were plenty of Barrack Bunnies sniffing around, looking for a soldier to spend the night with, but they weren't all that picky. Sure, you had the ones who could spot a Ranger or Spec Ops guy, but for the most part they were after any hot guy in a uniform.

But the women who sought out Frogmen were a whole different breed. They could spot a color or a number from a mile away. Though West Coast Frog Hogs didn't need that added sixth sense, seeing as Group One only had numbered teams. The East Coast women were like heat-seeking missiles with the accuracy of their hunt. There was Group Two, whose teams were numbered, then there was DEVGRU—the holy grail for a Frog Hog—and they were grouped into colors. If a woman could sniff out a Red Team guy and get him to take her home, that would be akin to winning a gold medal.

No joke.

They took the hunt to an extreme.

My eyes skated back to Jack, my head tipped, then I asked the stupidest question a woman could ask her man. "How many women have you—"

"None."

"You didn't let me finish."

"Don't need to. I've never taken a woman home from this bar."

I didn't need to probe or prod, I believed him.

But he'd said "this bar."

"Will I be running into your women from other bars—"

"There were no other women. Not in Idaho and not here, not since I met you. There was only my hand and you in my mind."

Nine months.

He'd gone nine months with no woman. And I didn't think it was because he was waiting for me, when he said himself he never thought he'd see me again.

"What about you?"

I didn't miss his hands on the table curling into fists, bracing for my answer. I'd be lying if I said that didn't send happy tingles up my arms.

"No one." His relief was palpable, but there was a small detail I needed to be honest about. "I did go out on a date." His gaze journeyed to mine, and his eyes narrowed. "Before I moved to Arizona. A friend asked me to go with her on a double date. I went, mainly because I was bored, but I also wanted to test the waters, see if I could get over you. He was a cool guy. Interesting, high-speed job, driven, ambitious. But five minutes into talking to him, there was nothing. Then I spent the rest of the dinner pissed off and missing you. We said goodbye at the restaurant with a handshake."

"High-speed job?"

"He flew Hornets out of Oceana."

"An F-18 pilot."

I didn't answer because there was no need. Jack obviously knew what a Hornet was.

A slow smile pulled at his lips. "Good to know I beat out the sky jockey."

I rolled my eyes.

"You ready to get out of here? Pete's place in Jamul is about forty-five minutes away."

No, I wasn't ready. This was nice, it was normal, just me and Jack eating lunch.

A date.

I was on a date with Jack Donovan.

The absurdity of that hit me. I'd slept with the man. I'd admitted I loved him, wanted to have his children, we'd already named one, and here we were on our first date.

He reached his hand across the table, pulled mine closer to the middle, and commenced tracing my fingers with his.

"It's funny," he said.

My eyes flicked from our hands to his face.

"We did it backward."

It was a little freaky how he could read my mind.

"We did," I confirmed.

"I like the way we did it."

My lips pulled up into a smile. "I bet. You didn't even have to buy me dinner before I gave up the goods."

Jack's eyelids slowly lowered. The gesture would've worried me if his shoulders weren't shaking with silent laughter.

"Smart-ass."

Yup.

That was me.

Totally a smart-ass with zero concern I had to pretend I was someone I wasn't.

I was me.

And Jack Donovan T-totally loved me.

Chapter Twenty-One

"It's beautiful up here," Cat said, craning her neck to look out her window down the steep ravine. "I know California's not the only state like this, but I've always found it interesting that you can be at the beach, then an hour later be deep into the mountains or a vineyard. You can see the most beautiful redwoods, then a few hours later see a castle."

She wasn't wrong; the juxtaposition was striking. The traffic was horrendous but the natural beauty was, in my opinion, only second to what Idaho had to offer. Though Idaho didn't have beaches, they had lakes, and it won out mainly because there were fewer people and less traffic. I'd give up the year-round nice weather and the beach not to spend my life stuck in gridlock.

"Have you spent much time here?"

"Not really. I did a temporary duty assignment at Fort Irwin and some training at NAS Lemoore and a two-week stopover at Travis. When I left Lemoore, I rented a convertible, took three days, and did the whole touristy thing. Drove PCH from San Francisco to San Diego and flew back to Bragg out of SD."

She paused, and I felt her gaze come to me.

"For the record, I rented a Ford. I fell in love with the Mustang and decided one day I would own one."

There was something behind the Ford comment that was more than a dig at car manufacturers.

"What about the Ford made you fall in love?"

"It was the first time I felt free."

My heart clutched at her soft admission.

"I went from . . . well, you know, I told you about it . . . to the Army. My life was not my own. I was told what to do, where to go, and when I got there I was given more orders. But I found I liked the structure. I needed it after so much disorder. I think that's what I saw in Steven when he came home to visit. He was settled, it changed everything about him. I wanted that. I needed a break from the chaos and worry about where I was going, who next was going to take in the poor orphan. Not that Lina ever gave me the impression she wanted me to go, but it was still in me.

"But those three days with the top down, cruising down PCH, my life was mine. I was in control. I stopped where I wanted, I saw what I wanted to see, I slept where I wanted. I was free. Every decision was mine. I had three days to think. Three days with myself to reflect on the life I'd been given—from my parents dying, losing my grandmother, to the assholes I was forced to live with. Lina, Steven, Lars. All of it. Somewhere around Morro Bay, things started to come clear. I stopped for the night in this place called Goleta. Before I left, I stopped at the beach. There's this long wooden pier. I walked to the end—mountains and ocean. It was so beautiful, I stayed out there for a long time thinking.

"It was there I realized that my breaths were finite. I only had so many of them before they were gone. I could spend the rest of them dwelling on the assholes in my life, or I could stop giving them precious headspace and move on. I gave them one final breath on that pier and moved on. I got back into the Mustang, turned the radio on for the first time since I'd started the drive, and spent the next two days with the music blaring, using my breath to sing at the top of my lungs.

"By the time I turned that rental in, it was gone. All the resentment, the bitterness, the anger. So while my life belonged to the Army, my breath belonged to me."

The puzzle that was Catarina Keys clicked into place, and the whole picture formed. And I wondered if she had any clue the strength of mind she possessed. With the way she'd told the story of a life-changing epiphany, I doubted it. She'd made it sound like her mental fortitude was commonplace instead of extraordinary. Most people did not have it in themselves to face the past—what'd been done to them, what hadn't happened, what they missed out on, regret. It's easier to bury the pain instead of facing it, reflecting, then freeing it from their minds. The problem with that was, it festered. The lesion was always there just under the surface, filling with poison. But the pain of bloodletting the trauma was so excruciating, for some, living with the toxin was easier.

I'd lived on both sides of that coin. I still had shit buried I would never unpack from my days in the Navy. Things I saw, but mostly what I'd heard—the screams, the sobs, the tremble in voices, the last breaths. Shit that I couldn't force my mind to relive.

"Favor, baby."

"What's that?"

"Twice now you've given me important pieces of you. Twice I've been driving and can't give you the attention I want when I learn more about your remarkable strength. Do me a favor and next time, wait until I'm not behind the wheel and I can properly tell you how fucking astoundingly special you are."

"I think you just told me," she whispered.

"I haven't scratched the surface, but as you wisely said last night, we're playing the long game, so I have a lifetime of showing you."

"And I'm not special," she parried.

"You are very wrong about that, Catarina," I told her and pulled onto the dirt road that led to Pete's mountain compound. "But we're here, and this is one of those conversations that shouldn't be had while I'm driving."

Cat leaned forward and stared out the windshield at the gateway sign.

"Downrange." She noted the sign. "That's . . . succinct."

"I think it says what it needs to say." I chuckled. "Pete's got eighty acres. We come up here to train."

"Where ya goin', honey?" she started in a fake and horrible Texan twang. Then switched to an equally fake but much worse male version of her exaggerated Texan accent. "Headed *downrange*, darlin'."

"You forgot the best part," I noted.

"What's that?"

"Headed downrange to blow shit up."

Cat sat back and crossed her arms over her chest. "You left that part out. What else does Pete have up here?"

"A shoot house, two pistol ranges, a sniper field, and long-range lanes set up. There are three houses—he lives in the main house, Beck lives in one of them, the other is guest quarters. There's three Quonset huts we use for storage for gear and several outbuildings."

"Who's Beck?"

"Beckett Yates. He's former DEA. I met him when I was up in Idaho with Takeback. He was undercover in a motorcycle club."

"The Horse Heads . . . or something like that?"

"The Horsemen," I corrected. "He was with them for years. I got no problem with MCs. A lot of clubs are geared toward former military or law enforcement. A brotherhood with a shared passion. But there are some, like the Horsemen, who are rotten. There wasn't a good man in that club. Drugs, prostitution, extortion. Beck lived and breathed depravity. That shit ended for him before Vegas, and he's adjusting to life outside that filth."

"Is he part of Pete's crew?"

"Yes and no. He lives up here and takes care of the gear, keeps the shooting ranges maintained, and other upkeep besides. What he doesn't do is go on ops with the guys. Neither does he go to the Dirty Plank to drink. If he makes the trek to IB, it's to come by my place or Mason's. The man doesn't do bars or restaurants. And Pete has told the rest of us Beck does his grocery shopping at night when it's less crowded."

"PTSD?"

We were approaching the main house, so I slowed.

"Not the way you're thinking, but yes. He lived so long with the stench of those assholes it seeped in. Part of that was submerging himself into the criminal lifestyle and living like one. He's having a hard time shaking it off. I get what he's going through, and I'm sure you do too. When you separate from the military, you lose a part of your identity. That transition is hard enough, but Beck's got that twofold; he has to shed the criminal he became *and* law enforcement officer."

Catarina was quiet for a moment.

"Duality," she murmured. "The lawman and the felon. Who does he shed first?"

"Yup. And how does he reconcile the crimes he committed, the laws he broke, when he'd taken an oath to protect and serve? It's easy to say he had to commit those crimes to keep his cover. It's harder to believe that to be true."

"Damn."

Damn was right.

I parked next to Mason's Ram and shut my Chevy down.

"If I told you to wait so I can come around to open your door, would you listen?"

When we'd stopped for lunch, she'd jumped out before I could get to her side of the truck.

"No, but if you *ask*, I'd consider it."

"How's this? Please keep your ass in the truck until I come around."

Cat rolled her eyes.

"That's not asking, that's using the word *please* in a command, and I only listen to those when I'm naked and promised orgasms."

Her eyes danced with humor—a stolen moment before we went inside to start planning a new op. A moment I didn't want to end, and not because I was worried about Catarina being a part of the mission. I just didn't want to have to share her. Not now, not so soon. I wanted more time before we were back at it again.

The long game.

"Good girls get good things."

The humor sped out of her eyes and desire sparked to life.

"What do bad girls get?"

"Spankings."

Cat opened her door, jumped down, and with a smile and a wink, she slammed it, effectively closing me in the truck while I roared with laughter.

Smart-ass.

Pete had just finished telling the team what had happened in Juárez with Rafael Quintero and the threats he'd unwisely made against my friend Cole's wife, Mia. Yes, she was Pete's sister, but the anger burning through me was for Cole. He should've been told. Takeback as a whole should've been told we needed to keep an eye on the situation, to make sure the danger in Mexico wasn't going to make its way up north. Further from that, they needed to know now, because Mia was currently operating with them.

"You need to tell Cole."

Pete's not-so-happy gaze landed on me. "Rafael's been taken care of."

"And Carlos? Unless Tom is full of shit, you have a credible threat gunning for your sister, yet you've got some hang-up about telling her team that I don't get."

"He'll *be* taken care of," Mason put in.

"As fun as it would be to tear through Juárez and liberate the people from the cartels, you know that's not gonna happen. Carlos goes down, within a week someone will take his place."

"It'll be—"

I cut Mason off. "Cut the shit, you're not a murderer. You're not gonna track down every male relative and preemptively kill them. There will always be a threat, and Cole needs to know. Again, I don't understand what the big fucking deal is."

"So your loyalty is with Cole?" Mason seethed.

From beside me on the couch, Catarina grabbed my forearm.

"That was way the fuck out of line," Fallon piped up. "Jack's right, Cole needs to be told. But you know who else needs to know? Mia. But, hey, you wanna talk about loyalty, Mase? You got Pete's back on this but don't talk to the rest of us?"

"Fuck," Pete growled and got to his feet. "This is on me, not Mason."

"You're right, it is," Ryan easily put in.

I glanced over to the table off to the side where Aiden and Gavin were sitting. Both had identical frowns.

Ryan and Fallon were sitting on a couch at opposite sides, an empty cushion separating them. Mason was in a chair next to Ryan, and Fallon across from where Cat and I were sitting.

Pete was now pacing.

The room wasn't huge, but it was big. Still, it was now suffocating. Every man in the room was giving off seriously pissed-off vibes.

"I fucked up," Pete admitted. Then growled, "She's my *sister*. She's all I have. Fuck." He tore his hands through his short-cropped hair. "I lost it. The women he had, and the little . . . fuck, she was a kid. A little fucking girl. I snapped. He had my sister's picture. He said . . . Christ . . . I came home, and that's when I fucked up. I should've gathered the rest of you and told you. I should've told Mia and Cole."

Pete stopped moving and dropped his head forward. After a pregnant pause, he confessed, "I couldn't repeat it. I didn't want Mase to know, but I was dying inside. I didn't want him telling the rest of you, speaking those words out loud into the universe. I don't know, I just wanted to pretend that some sick fuck hadn't gone into great detail, telling me all the ways he was going to violate and rape my baby sister, then rent her out before he sold her to another sick fuck who would do the same."

I thought about my sister and my nieces. As soon as the thoughts flitted in, I shoved them away before the bile rose any higher.

"You did what you had to do, and that includes taking the time you did to process what happened," I began. "That's done. Now, Cole and the others need to be told to keep an eye. It's not like they don't already, but still, they need this intel." I stopped to look at Mason. "We've got an op to plan. Are we good to do that, or do you and I need to talk?"

Mason lounged in his chair, holding my gaze.

"Fallon's right, that was a shit thing to say," Mase admitted.

"It was. But just so we're clear, the loyalty you brought into question was for *Mia*. And to be clear on one more point, my loyalty doesn't extend only to one person or team, nor does it end. When you have it, you got it for life. Just because I no longer work with those men, they are still my brothers, and I will never not have their backs. But make no mistake, this team has my full commitment *and* loyalty too."

"You're heard," Mase said.

Good.

Time to move on.

"I love my sister," Pete unnecessarily clarified.

"Never thought you didn't. Which again begs the question why you wouldn't want more eyes on her."

"Because for as long as I can remember it's been *me* taking care of my sister. *Me* making sure she's safe. *Me* protecting her." Pete stopped, glanced at Mason, then continued. "Me and Mase. I know Cole loves her, I know he'd give his life to protect her, but that doesn't mean she's still not mine. I've never had to answer to anyone about how I provided for my sister. Further from that, Cole is my friend too. They spent a long time apart, and I didn't want anything fucking up them getting back together.

"But you're right. With Carlos in play, they need to know. I'm being a stubborn asshole about this. I don't want my sister worried when, after twenty years of living in misery, she's finally happy." Pete paused again to suck in a deep breath. "I screwed up. You all have my apologies. Before we get back to it, I have to call my sister. Then I need to talk to my brother-in-law and endure a well-deserved ass chewing. If anyone has something to say, now's the time to say it."

No one said anything, yet the room remained stifling.

Chapter Twenty-Two

The guys had left me with Shep's intel in favor of maps.

Ryan and Aiden were planning the route we'd take to get to Juárez. Mason, Pete, and Jack were leaning over a large map of Juárez while at the same time using a tablet to enlarge areas of interest.

Fallon, Gavin, and Beck had been working with Pete and the guys, pinpointing possible places Carlos could be holding Calista, but they'd gone out when a box truck pulled up. Pete had been expecting the delivery—Tom's ammo had arrived.

That left me to go over a very detailed report on Carlos Quintero and his operation, as well as his cousin Rafael. Between my stomach churning in disgust and my temper flaring with every sentence I read, I was having trouble seeing the bigger picture.

Jack had told us he'd spoken to Lincoln Parker, and he relayed Linc's thoughts on Tom, his reasoning for conning me and cornering Pete and his guys, not to mention Berta. I could have bought Tom's reasoning if the Honduran president's wife and kids had not been among the women and children smuggled out.

I could see Tom wanting to know the whereabouts of this woman in case he needed to use her location in the future. Information was power. The whereabouts of a runaway wife could buy Tom the upper hand should he need to control the president. I didn't like it; the thought of using humans like disposable pieces on a game board made me sick, but that was the way of the world. Especially in the CIA.

There wasn't much information on the men Calista had supposedly killed—I was reserving judgment until I met her. It was easy to set someone up. There was even less information about Calista herself and her family. Specifically her father, the man who Tom said had saved his life. How did a man who owned three dry cleaners save a CIA officer's life? Unless that man was using his businesses to clean more than clothes. Unless that was a cover for something else.

"Shepherd Drexel is supposed to be the best, right?" I asked the room.

"Can't say I've worked with every hacker out there," Pete said. "But he's the best I've personally worked with."

"Then why is my intel light on Calista and the assholes she supposedly killed?"

"What makes you think they're assholes?" Aiden inquired.

"Typically, women don't kill men for no reason. They're emotionally driven to kill."

"Puts a whole new spin on turning feelings into felonies," Ryan muttered.

"You need a coffee mug with that on it," I told him. "Instead of 'fuck your feelings,' you need one that says 'don't make me turn my feelings into felonies.'"

I heard some chuckles but didn't look up to see who I'd amused.

"Where the hell did you find this chick?" Ryan went on.

I felt my shoulders stiffen.

"What?" Jack's grunt was a warning.

"Where'd you find this chick?" Ryan repeated. "I need the coordinates, ASAP, so I can see if there are more of her there."

Oh . . .

Well . . .

That was a nice thing to say.

"No dice, my good fellow. I am my own special brand. A one-off, never to be made again."

"So what you're saying is, I have to challenge Jack to a duel at dawn and hope I'm quicker on the draw so I can take you from him and not look over my shoulder every day for the rest of my life."

Jack growled.

I smiled.

"You could hope you're quicker than Jack, but I guarantee you I'm faster than the both of you, so you'd lose the duel and I'd ride off into the sunset with Jack."

I dreamed of us horseback riding—and baby, I gotta admit, that one threw me. My ass has never been on the back of a horse, and I have no interest in ever riding.

My smile got bigger.

The laughter I heard that time was definitely Jack.

"You think you're faster on the draw than me?"

"No doubt. When we get back from Mexico, I'll prove it to you."

"Ten bucks says I'll smoke your ass."

That made me crane my neck and look over at the makeshift workstation—a.k.a. two end tables pushed together so Ryan and Aiden could open two spiral-bound road atlases.

Ryan looked smug and sure of himself. Aiden was giving me a 'you don't wanna make this bet' look. I glanced at Jack, and his features were neutral.

"Twenty bucks says I can draw from the hip and put a bullet downrange faster than you. Another twenty says I can clear a course faster than you. I'll throw in another ten that I score higher on accuracy too."

Suddenly, Ryan didn't look so sure. "I feel a moral obligation to warn—"

"You're not morally obligated to tell me anything," I cut him off.

"Because you don't want to have to reciprocate and tell me your quals."

He was correct.

I shrugged.

"You're on."

I nodded and looked back at the tablet with Shep's report. "Just don't be a sore loser and bellyache when I take your fifty bucks."

"I never lose."

Famous last words.

"Oh, and I don't take ones. My name's not Candy, and I don't wear glitter and clear platform heels."

"Do strippers still accept dollar bills?" Mason joined, because of course he wouldn't miss out on a stripper conversation. "I thought with inflation they were up to fives."

"Like you don't know," Aiden threw in.

"Never been to a strip club. What, do they only accept Venmo and Cash App now?"

Mason had never been to a strip club? On one hand, the guy was extremely good looking. He wouldn't need to buy a lap dance to see some action. But I knew plenty of good-looking men and women who'd visited strip clubs.

"You've never been to a gentlemen's club?" Ryan asked.

Out of the corner of my eye, I caught Mason arrogantly waving a hand from his face down his body.

"Do I look like I need to visit a gentlemen's club?" Mason voiced my thought.

I left them to the squabble I'd inadvertently started and tuned them out.

Carlos Quintero was your typical gangster—wannabe warlord, clawing his way up the criminal ladder. He'd expanded his cousin's prostitution ring and now controlled more than double the bars and hot spots than Rafael had. He might've cut out the high-interest-loan portion of the old regime, but he'd expanded the gambling.

"Why hasn't the cartel just gobbled up Carlos's territory?" I again asked out loud but to no one in particular.

Pete again was the one to answer, or in this case, question. "What do you mean?"

"For that matter, why did they allow Rafael to operate? Juárez is a cartel stronghold. Big players. And here's this small-time gangbanger."

"They take their cut," Pete told me.

"Think about it like this," Aiden started. "The cartel is McDonald's—it's easier to franchise. They get to take their cut without the hassle of ownership."

That analogy only sort of worked. But I caught his meaning.

"The cartel lets him rent space and do his business, and they collect a percentage of his earnings?"

"Yup."

"So, if Carlos has this beautiful Russian woman—who, as Mason pointed out, would get top dollar—would he share the news of his good fortune with the cartel, or would he move her out of Juárez, sell her privately, and keep all the money for himself?"

"Fucking shit," Pete growled.

"He'd move her before the cartel caught wind he had her," Mason said. "Either to keep the money or to stop the cartel from coming and getting her so they could sell her to one of their contacts. We're looking in the wrong spot."

Well, damn.

I heard chairs scraping against the floor and paper rustling as the men moved from their positions to join me back in the living room. Not that the dining room and sitting area off to the side weren't one big room, it was just that the furniture—and there was a lot of it—delineated the spaces.

The men immediately started brainstorming.

Aiden began. "He wouldn't bring her into the US."

Ryan then took over. "He'd take her out of Chihuahua, and the cartel has ties to Michoacán. Those two states are out."

"The Sinaloa Cartel would eat him alive," Jack put in. "That state's out."

How many states did Mexico have? Thirty-one? Thirty-two? At this rate, we'd be here all night.

"Tom's source in Juárez said there was a Russian going up for auction. If that intel is out, there's a good chance the cartel already knows," I said, contradicting my own theory.

"Not if Tom's source is inside Carlos's organization," Pete answered. "Cat, you call him and ask who his source is and if he has any idea where Carlos would take her."

I fought back a salute as I stood to get my phone out of my backpack. I really needed to find the time to go back to Arizona and pack. "I know the timing sucks, but I only have two days' worth of clothes with me. I left my suitcase back in the hotel in Honduras—"

"I asked—"

I interrupted Jack right back. "If I had anything important in my room. The answer is still no. I had clothes, nothing else. But we're gonna have to stop at a mall or something on the way home."

"I got a tee you can have, Kitty," Mason goaded Jack.

"Yeah, yours would probably fit me better than Jack's." That was a lie. Mason was way broader than Jack. "I could also use some pants. What size shorts do you wear, extra-shlong-long?"

I was digging through my bag when my joke landed.

The room exploded in laughter. As any good teller of a joke that had landed perfectly, I did not laugh. I smugly found Tom's number and put my phone to my ear. I was walking out of the room to get away from all the chortling when Tom answered.

"Catarina."

I didn't know what part of the world he was in, but it sounded like I'd woken him up.

"Is now a good time?"

"I'll call you right back."

The line disconnected, and a moment later, an unknown number called back.

"Are we secure?" I asked.

"Yes."

"Is your source inside Carlos's crew?"

"I can't say. Why?"

Typical.

"If he's not on the inside, then the cartel knows Carlos has the girl. If he's on the inside and this information hasn't been leaked, then Carlos has moved the girl."

"Goddamnit. I didn't think of that."

"So? Is he in or out?"

"Inside."

Great, now we were looking for a needle in a haystack.

"Any ideas where he'd take her?"

"The Sinaloa—"

"Not to be rude, Tom, but we've already scratched the places he *wouldn't* take her off the list. We need intel on where he would."

The laughter in the other room had quieted. I could now hear faint murmurs, but I couldn't make out what they were saying.

"Carlos has ties in Baja Sur. A cousin in Tortuga Bay."

"Anywhere else? Out of Mexico?"

"Not that I know of."

"Did Calista kill Victor Stone and the two lawyers?"

Silence.

"If she *had* killed him, *why* would she kill him?"

More silence.

"You're asking a lot of this team, of Berta. If she murdered them in cold—"

"Victor Stone was a pissant who had issues with the word *no*. He also had a reputation for certain . . . proclivities. One of those kinks was inviting his friends to the festivities. Consenting adults do what consenting adults do, and that's no one's business. However, without the consent, that's something else entirely. And let's just say there was no consent."

I hadn't realized I was grinding my molars until my jaw started to ache.

"Did he—"

"No. Not her. If she did kill Stone, it was because she walked in on him forcefully taking something that was not offered."

I had yet to meet this woman and I already liked her.

"What do you want with the Honduran president's wife and children?"

"Nothing," he bit out.

That was a lie.

"You know, in the Army, I was called a human lie detector, and I didn't need to be in the same room as the subject to pick up on an untruth. You of all people should remember this about me, seeing as you've used my skills in the past. Which I've thought about, and it annoys me to no end that you played me and I didn't catch your lie. But I've come to the realization it's because you didn't fully lie. You did want me to find Berta and give her your intel. You simply omitted the truth behind why you wanted that, and your intel was bogus. You played me once, Tom. It won't ever happen again. What do you want with the wife?"

"Nothing."

"Bullshit—"

"You're highly intelligent. I wanted you with me at the Agency. I knew I'd never get that. I want your skills available to me in the future, so I say this with respect, but leave it the fuck alone."

That last part was said with authority but was tinged with melancholy.

There was a connection.

"Do you love her?"

"Leave it alone, Catarina."

He loved her.

"Sure," I lied. "One last thing. You said Calista's father saved your life. He owned—"

"His father cleaned money for the Irish mob. When the time came for him to take over the family business, he found he couldn't stomach it, and he approached the CIA."

"You turned him into an agent?"

"Yes. He was assigned to me because I'd been tracking a bomb maker with ties to an Irish crime syndicate. I was in Liverpool. My intel said Danny was visiting a church. I was on my way there when Calista's father called to warn me I was walking into an ambush. Fifteen minutes later the church blew up. If he hadn't called, I would've been inside."

"Does Calista know about her father?"

"No. Neither does his widow, and I'm trusting you not to tarnish the man's memory. He didn't volunteer to clean the mob's money. And as you know, when you're in, you're in for life. Generations. His father made that deal. In the end, he did the right thing."

And as his reward, his daughter had been kidnapped and trafficked.

"You have my word I will not tell her, and I'll inform the team—"

"Keep that to yourself."

I felt a prickle hit the base of my spine. He was asking me to keep something from a group of men whom I was bonding with. We were learning to trust each other. One of those men was Jack, who I trusted implicitly and would not keep secrets from.

"I can't do that, Tom. I won't keep something from my team. I trust them, and they will not betray my request and speak to Calista about this."

"Catarina—"

"There is nothing you can say that will make me change my mind. I will not keep this from them."

I waited a few moments for him to say something.

When he remained silent, I went on, "Call me if you get anything about the location of the auction."

"I will."

I disconnected the call, turned to get back to the team, and found Mason leaning against the wall, listening to my conversation.

Warfighter Mason was in the house. His stare was blank, mask fully in place, a thousand-yard stare that gave away nothing. This state, absolutely devoid of any emotion, was different from the other times he'd slipped into this persona.

Dead man walking.

That's what he looked like—dead in the eyes.

I lifted a brow, inviting him to speak first.

"What did he want you to lie to us about?" Mason asked.

Tom hadn't asked me to lie. He'd asked me to keep a secret, but I figured that to Mason, they'd be one and the same. So I answered.

"Calista's grandfather made a deal with the Irish to clean their money. When her dad took over the laundering, he called the CIA. They turned him, and he became Tom's informant. Her dad warned Tom he was walking into an ambush and saved his life."

Mason was silent.

"Did I pass?"

"What?"

God, now the man was going to play dumb.

"Don't," I hissed. "Be honest about it. You heard what I said to Tom. You knew he wanted me to keep something from you. You heard me tell him I wouldn't. You asked what that was. I told you. So, did I pass?"

"You're asking me if you passed, not if I trust you."

"We've already established this. I know you don't trust me, and that's okay. I get it. You trust me not to let you get shot. I trust you won't tell someone to knife me to death. So we're good."

Mason's mask bled away.

God, who hurt this man?

I understood being private. I understood holding your cards close to your vest. I knew what it meant to turn battle time on and, when it was over, turn it back off. But I had never seen someone break so hard, so fast, that the mask slipped on and off like his did.

"I promise I'll step in front of a knife for you."

I shook my head. "Great."

"I . . ." Mason trailed off. "It takes me a while. Especially with women." He paused again. "I've known Mia most of my adult life and trust her, but . . . I don't. I love her more than anyone, including Pete. She's not my blood, but she's my sister, and I still can't allow myself to get too close. So . . ."

So there was no chance he'd ever trust me.

That was sad. I didn't like it. But that didn't mean we couldn't be friends.

"You don't need to spill your deepest, darkest secrets for me to be your friend."

Relief and pain and panic melted together.

It was time to change the subject.

"We need to call Shep. I think Tom's in love with the president's wife. Or maybe not *in* love, but there is an emotional connection."

The look of shock on Mase's face was hilarious, but I didn't have time to marvel. "Mason!" I snapped.

"Right. We need to call Shep."

I started his way. He pushed off the wall, and I got no farther. He grabbed my arm to stop me.

"Don't let me do to you what I do with the others."

Was he giving me permission to pry? And why me?

"I'll dust off my crowbar when we get home and start chipping away."

"You might need an excavator," he mumbled under his breath.

He was. He was giving me permission.

And I wouldn't waste the opportunity by asking questions that did not matter. If Mason Hughes had picked me to break through his walls, and that might help him open himself up to the others—I'd learn to drive an excavator, and I'd dig.

Chapter Twenty-Three

Pete had called Shep. We were running through possible locations when Catarina walked into the living room with Mason on her heels.

"Carlos has a cousin in Baja," Shep was saying. "Hold on."

Catarina stutter-stepped to a halt, tilted her head, and narrowed her eyes. I didn't get the chance to remark on her strange entrance before she shook the look free and filled us in. "The cousin lives in Tortuga Bay."

All eyes went to her.

"That was all Tom had on the cousin's location. And his informant is on the inside."

"What else did Tom give you?" Pete inquired.

She filled us in on Calista's father and Tom's request to keep it from us. I glanced around the room and saw near-identical expressions on all the men's faces—respect.

"Something wasn't sitting well with the president's wife, so I pushed him about it. He told me to drop it. It wasn't evasion, it went deeper. There's an emotional connection."

"Why do you think that?" Shep asked.

Cat stared at Pete's phone on the coffee table for a second in what appeared to be disbelief before she answered, "It was in his tone. There was a sadness there. The way a man whose heart was broken would not want to talk about the woman who broke it. I asked him if he loved her, and he told me to drop it. The demand was forceful but, again, mixed with sorrow."

I didn't know how old Tom was. He looked older than I was, and Maria was a few years older than Catarina—an age gap but not one that would make Tom look like a dirty grandpa panting after a young girl.

"Has Tom spent any significant time in Honduras?" Fallon asked, looking around.

"That would take me weeks' worth of digging through his aliases. Hold on a second."

Keys could be heard pounding in the background.

"Jesus," Shep muttered.

"What?" Pete looked just as impatient as he sounded.

"Guess who was the ambassador extraordinary and plenipotentiary to Honduras?" Shep asked and continued to pound on his keyboard, then went on to answer his own question. "Charles F. Washington."

"Tom's father was the ambassador?" Catarina inquired. "Could he have met her when he was a kid? When was this?"

"Two years before Maria was born. His mission ended the year after her birth. According to her birth records, Maria's mother was unwed. No father listed."

"Sister," Pete, Catarina, and Ryan all said at the same time.

"Would be his half sister," Shep corrected. "The timing matches. And if Sphynx thinks she heard an emotional connection, half sister would explain it."

Sphynx?

Catarina's torso swung back, and her gaze remained glued to the phone.

Apparently, no one else in the room caught the slip, nor did they catch Catarina's reaction. Not to Shep's voice when she'd first heard him, and not to the use of a nickname no one had heard.

Catarina pulled herself together and asked, "Was Charles married to Tom's mother?"

"Yes, until he died two years ago."

"Deathbed confession?" Mason muttered.

"Doesn't matter," Pete cut in. "We'll ask Berta what she knows about Maria's family. If she knows that Tom is her half brother, that'll tip her off that we figured it out, and she can confirm. But if she doesn't know, for Maria and the kids' safety, I think we should keep that to ourselves."

Before anyone could give their opinion on the matter, Aiden strangely blurted, "Isla Natividad."

"What?" Ryan got in there before I could.

"Isla Natividad, six kilometers off the mainland. It's a small fishing town, mostly uninhabited, with a dirt airstrip. Twenty-three nautical miles from Tortuga Bay. If I had a pretty Russian for sale and I didn't want the cartel getting their hands on her, I'd take her to family to hide, then a small island with a few fishermen living there. If payoffs needed to be made, it'd come cheap."

"Shep can track—"

He cut Pete off. "Already on it. Give me twenty minutes to see if I can get a lock on Carlos and what I can pull up on the cousin."

"Thanks, we'll be waiting." With that, Pete disconnected.

I wove around the furniture to get to Catarina.

"Are we pretending that Cat didn't have a weird reaction to Shep?" Mason asked. "And Sphynx, what the hell is that?"

Fuck.

"Mase—"

"What? You were across the room, and I know you didn't miss it. So me standing next to her, I sure as shit didn't."

I wasn't a fan of Catarina being put on the spot. Though after she blew out a breath, she didn't seem to mind.

"His voice . . . he sounded familiar. I thought I was wrong, then he called me Sphynx . . ." She didn't finish her thought.

Ryan looked up from his tablet to ask, "Do you know him? Like in real life?"

Cat rolled her eyes.

I knew she refrained from a snappy comeback when all she said was "Yes."

Mason looked around the room. "Does anyone know Shep in real life?"

There were head shakes and noes all around.

Pete added, "Never met him, and I don't know anyone who has."

"Where's Shep get the money to bankroll the ops?" Cat asked.

"He steals it. And before you ask, that same money pays our salary." He looked at Catarina. "And now yours. It pays all of our bills. Not a single person we rescue pays—not for the exfil and not for the safe house. Their captors do. Shep drains all their accounts. If he's bored, he finds other criminals doing jacked-up shit and takes their money too."

I knew Shep paid my salary. I didn't give two shits it came from stolen funds for criminals.

"You got a problem with that?" Pete finished by asking.

"Me?"

Pete dipped his chin.

Cat thought about it for a moment. Then she smiled.

"Nope. I actually love that the assholes who cause so much pain and destruction with their greed will now be paying my car payment."

Pete looked at me and smiled.

"Good. Now, Ryan, tell us about this island."

By the time Shep called back, we'd thoroughly checked out the island the best we could electronically. We'd also looked into Tortuga Bay and the ocean route to get to the island. The seaside town was small but had an airfield. Pete had also called Berta to ask her if she had any allies in that area. Unfortunately she didn't. He didn't ask about Tom's connection to Maria; that was for a different day when we weren't on the clock.

"I got two things for you. I ran some of Carlos's known associates. You won't be surprised to know they're not big into credit, banking, or credit cards. But I found one, a woman, Gloria Alverez. She charged gas in El Riito. Then again southwest in Santa Ana. Again in Mexicali. From there, she caught the 5 and headed south. I got another charge in Playa Hermosa. The last charge is in Chapala, where the 5 turns into the 1. That highway dead-ends in Tortuga. It's a twenty-two-hour drive. I can't get her all the way, but in the vicinity. The rest of the gas would've been paid in cash.

"I called Tom. He reached out to his insider in Carlos's organization and got back to me. First, Gloria is Carlos's woman—as in, his girlfriend and also the woman who runs his stable. She takes care of the girls, and I use that term loosely, but Gloria oversees the prostitutes. Second, the auction in Juárez is set. Carlos's second-in-command is handling the sale since he's not there, and there are no out-of-town buyers coming in, which confirms Calista isn't there. I think it's a safe bet Carlos and Gloria took Calista to Tortuga."

"Any word in any of those dark holes you peruse about a Russian being sold in Mexico?" Aiden asked.

"I don't bury the lede." Shep blew out a breath. "I would've led with that."

Pete looked like he was deep in thought.

"What's on your mind?" Mase asked Pete.

"I don't like leaving those other women up for auction."

"We can't save—"

"Them all, yeah, Mase, I know. But I know there's an auction; it's sitting heavy in my gut."

I was about to suggest calling Takeback, but then I remembered Mia shouldn't go anywhere near Juárez, and getting her to stay behind would be like me convincing Catarina to sit this op out.

It just wasn't going to happen.

"Me, Ryan, Gavin, and Fallon hit Juárez," Aiden suggested. "You, Mase, Cat, and Jack hit the island."

"Shep, what's your intel on the auction?"

"I don't have much. Word is there are ten girls. They're from Carlos's stable. He's rotating out."

I wasn't the only one who grunted in disgust.

"I can have a workup in a few hours. First I need to make the arrangements for the flight down to Baja. There's a larger island north of Natividad. Cedros. It has an airport. It would also be a good place to handle the sale. It's worth checking out the island before you head to Natividad."

"El Morro," Ryan confirmed. "Fifteen kilometers."

"Correct. Did you get the workup I sent over on Calista Ventura?" Shep inquired.

"Yeah. Thanks for that," Pete answered.

I still didn't know who the model Tom had referenced was, but the pictures Shep had sent over, along with a full dossier on Calista, proved she was pretty enough to be a model. Long blonde hair, blue eyes. I thought she resembled Kate Hudson if Kate had longer hair.

The report also included her occupation—freelance investigative journalist. Something Tom had conveniently left out. She had written numerous articles on the sex trade and an exposé on Washington elites using high-dollar escorts, and the women who serviced these men. She hadn't named any of the men but gave enough detail that it didn't take a rocket scientist to figure out who the piece was about.

She also smartly wrote under pseudonyms—three of them to be exact. And she didn't only report on trafficking; under one of the pen names, she exposed corruption. Meaning if her pseudos ever got out, she'd be in danger. Which seemed moot seeing as she'd already been kidnapped.

"Good. I'll hit you back soon."

"We have a plan," Pete announced. "We hit both targets."

"Copy."

"Wait." Mason stopped Shep from disconnecting. "Are we just going to pretend that Cat and Shep don't know each other?"

Catarina's hand shot to the side so fast, Mason didn't have time to stop her backhand to the solar plexus.

"Damn, woman," he grunted.

Shep said nothing.

"You do know her, right?" Mase continued, like he hadn't just had the wind knocked out of him.

"Sphynx," Shep said.

Catarina went statue still.

"I'm calling my marker." With that, Shep disconnected.

Catarina frowned. Then her lips twitched. After that, her eyes went to the floor.

"What the hell was that about? What's sphynx?" Mase pushed.

"I'm Sphynx. Or that's what some of the guys called me. It's a hairless cat."

"Like that grumpy cat with no fur?" Aiden asked.

"Yes, Aiden, that's what hairless means." Cat offered no more explanation.

"So you know Shep," Mase continued.

She lifted her eyes, but her gaze was faraway.

"In another life, yes." Her tone sounded wistful.

My gut twisted. "And the marker?"

"To keep his secret."

"Were you two . . . did you . . ." Ryan stumbled, then put up his hands. "None of my business. Sorry."

It was my business, but I wasn't going to ask her in front of the team.

Thankfully, she put me out of my misery.

She glanced over at me and answered, "Never."

That was good enough for me. Cat wouldn't lie. She'd evade if she didn't want to answer but she'd never flat-out lie.

"I'm not sure if I'm pissed or jealous Cat knows Shep," Mason muttered.

"We got work to do," Pete reminded him.

Right.

Everyone scattered except for Catarina.

She turned to face me, and I knew what was coming.

"You don't have to convince me."

"I can't betray his trust and tell you who he is."

"Baby, I'd never ask you to break anyone's trust."

"Okay. It's just, it's the same as Tom asking to keep a secret—"

Before she could finish, I tagged her around the waist and hauled her close.

"It's not remotely the same, and I get it, baby. Stop worrying."

She leaned closer and relaxed.

"Kiss me so we can get to work."

"Are you asking or commanding?" she sniped.

"Commanding."

Her eyes narrowed. "Jack."

"Catarina."

One side of her mouth hitched up.

Fuck it.

I bent forward and kissed my woman.

Chapter Twenty-Four

"Has it been twenty-four hours since our last flight?" I grumbled as we disembarked the plane on Cedros Island.

The airfield was nothing more than a long runway. No tower. No hangars. One end of the runway was feet away from a bluff that went straight down into the ocean. I was not afraid of flying. I wasn't a fan of back-to-back flights, but planes didn't bother me. However, I'd closed my eyes when we came in for landing. Taking off would be worse.

"Just barely." Jack transferred his duffel to his other hand.

Before we'd boarded the flight, which departed from the same airport we'd flown into yesterday, Jack took me to a mall so I could pick up a few things before we went back to his . . . our house so he could get packed. We'd also made a stop at a Walgreens so I could get toiletries.

He hadn't probed or given me any weird sidelong glances after the whole Shep incident. He'd said he believed I'd never been with Shep in a romantic way. But sometimes people say one thing but really feel another way. Jack didn't.

On the plane while Jack was snoozing, I thought about the man who had once upon a time been my friend. A man who had caught me by the ankle before I rolled off the roof of a three-story building. A man who'd kicked in doors and cleared my way so I could gather intel that would further help his team track terrorists. A good man who had fallen on hard times, then disappeared. Over the years, I'd thought a lot about him. Where he was, if he'd recovered, what he was doing.

Never in my wildest dreams did I think he was the infamous Shepherd Drexel.

Though, I should've put two and two together. But this was one of those times when it only hit you in the face *after* you knew. If Jack and the rest of the guys knew, they'd probably laugh their asses off.

My friend's beloved German Shepherd's name was Drexel.

But I owed him my life. He'd called that marker. I would never breathe his real name to anyone, thus they'd never know how Shep Drexel got his name. But I knew, and I loved that was the name he picked.

"Why does it raise the pucker factor when the plane that dropped you off taxis away?" Mase asked.

"Because your ride dumped you and now you got no way home," Pete offered.

"Before we hit the hotel, I wanna stop at the grocery store," Mason announced.

Of course he did.

"I saw the five SNICKERS you put in your pack," I noted. "Do you really need more candy?"

"Yes, Kitty Cat. I prefer local chocolate when I'm traveling."

Pete was a few feet in front of us. He didn't break stride when he confirmed, "He's not lying. Every country, multiple stops for candy bars."

"Some of us like foreign chocolate. Some of us like foreign women. But one of those things doesn't steal your wallet and watch." I heard a loud snap. "Oh, and your passport."

Jack chuckled. Pete did not.

"Did you buy a hooker and she pulled the ole 'wait until you pass out, then steal all your shit'?" I asked.

"No. I did not buy a hooker. I met a woman in a bar and took her back to my hotel room," Pete disgruntledly mumbled.

I bit my lip to stop myself from laughing. "Where was this?"

"Saint Petersburg."

And then it hit me. "Your nickname."

"Yup."

"Russia or Florida?"

There was a beat of silence.

"The Sunshine City in the Sunshine State," Mason answered. "Had to explain to the Master Chief why he was missing our flight out of Tampa."

"I was twenty-three," Pete defended himself. "And the woman had this British accent that drove me wild. Totally lost my head."

"Lost your head and your wallet," I noted. "Are we walking across the street to the grocery store here or the one by the hotel?"

We'd all studied the map of the island. There was a tiny village next to the airfield. It had a few stores and a church. Our hotel was seven kilometers up the road. We could hoof it, and with the clean, cool night air after being in a stuffy plane, I would've suggested ditching the car and walking, but I was ready to sleep. We had an early morning tomorrow. Before we left for Natividad Island, we needed to make sure Carlos hadn't brought Calista here. If she wasn't on either island, we'd head to the mainland.

"Hold up," Pete said as he pulled his phone out of his pocket. "It's Shep." There was a brief pause before "We've landed." Another pause, this one longer and accompanied by Pete's gaze sliding around the group. "Right. We'll pivot. Thanks for the update."

Pete pocketed his phone and announced, "A plane registered in the United Arab Emirates filed a flight plan to Mexico City. The plane is still there, but the pilot and the four occupants of that flight boarded a smaller aircraft. Flight plan has them landing here on Cedros. Shep missed it earlier, but Gloria Alverez checked into a hotel here two days ago and hasn't checked out."

I guess I wasn't getting into bed anytime soon.

"Well, that fucks up tonight's plans of kicking back and eating chocolate," Mason grumbled my thought.

"I feel like I should ask if eating chocolate is a euphemism for something. But I'm afraid that's what you call a combat jack and I'll be scarred for life, so I'm not going to ask."

Mason's smile was wicked.

Thankfully Pete cut in before Mason could confirm my suspicion. "We've got five unknowns, Gloria, and Carlos on the island. The hotel Gloria checked in to is in the same village where our hotel is, near the fishing port and pier. We're hoofing it, using the beach until we hit the bluffs, then we'll use the dirt access roads to Ghost Town. That puts us three klicks from the hotel."

The beach route was the long way to the village north of the airport, where the hotels and pier were. It would add forty minutes to our walk.

"Are we hitting the hotel tonight or waiting until dawn?" Jack asked.

"My vote is tonight," Mason declared. "I'm not all that fired up about hanging out for longer than needed in a place named Ghost Town."

I couldn't stop my smirk.

"Scaredy cat."

Mason lifted his right hand and flipped me off. What he didn't do was deny he was scared.

"Does this mean I'm shit out of luck?" Mason asked. "You know chocolate helps me concentrate during a—"

"Stop talking," Jack interrupted Mason. "The last time you complained about something, we engaged in an all-night battle. Can we just get to the hotel without having to draw our weapons?"

The rat-a-tat-tat of gunfire had us all stopping.

"Goddamnit," Jack snarled.

"Visual?" Pete asked.

I scanned the runway and didn't see anything. "Negative."

I was already pulling my pack off to grab my vest.

An advantage to Shep chartering us a private plane was no one said anything when we walked on strapped. However, I didn't want to wear uncomfortable ballistic plates on a flight. But I sure as shit wanted them on with the sound of bullets popping off.

I dropped my bag, crouched in front of it, and was unzipping it when I saw movement on the opposite side of the runway nearest the beach.

I watched and waited.

There were neat rows of sand or aggregate piled high. Beyond that there was a long shipping dock. It was night, the business was closed, there were lights at the end of the dock, but otherwise the staging area was dark.

I went back to unpacking my vest. I had it over my head when I saw another dark shadow.

"White sedan rolling in hot. We need to move."

Pete was right. We were sitting ducks with no cover.

Just as I was standing, I caught a flash of someone running from behind a pile of sand and making a mad dash to a cluster of shipping containers. There was a full moon, not enough light to make out facial features but enough to know the long ponytail whipping around as she ran was blonde.

"Is that her?"

How many blonde-haired women could there possibly be on this island? And a blonde running from someone shooting at her . . . it had to be Calista.

"Who?"

"Calista! I think that's her behind the shipping containers."

Engines roared closer.

The woman dashed across an open space headed for another container. She turned her head to look over her shoulder, and I still couldn't be a hundred percent sure it was Calista, but damn if she didn't have the same build as the description Shep had sent—tall and slim.

"Cat—"

"It has to be her. Cover me!"

I yanked the Sig P226 Pete let me borrow out of my holster and ran as fast as I could across the tarmac. I was on the other side, back on the dirt, and beelining for the shipping containers. I heard the guys laying down cover fire. I had five feet left to go when a barrage of gunfire rang out, forcing me to do a running dive for cover. I rolled, came up on my hip, and cursed Tom Washington's name when the incision from removing the tracker reminded me that Jack had only cut into my flesh a few days ago and it was not healed.

I forgot about the pain in my hip when I pulled up on my knees and felt the barrel of a gun pressed to my forehead.

"Calista Ventura?" I asked, even though I knew it was her.

"Who are you?"

"Tom Washington sent me to find you."

"How do you know Tom?"

"I'll tell you, but can you please lower your weapon?"

"No."

Shit. I did not want to hurt this woman. Berta respected her. Tom cared about her. Her sister had been murdered. And Carlos had brought her to an island to sell her.

But still . . .

"Really, Calista, Berta thinks highly of you, but I need you to get your gun out of my face."

"Berta?"

Fucking hell, I was done. My left hand went to the outside of her wrist. I pushed the barrel away from my head and lunged while holding her hand with the gun in the air. I landed on top of her with a thud. I heard the air leave her lungs in a whoosh. A second later, I'd successfully disarmed her.

I pushed up on my knees, straddling her tiny waist, and told her, "We need to get back to my team."

"Who are you?" she pushed out while trying to suck in air.

I climbed off her.

A loud explosion rocked the earth. I looked up and flames licked the night sky.

I held the gun back out to Calista. "Don't shoot my team. Three men. All in black tees."

"Got it."

"Follow me."

I crept to the end container and peeked around it. A gas station was fully engulfed in flames. There was a car on fire. But no guys.

Instinctively, I reached for my ear.

No comms. My phone was in my pack.

The guys would need to fall back and find cover before the fire drew a crowd. I thought about the map. The church at the end of the runway was too far away. They'd lose visual of me. The grocery store could be seen when we exited the plane, meaning the rooftop would be a good perch for overwatch.

Jack was for sure going to redden my ass for this.

"We have to get across the street to the grocery store."

"Are you insane? I just spent two days tied to a bed in a hotel. You're crazy if you think I'm taking a chance of being seen and taken again."

"You'll be safe. My team will be there to meet up with us."

I didn't have time to argue with her. We had to get back to the guys before people flooded the streets, making it harder to go unnoticed.

"You go," she told me.

This was one of the many times I wished I was male. I was not big enough to toss her over my shoulder and carry her. Nor was I strong enough to do that even for the short distance to the grocery store.

"I'm not leaving you."

"I appreciate you—"

She clamped her mouth shut when angry male voices sounded close.

Too close.

We turned at the same time.

Three men were running from the dock in our direction.

"Run!"

Calista took off. I followed. We made it to an office trailer as shots started flying.

I had a fifteen-round magazine and one in the chamber, then I would be out of ammo. Oh yeah, Jack was going to go apeshit.

"Is your mag full?"

"No clue. It's not mine."

I didn't get a chance to ask her whose it was before bullets started pinging the trailer. I glanced around the corner. The guys were still coming.

"Are you a good shot?"

"Yeah."

"We've got three coming our way," I told her. "You take the right. I'll cover left."

"Got it."

"Ready?"

Calista didn't verbally answer. She stepped out from behind the trailer and aimed right. I did the same but went left.

My first shot was low and to the left. I adjusted, pulled the trigger, and before my first target hit the ground I moved to my second. Calista fired twice and all three were down.

Now we really had to move.

"See the building on the other side of the tarmac?"

"Yeah."

"That's where we're headed."

She didn't wait for me. I took a second to make sure no one was coming up on our six, then sprinted after her.

I needed to get back to Jack and the guys. And one way or another, Calista was coming with me.

Chapter Twenty-Five

The street was now filled with people.

A fire truck—with no lights or sirens, just a tanker and three men—rolled up to put the fire out. The car that had ignited the explosion was on its side, where it had landed after careening into a pump.

But that was not what had my attention. Pete would handle the ground. I was on the roof of a goddamn grocery store, peering through the scope of my M4, looking for my crazy woman. Mason had taken off toward the dock to circle around to where Cat had disappeared. I saw three men drop, that was the only reason I wasn't pissed and out-of-my-brain terrified.

I blew out a slow breath to calm my heart rate.

It was there I realized that my breaths were finite.

Yeah, baby, and I'm gonna be mad if you lose yours tonight.

I exhaled again.

Where the hell are you, Catarina?

I caught a heat signature through my scope. A second later there was another. Two figures running. From this distance I couldn't see faces, but they were definitely women. A third figure came around the structure. My finger gently pressed down, taking the slack out of my trigger, and paused. Mason was wearing a chem light. I didn't see the hot spot from the stick.

I fired.

The woman in the back looked behind her. Faced front and continued to run but lifted her arm. The second woman was Cat. I watched Mason round the building the women had come from and pick up speed to catch up to Cat and Calista.

I lost sight of the women first, then Mason. I let out a sharp whistle to let Pete know I was coming down. I got one in return. By the time I made it off the roof, Pete had moved to the front of the grocer. Catarina and Mason were flanking Calista Ventura as they jogged across the street.

Pete did not delay in ordering, "We gotta move."

"She won't go back to the hotel," Catarina announced, but did not stop until she walked directly into my arms.

Smart woman.

"You good?"

"How much trouble am I in?"

Together you make the sword. Two shields cover front and back.

I blew out a breath.

"Next time, can you at least take your goddamn phone and wait until I can cover you before you take off?"

Catarina jolted, then she relaxed into me. "Yeah, honey."

"That's not an option," I heard Pete say.

"I don't mean to sound ungrateful, but I was the one who jumped out of a car to escape. I think I get to say where I'm going and where I'm *not* going. And I don't know who any of you are."

It was like Calista hadn't spoken when Pete asked Mase, "Were there any boats down at the dock?"

"Yeah."

"Fuck," Pete sighed. "Let's go."

Calista's shoulders snapped back, her chin jutted out, and she all but growled, "Again, really grateful for the assist, but I'm not going anywhere—"

"Tom Washington sent us," Pete explained.

"She already said that," Calista said as she pointed at Cat. "But who are you, and how do I know I didn't escape one hell just to walk into another?"

Mason looked thoroughly offended. I wasn't all that pleased at the inference, but to be fair, the woman didn't know us.

"I'm Catarina. This is Jack, Mason, and Pete." Cat pointed to each of us as she announced our names. "Tom went out of his way to track us down in Honduras to ask us to find you and get you safe. You're obviously important to him—"

"You mean my father was important to him," she corrected. "He doesn't think I know what my dad did for him, but I do."

"Just a suggestion," Mason started. "Can we please finish this conversation someplace else that's not on a street next to a burning gas station with bad guys roaming around? We've had a good run, but I'd prefer not to get shot at anymore tonight."

Calista's gaze was parked on Mase, but the sound of screeching tires pulled her attention to the road.

Obviously she'd made her decision when she declared, "I'll shoot you if you try—"

Mase jerked his head down toward her hand. "Hate to be the one to tell you this, but you're out of ammo."

"Shit."

"Once we're on the boat, I'll reload your magazine," Mase offered.

"How do I know you're telling me the truth?"

Mason shrugged. "You don't. You'll just have to trust me."

That was rich coming from the untrusting Mason.

"Let's go," Pete ordered.

With a kiss to the top of Cat's head, I stepped away from her.

"Where's my bag?"

"Gone."

"Bummer. My burner was in there. Now I need a new one."

I gritted my teeth.

"I think I might vomit," Cat complained.

"For a badass, you sure do have a weak stomach."

Cat was sitting with her head between her legs. This time I couldn't make any excuses for her. At the speed Pete had us at, the boat was barely rocking.

"Almost there," I told her.

"What happened back there?" Pete asked.

"Which part?" Calista returned.

"Start with how you escaped the hotel."

"Carlos had me at the hotel. He had two guys with him and a woman. One second I'm tied to a bed, they're watching TV, the next second the door's kicked in and four men come in. They shot Carlos, the woman, and his pals. Then one of them untied me and dragged me out to a car."

"And you jumped from the car?" Pete continued to question.

"Yep."

"You jumped from a *moving* car?" he asked again.

"Yeah, after I punched the guy next to me in his dick and took his gun."

Catarina lifted her head, turned to look at Calista, and smiled.

"I think I like you. That is, when you're not pointing a gun at my head."

What. The. Fuck.

"Come again?"

"Don't worry, it was a misunderstanding. We worked it out."

My eyelids drifted closed.

I tried and failed to pull up Lincoln's wisdom.

My hands balled into fists.

Catarina reached over, peeled back my fingers, and laced hers through mine.

"Your palm getting twitchy?"

She thought she was being cute.

For once, she was not.

"Twitchy doesn't cover it," I growled.

"Do you have any idea who those men were?" Mason picked up the interrogation.

"No. And no one spoke."

Well, that was unhelpful.

"Where are you taking me?"

"There's an airport in Tortuga—"

"Carlos has friends there. Before one of them took us to the dock and gave him a boat, we were at a house near the water. I counted fourteen men there. Two of them came with us to the island."

The cousin.

Pete slowed the boat as we neared the peninsula of the mainland.

"Jack, check and see if there are any airstrips north."

I took out my phone and pulled up the map.

"Nothing. We'd have to go thirty miles south of Tortuga. It's a dirt runway."

"Not enough gas."

"Tortuga it is," Mason decided.

"We'll pull into the bay and check it out. We could anchor and stay on the boat. Shep said our ride would be here in an hour."

Catarina groaned at Pete's declaration.

"Gotta learn to embrace the suck, Kitty Cat," Mason unwisely remarked.

"I swear on all things holy if you come at me with any more Navy SEAL sayings, I'm tossing you overboard. The only easy day was not yesterday. I'm already someone special, and I don't need to *not* back down from sharks because I'm never getting into shark-infested waters. I'm woman enough to admit I'm afraid of them. But if you want to test the waters and take a swim, by all means, buddy, keep talking."

Mason smiled at Cat, then he turned his attention to Calista.

"Hand me your mag. I'll reload it."

"Seriously?"

"I'm a man of my word."

Calista dropped the mag out of the pistol and handed it to Mason.

With nothing but the sound of the engine and the waves lapping against the hull, I blew a breath.

Cat was sitting next to me.

Safe.

But I was still reddening her ass the first chance I got.

Chapter Twenty-Six

As much as I hated boats, I had to admit the moonlight reflecting off the water was beautiful as Pete navigated the rocky shoreline on our way to Tortuga Bay. I sucked in a deep breath of sea air in an attempt to quell the churning in my stomach. Now was not the time to get sick—for obvious reasons—but beyond that, I was a hundred percent sure Mason would never let me live it down. Me throwing up would give the man years of ammunition I'd rather him not have. I was good with being on the receiving end of a teasing session. Though I preferred to be the one doing the ribbing, I was a good sport and took my knocks.

I just didn't want those to include me expelling the contents of my stomach into the water. I'd take a firefight over the rocking of a boat or a drop of a roller coaster any day of the week. And, now that Pete had slowed, the way we were rocking . . .

Gah.

Needing to get my mind off the seasickness, I asked, "How did Carlos's men find you?"

Obviously my question was directed at Calista, and she didn't delay in her response. "My best guess is a woman I'd been in contact with. I promised her safe passage out of Mexico for information on Carlos."

"Come again?" Even over the whine of the engine, I could hear Mason's incredulous tone.

"I made a deal with a woman—"

"You made a deal with an unknown?"

Calista looked highly offended at Mason's probing.

"You do realize that ninety-nine percent of my interactions start with a cold lead. Most are *ice* cold. It's my job to turn those warm, then hot, and get an unknown to turn into an informant or whistleblower. I'd assume the same goes for your profession. I'm not stupid, nor am I careless. Obviously I thought this woman was ripe or I wouldn't've approached her in the first place."

I really, really wished this conversation wasn't taking place when my tummy was staging a revolt so I could cheer Calista on. I'd come to adore Mason in a short amount of time, and part of that adoration included me wanting to see him happy. Not that I was under any illusion it would be Calista who would be that woman for him, but that didn't mean I wasn't thoroughly enjoying her standing up for herself. With Mason's good looks, he needed someone like Calista, who wouldn't be taken in by his pretty-boy charm and would shovel shit right back at him.

"Clearly you thought wrong," Mason remarked as he handed her back her now fully loaded pistol.

I wasn't sure if that was smart. Calista looked like she was ready to put Mason's bullets to good use.

"No shit, Captain Sherlock. Tell me, did you figure that out all on your own with your superior abilities of deduction or did you need help drawing that very obvious conclusion?"

Mason's face turned to granite and suddenly this was no longer fun.

"Tone it down, woman."

Yep. The mood shifted and Mason had gone from being mildly ticked to seriously pissed. It was time for a subject change.

"Did you get anything useful during the car ride down here?" I interjected. "Anything on who Carlos had set a meeting with?"

"You mean, who was coming to *buy* me?"

Well . . . yeah, but I'd been trying to be sensitive.

She'd made it clear she preferred the direct approach, so instead of beating around the bush, which I figured she'd find insulting, I answered honestly. "Yes."

"No. Carlos and the woman mostly argued. I wasn't sure which one of them I wanted to knock out first. Him for being a repulsive human or her for being equally as repulsive but worse, because she was a woman holding other women against their will. I had a lot of time to think on this while they fought about Carlos being a slob, to which he parried with her being a shit cook. Let's just say the two of them were a match made in hell, and there were times I wished I had an ice pick to drive into my eardrums to silence their stupidity."

"Which one did you pick?" Mason rejoined with a much calmer manner.

Calista's attention went to Mason. I had her mostly in silhouette, but I didn't miss the way she stared at him.

"Her. Women should look out for other women. So if I had to choose between the two of them, I would've knocked the bitch out before I strangled the life out of her. In the end, she got what she deserved. Carlos did too."

I wholeheartedly agreed with Calista.

It was clear Mason did too. Though he didn't verbally confirm, his nod of approval did the job. However, he did go on to ask, "Why'd you kill Stone and his pals?"

The question was mostly superfluous. One I would've asked her myself even though Tom had already told us why Calista had *allegedly* killed the men, and Jasmin's husband Lincoln had corroborated Tom's assertion Stone was a full-fledged douchebag.

Trust but verify . . . as the saying goes.

It was either the droning of the engine or the waves hitting the side of the boat or the rumbling in my stomach or a combination of all three that had me off my game. So, I couldn't get a read, and Calista's body language said one thing, but the tone of her voice said another, and her words contradicted both—that being she wore a sneer that clearly stated she gave zero fucks, her tone aggressive, her explanation foul.

"I walked in on him violating a friend," Calista spat. "I've never had a man take me against my will, but still, I can imagine having it done is the worst thing that can happen to a woman. Add in two other men being present, lounging back on a couch like they don't have a care in the world while you're begging for help, takes the worst thing that can happen to you and ratchets that shit up a few hundred notches."

"Jesus fuck, I hope you made it painful," Pete interjected.

"Unfortunately, no," Calista told him. "At the time, I was more concerned with getting my friend out of the hell Stone had put her in than I was with making them pay. It wasn't until I had Diane safely back at her place and I'd spent the next eight hours holding my girl while she sobbed and violently shook in my arms that I wished I'd had time to get creative."

I seriously liked this woman.

"How'd you get tagged for the murder?"

"I wasn't exactly careful when I broke a window to gain entry into Victor's home. I cut my hand on the broken glass. What's funny—and not in a ha-ha way—is Diane's DNA was all over Stone, if you get what I'm saying, and the police have never once questioned her. Explain to me how a dead man's dick can be covered in body fluids and that woman isn't a suspect, but a random drop of blood found on the floor is.

"Don't bother taxing your brain, I'll tell you why. Victor is known to take what he wants, but more, he likes to be watched. The two other men were prominent attorneys. Victor was the aide of a senator, and that piece of shit liked to watch Victor. No one wants the woman connected to those fluids to be found. Hell, I'd bet my savings account the condom I left on his dead dick magically disappeared before the ME was on scene. Now, don't mistake me. I don't want Diane anywhere near this. I'm happy she hasn't been dragged into the fallout."

"Even if it means helping you with a defense—"

If Mason meant to say more, he didn't get the chance before Calista cut him off.

"Revictimize the victim so I get a lesser sentence. No thanks."

Apparently no one had anything to say to that. After a few beats of silence, Calista said, "I was in a snit when I thanked you all for the save, but I really did mean it. And Catarina, I'm sorry about the whole gun in your face."

I waved the apology off.

"All in a day's work."

I heard Jack growl, and I leaned into his side and tipped my head back to smile at him.

He wasn't smiling. But he no longer looked red-hot pissed, so I was considering it a win.

"We're coming up on the bay," Pete announced.

The boat slowed. Bad news for me and my stomach was, at this new speed, the boat rocked *more*. The mouth of the bay came into view, no lighthouse to guide vessels into the harbor, just a wide opening with a lonely, low-lit building up on the bluff. A church, maybe. Either that or someone had prime real estate overlooking the water and the village farther off in the distance. And that village was lit up like a beacon in dark moonlight.

"Jack, pull up the map. What's the terrain north of the pier look like?" Pete asked.

Jack shifted to get his phone back out. He pulled up the map, angling the screen so I could see too. There was a mountain—okay, more like a very tall hill—that cut off the beach from the village proper. It'd be a trek to traverse it, and it would also put us on the only road entering the village. Jack used his finger to move the map south of the pier. More of the same rocky shoreline.

"I think it's a safer bet pulling into that alcove there." I pointed at the map. "And coming up from the south. The terrain's not much better, but we'll avoid the road. We can stay on the outskirt of town."

"Too rocky," Jack denied. "We'd have to anchor and swim in."

"You got a problem getting wet, sailor?"

"No. I gotta problem with you getting smashed against jagged boulders."

I had a problem with that too. But it was still the best course of action.

"I *can* swim," I told him. "And the water's calm."

Though my roiling stomach belied my statement.

"I thought you said you were afraid of sharks," Mason unhelpfully put in.

"It's called Bahia Tortuga, not Bahia Tiburón," I reminded him.

However, I wasn't sure I wanted to swim with sea turtles either. I'd never seen one in real life, but like two-thirds—that was a rough guesstimate, but I figured it was close enough—of the population had seen them on TV. Those fuckers were huge. I couldn't remember the size of their mouths, and with a possible dip into the water on the horizon, I wasn't going to think about it.

"If you looked at the map, would you be able to locate the house Carlos took you to?"

I glanced at Calista. She was nodding and holding her hand out to Jack.

"Here, take my seat," I offered, so she could sit next to Jack.

As soon as I pushed to a stand, a wave of nausea hit, and I swayed.

"Jesus," Mason mumbled. "We need to get her off this boat."

I barely fought back repeating Calista's earlier retort—no shit, Captain Sherlock. Instead I opted to flip him the bird.

"I'm fine."

I wasn't.

I was ready to jump overboard and take my chances swimming with the turtles.

Mason took pity on me and grabbed my arm to steady me. "Here, sit by me."

Calista moved from the port side to sit next to Jack. Mason guided me starboard. For the record, "guided" was an understatement. He practically dragged me to his side.

Once I was seated, Mason leaned close and whispered, "The trick is to focus on something stationary in the distance."

The only trick that was going to work was getting off the rocking boat.

I didn't say that. I stared at the lights coming from the village and breathed deep while I listened to Calista tell Jack about what she saw and what turns she remembered before she'd arrived at Carlos's cousin's house. At least, we assumed it was the cousin's place, though it could've been anyone's. But the bottom line of it was, it was a house we wanted to avoid.

"Water infill," Jack announced. "The house is on the north end of town."

I practically groaned my relief.

Mason chuckled from beside me. "One day you'll get your sea legs, Kitty Cat."

When I'd moved to Virginia, the people there had told me my Texan blood would thicken and I'd get used to the cold. That hadn't happened, so I wasn't holding out for sea legs.

"Doubtful," I muttered as I watched the rocky shoreline for the alcove, counting down the seconds before I got to get off this puke bucket.

Thankfully, a few minutes later, Pete was pulling back on the throttle.

Nope. Scratch that, now that the boat was no longer in motion, it was bobbing side to side.

"Everyone ready?" Pete asked.

Hell. To. The. Yes.

"Whoa there, Kitty." Mason grabbed my shoulder before I could bolt. "Pete goes first. Then you and Jack. Calista and I take up the rear."

I wasn't so seasick I didn't smirk at his comment.

With a shake of his head, Mason cut off my retort. "Don't."

I didn't have time to evaluate Mason's stern tone before Pete was shuffling forward. Jack and Calista were on their feet, with Jack swinging his dry pack over his shoulder. When Jack had his gear adjusted the way he wanted, he took a step closer to me and offered his hand. Once I was tucked to Jack's side, Mason got himself ready.

Next thing I knew, Pete was in the water. He dove under and a few seconds later popped back up.

"Maybe ten feet deep," Pete called back.

"Sit on the edge and push off. Not straight down," Jack instructed.

I followed his unnecessary orders without comment. Mostly because I was eager to get off the boat but also partly because if he hadn't told me to push off, I might've just dropped straight down.

What can I say? I'm not a boat person.

Seeing as I'd been sitting on the edge when I pushed off, my head barely went under water. But when I popped up, Pete was right next to me with a hand around my upper arm, guiding me away from the boat and the rocks.

Jack jumped in next and came right to me, followed by Calista, with Mason indeed taking up the rear.

"Do you know how to sidestroke?" Jack asked.

"That's the doggy-paddle thing on your side, right?"

"I thought you said you knew how to swim?"

"Yeah, in a pool."

Jack let out a string of expletives.

"I'm screwing with you," I told him.

In the moonlight, treading water, I watched Jack shake his head in exasperation.

"Ready?"

I ignored his question and kept staring.

"Baby?"

The timing was strange, but the feeling wasn't. It was the kind that dug in and settled deep. The kind that warmed you to your core. Not contentment or happiness or anything as simple as that. It was bigger than that, so huge it filled my lungs and fed my soul.

This was life—*my* life—it was unpredictable at best. After losing my grandmother and the foundation she'd given me, moving on to not so great until Lina, I'd never been settled. When I got older that had translated into me craving the thrill of the chase. I didn't know why and it didn't much matter, I just knew I liked the excitement of the hunt. I liked moving around. I liked knowing I did a job that made a difference. I needed these things to define me. My job was my identity.

But right then, treading water off the rocky shore of a Mexican village, I came to the realization I no longer *needed* the chase or the rush. I wasn't ready to give it up, I loved what I did, but I didn't *need* it—I wanted to continue because it helped good people who'd found themselves in impossibly heinous situations, but I was more than the human-lie-detector soldier, the agent, the federal law enforcement officer.

I was just me.

Catarina, the friend, the daughter, the granddaughter, Jack's woman.

There was nothing to prove to anyone.

Not even myself.

I sucked in a breath . . . all mine.

The feeling of freedom I'd discovered all those years back was now accompanied with a sense of completeness.

I was whole without Jack.

But with him, I was complete.

"Ready," I told him.

It was his turn to stare at me.

"Move it, Donovan. We don't have all night, and now my jeans are wet and sticking to all the wrong places," I bitched.

"Catarina—"

"Jack."

His lips tipped up into a smile.

And there it was again, total and absolute completeness.

Chapter Twenty-Seven

The swim to shore was quick and thankfully uneventful.

However, something happened out there in the water. Unfortunately I didn't have time to ask her about it, but whatever it was looked important—like she'd had a revelation.

But that would have to wait. We had a plane to catch and an uncertain route to get there.

"New grievance unlocked," Cat started. "Or maybe it's not a complaint and more of an unhappy observation. Swimming with a vest on sucks."

Pete was digging through his SealLine pack but looked up at Cat to say, "True story."

Her expression was comical when she asked, "What, no tough-guy Team Guy recounting of how you swam ten miles upstream in frigid water with a vest and a fifty-pound ruck? All of this before you ate snails for breakfast."

Pete pulled his phone out and began rolling the top on the pack closed. "Tough guys don't need to tell fish tales."

"Why's that?" she asked.

"Because the shit we do doesn't require exaggeration."

"What he means is," Mase interjected, "the *cool-guy shit* we do gives regular men boners."

Fucking Mason.

"Are you always this full of yourself?" Calista inquired.

"If by full of myself you mean confident, then yeah, sweetheart. All the fucking time." Mason shrugged. "And before you ask, yes, my confidence skirts arrogance, but only because I can back my shit up. Most people like to think they're better than they really are. I know I'm better—not because of the cool shit I've done. Not because I think I'm a tough guy. But because when the call comes, I'm out the fucking door no questions asked."

Without missing a beat, Calista remarked, "And that's why Tom sent you to find me, because you wouldn't ask uncomfortable questions."

I wasn't sure if that was an accusation or a statement of fact, but still Mase fielded it. "What questions would Tom find uncomfortable?"

Calista closed down. "Forget I said that."

"Sure," Mason magnanimously agreed, even though it was a flat-out lie.

He might drop the line of questioning with Calista, but he wouldn't forget to dig in when we got home.

"Three missed calls," Pete announced. "Shep. Fallon. Tom."

Well, fuck.

Fun-time Mason fled, replaced by pissed-off warfighter.

"Call Fallon."

Pete didn't need Mason's directive. He'd already engaged his phone and was lifting it to his ear.

"You good?" Pete asked into the phone. "Right. Good work." Pause. "Yeah. We got the package, tangos are down, on the way to the mainland airport now. We'll debrief when we get on the plane." Another pause. "Later." Pete lowered his phone but didn't look up as he slid his finger across the screen again and told us, "Mission success."

"Righteous," Mason muttered, and his shoulders relaxed now that he knew the team was safe.

If they weren't, Pete would've led with injuries.

Pete's phone was back at his ear. "Whatcha got, Shep?"

Mason's gaze jerked over his shoulder. Cat's hand landed on my forearm and squeezed. My other hand shot up to silence Pete.

They'd heard it too. Voices in the distance.

"Yep," Pete whispered. "We got incoming."

Cat dropped her hand, and out of the corner of my eye I saw her pull her pistol from her holster as she stepped next to Calista and whispered something to her as I swung my M4 up, the buttstock of the rifle pressed tight against my shoulder, ears straining to hear, eyes scanning the hilly terrain.

Mason had his dry pack hanging from one shoulder. Using his opposite hand, he unzipped and reached into the side pocket, pulling out a pistol. Wordlessly he handed Calista the weapon he'd obviously stowed for the swim. As soon as Calista retrieved her weapon, Mase secured his bag and pulled up his M4.

Without needing verbal commands, Mase moved left, I stepped right, and we took our watch positions, leaving Pete and the women between us.

"Copy that." Pete spoke quietly, ending the call. Then to the rest of us, "Carlos's cousin got word Calista escaped, and he knows she had help."

Fuck.

Not surprising but still fucking hell.

Pete quietly went on. "He knows she fled on a boat and is sending men out on the water. Airport's gonna be hot."

No, *now* fucking hell.

"New exfil?" Mase asked.

"No. Shep said we'd have backup. The plane's thirty minutes out."

Fuck, fuck, *fucking* hell.

We were in an alcove with a small beach that would open up to a ravine. We needed to hurry up and get to higher ground.

I glanced down at my Suunto, checked where we were on the GPS, and motioned forward. Pete led, taking the western route avoiding the structure to the east. It was the longer route, but safer.

Calista dogged Pete's heels, Catarina behind her, with me after Cat, and Mase taking our six. Single file, we trekked the valley—a fetal funnel with a pucker factor of ten. I felt sweat trickle down my back and didn't breathe a full breath until we climbed a small hill.

My relief of being out of the ravine was short-lived—not a single tree, bush, or building for cover. The lights of the village shone to the north, then total darkness beyond. It was eerie as fuck, a fishing village in the middle of nowhere surrounded by inky black.

The next twenty minutes were silent.

Utterly so.

As the silence stretched, the sweat continued to trickle down my neck, and a ball of unease formed in my gut.

It was too quiet—like an ambush you didn't see coming.

As soon as the thought crossed my mind, Murphy's Law of Combat number two kicked in: *incoming fire has the right of way*. Or was it fifteen: *anything you do can get you shot, including nothing.*

Either or, shots rang out.

Catarina dove forward, taking Calista to the dirt. From behind me, Mase blindly returned fire. I hit my knees and did the same. Pete was on his stomach diagonally in front of the woman, barrel of his rifle pointing behind Mase's position, now covering our backs.

"Come on, fuckers," Mason grumbled. "Show daddy where you are."

"Did Mason just call himself *daddy*?" Calista snickered.

It didn't take long for more shots to pop off, the muzzle blasts giving away the enemies' location on the eastern hilltop. Which brought us to Murphy's Law of Combat number one: if the enemy is in range, so are you.

"Cover me," Pete ordered. "I'll meet you at the cemetery."

Before I could reject Pete's plan for a solo mission to get to the enemy, he was up and running.

Fuck.

I laid down cover fire until Pete disappeared down the side of the hill.

"Get up, baby," I demanded. "Take Calista and find cover."

"Not a chance, hotshot."

"Catarina."

"Jack."

"Baby, get the package secure. We'll catch up."

"Goddamnit, Jack," Cat snarled. "I don't like—"

"We'll be right behind you," Mase put in.

Cat rolled to her hip, then up to her knees, her right arm straight out, holding her Sig pointed toward where the enemy was holed up, her other hand reaching for Calista.

"If you're not at the airport right after we get there, I'm coming back to find you," Catarina angrily clipped.

Of course she would.

At one time, I would've called that reckless. Now I understood it for what it was—loyalty. She'd never leave me behind, or anyone on the team.

"Got it. Now go, baby."

Catarina let out a colorful string of obscenities that in no way made sense, though I couldn't miss their meaning or her level of displeasure.

"See you soon, Kitty Cat."

Cat shot me an unhappy look before her anger cleared and her hand wrapped around my wrist.

"Be safe."

"That's my line."

Then because that knot in the pit of my gut was twisting, I took the time we didn't have to tug her close and press a hard kiss to her mouth.

"Get on that plane no matter—"

"Save your breath. I'm not leaving you."

Fuck.

I lost her hand when she stepped away, then I lost sight of her when she took off in a sprint, and I turned back to the direction the gunfire was coming from and unloaded half a mag.

"Reload," Mase called out. A moment later I heard him reengage.

I quickly glanced to the left. Cat and Calista were nowhere in sight.

"Ready?" I asked Mase.

"Yep."

Mase took off in the same direction as Pete. The decline wasn't steep, but it was unsteady. Rocks and sand made it possible to slide most of the way down.

"This shit was easier when I was twenty," Mason griped.

He wasn't wrong.

"True story."

We hit the valley, slowed to a walk, and Mason came up next to me.

"I can't believe she actually followed orders."

He was talking about Catarina.

"She's not dumb. She knows Calista's the mission."

"Fuck you very much," Mase huffed. "I wasn't implying she's stupid. I'm just surprised she left you under my protection."

I snorted.

Mase finished, "But it's good to know she trusts me to keep you safe."

I hated to say it, but damn if I could shake this feeling.

"Something's off," I told Mase.

"What kind of something?"

I couldn't answer that.

"Pete never called Tom back."

"You think Tom fucked us?"

Did I?

He was the one who'd sent us to find Calista, but Shep had been the one to get us the intel.

"Calista didn't know who broke into the hotel room and killed Carlos and Gloria. We don't know who was driving the Toyota that hit the gas pump. We don't know who was on the plane from the UAE to Mexico City. Too many unknowns. I have a bad feeling Pete did exactly what they wanted him to do."

Mason didn't need me to explain. "If I wanted to draw the enemy into an ambush, I'd give away my location and wait."

Firing across the valley wasn't an impossible distance if the shooter was a good marksman who understood bullet drop, crosswind, powder load, and a slew of other shit that made long-distance shooting an art form. That was not who had been shooting at us. And I knew because we were all still alive. A good marksman would've been able to pick us off.

But they got their desired outcome.

Pete had run toward the danger to eliminate it.

"Watch my back," I said as I let my M4 go.

It caught on the sling, and I shrugged my pack off to get my phone out.

Thank fuck for dry bags.

As soon as I had my phone out, I was reminded Cat's bag was still on the runway back on Cedros.

Motherfucking shit.

"Cat has no comms," I mumbled, and scrolled to find Tom's contact.

"I'm getting the woman a fanny pack," Mase returned.

I was thinking more along the lines of asking Tom for another subcutaneous tracker.

The call went to voicemail. I disconnected and dialed again. I was getting ready to try again when Tom picked up.

"Who is this?" he clipped.

"Jack. You called—"

"You've got two Emiratis there and two former . . ."

"Tom?"

"Watch your back . . ." The connection cut off again. ". . . here . . ."

"You're breaking up."

I heard three tones indicating the call dropped. I looked at my screen. Full bars. That meant Tom had shit service.

"Bad copy," I told Mase. "All I got was two guys from the UAE and two former *something* before he broke up. He said to watch our back and the word *here*."

For a long moment, Mase didn't say anything, though he didn't need to.

It was one thing to be dealing with the cousin of a gangster who thought he was a predator—and he was to women and children—but the big dogs in the cartel would eat him alive. It was another to be dealing with professionals.

Pete thought we were dealing with locals, so he made the call to eliminate the threat.

He would've made a different choice if he'd spoken to Tom before he'd taken off.

"Let's hope Pete didn't just step into a heaping pile of shit."

We could hope.

But my gut said we'd be buried in shit before the night was over. And part of that was missing Catarina's deadline, then my woman would circle back.

"We need to get to the airport before Cat comes looking for us."

A look I couldn't decipher flooded Mason's features, and before I got a lock on it, his mask fell back into place.

But it looked a lot like panic and his voice was tight when he said, "Let's hit it."

"Mase—"

"She'll be fine. The woman's tough as fuck."

I wasn't sure if he was trying to convince me or himself.

But right then I didn't have the time nor the headspace for contemplation.

We needed to get to Pete, then haul ass to the airport.

The knot sinched tighter.

Chapter Twenty-Eight

"Is that the cemetery?" Calista asked.

There hadn't been a tree or bush in sight for the last thirty minutes we'd been walking. Which made the aboveground tombs stand out in stark relief.

Rows and rows of them. Some with tall monuments, others just the vault. It was an odd place for a cemetery—on top of a hill in the middle of nowhere. Then again, it wasn't. It was peaceful up here. A place to come and mourn with a view of the sea. If we were in the States, houses would dot these hilltops, the bluffs would be littered with homes, the natural beauty decimated, the tranquility lost to mankind.

But right then, all was peaceful. I hadn't heard gunfire since I'd left the guys. For my mental health I wasn't going to contemplate what that could mean—at least not right now. I had a mission: get Calista to the airport and find a safe place to wait. If the guys were a no-show, I'd figure it out then.

I hadn't answered Calista when she went on, "It's kinda creepy in a beautiful sorta way."

"I'm not a fan of cemeteries in general," I told her.

"So you'd never go on one of those ghost tours of an old graveyard."

That was a hell to the no!

"Hard pass."

I stayed well away from the tombs as we walked the dirt path toward the village.

"How much farther?"

I was impressed Calista hadn't asked sooner. Although she hadn't complained once since her initial squabble about coming with us.

"About twenty minutes. But in three hundred meters we'll hit a street with houses."

"Pete said the airport was hot," she unnecessarily reminded me.

I hadn't forgotten what Pete had relayed from Shep, nor had I forgotten the part about Shep telling Pete we'd have backup. Which was both good and bad. The good was obvious, the bad was I didn't know who the backup was or where they were, and with no phone and no comms I couldn't shoot first, ask questions later.

"We'll get as close as we can and wait."

"Were you in the military?"

Her question came from left field, but I got it. This wasn't my first long walk in enemy territory. Some of *those* conversations had been off-the-wall strange. Others had been informative. There was something about trekking through the desert with thirty pounds of kit on with your mortality top of mind—not knowing if you'd be returning back to post with your team, or worse, the person next to you wouldn't—that loosened your lips. It had also been a way to cut through some of the tension.

"Yeah, Army."

"Good thing you didn't go with the Navy," she teased.

"Right, I would've gone AWOL the first time I got assigned to a carrier group. You're a journalist," I prompted.

There was a moment of hesitation before she answered. A moment I didn't quite understand.

"Yeah."

One word, no elaboration.

"Do you like it?"

"It's a means to an end."

Her sister.

I changed the subject. "Do you know where you'll go after here?"

"You mean since I can't go back to the US?" she asked, but didn't wait for confirmation. "Probably Canada."

If I was wanted for murder, Canada wouldn't be my first choice, but to each their own.

The first house of the neighborhood—if you could call it that—we had to walk through came into view. I stopped to get my bearings; Calista did the same beside me. The village was lit up to my far right. A pier jutted out into the bay with a bright light at the end of it. In front of us, there were fifteen structures on the road we needed to travel. Behind ten of those homes was a steep hill. The other side of the street had five homes spaced a good distance apart. There was no good way to do this. We couldn't skirt the town. The terrain to my left became too extreme.

I had yet to decide the best way to get around the houses unseen when four dark figures appeared on the path in front of us.

Fuck.

"Down," I clipped.

Calista immediately dropped.

If I can see them, they can see me.

I did not want to fire my weapon this close to the village and alert everyone to our presence. Which would mean we'd have to take our chances traversing the mountains. That was going to seriously suck. With no choice, I gently pulled the slack out of my trigger, chose a target, let out a breath, and . . .

"Don't shoot me."

Tom?

Three of the men fanned out, taking a defensive position to guard the man in the middle, who was now coming at us at a fast clip.

Calista got to her feet and voiced my thought. "That's Tom."

What the hell was he doing here? And how did he find us?

"Stand down," he commanded.

Screw that.

I kept my Sig leveled and at the ready.

And Christ, he needed to stop yelling before he woke up the whole damn town.

"Get behind me," I told Calista.

"But Tom—"

"We don't know why he's here or who those men are."

"They're Tom's team."

Tom's team?

Since when did CIA officers have teams? And how the hell did Calista know Tom had a team?

"Tell them to lower their weapons," I called out when Tom was close enough I didn't have to shout.

Tom waved a hand. The men followed his silent order and lowered their rifles.

"Your turn," he returned.

"First tell me why you're here."

"To get Calista."

"Are they our backup?" I motioned to the men with the barrel of my Sig.

"No. They're here with me."

Of course Tom would only be out for himself.

"Here." Tom held out his hand when he stopped in front of me. "This is for you."

He opened his palm, presenting me with a white earbud.

"What's that?"

"Your backup." When I didn't immediately take Tom's offering, he continued. "Jack called in, but we were still in the air. Service was cutting in and out, so I don't know how much he heard. Ahmad Sindi sent two of his people along with two guards to retrieve Calista. Those guards are former British Special Air Service. Only one of those men went to the island. The other one is still here."

Well, fuck a duck.

"Who is Ahmad Sindi?"

"An Emirati real estate billionaire and known trafficker. He's also untouchable."

No one was untouchable.

"How did you find us?"

"I didn't. Shepherd Drexel told me where to find you, and he asked me to give you this." Tom shook his hand again. "Your plane's on the tarmac. It landed right after we did."

I took the earpiece from Tom with my left hand and awkwardly placed it in my right ear while still pointing my Sig at one of Tom's men.

As soon as it was in my ear, I heard, "Let them leave. We need to move."

Shep.

Just hearing his voice calmed my nerves I'd been working overtime to suppress.

"Copy."

"It's time to leave," Tom said, and motioned again to one of his men.

The man stepped forward, swung a rifle off his shoulder, and handed it to Tom.

"Here."

I took the SBR from Tom and hooked the sling over my shoulder. He immediately held out another hand and two magazines were handed to Tom, who held them out to me. I took those too.

"Thank your team for the assist."

The assist.

Typical.

I probably should've thanked him for the rifle and extra ammo, but I wasn't going to. What could I say, I was a petty bitch and didn't like to be used and lied to. As sweet as the 300 Blackout he'd handed over was, it didn't come close to making up for his bullshit.

Calista grabbed my arm and squeezed.

"Thanks for the ride. And again, sorry for the whole gun-in-the-face thing."

"No worries. Good luck, and be safe out there."

"You too."

With that, Calista moved to stand beside Tom, then they moved out, with Tom's guards circling them, turning their backs on me. Not the smartest move when I could've shot them in the back, but whatever.

"SITREP," I asked Shep through the earpiece as I jammed my new magazines into the empty pockets on my vest.

"Pete walked into a trap."

My heart sank before it started pounding in my chest so hard, I feared cracking a rib.

"Where's my team?"

"At the dock."

If Pete was captured, Jack and Mason would already be there to rescue him.

"Where are you?"

"At your back."

I spun to look behind me. Nothing. I looked left, then right, and still nothing.

"You know better than that, Sphynx."

Damn, he was right. If Phantom didn't want to be seen, he wasn't seen. Further from that, the man could materialize and dematerialize right before your eyes.

Like vapor.

"How are we doing this?" I asked.

"East to the dock. It's less than two klicks. I got your back."

I continued walking toward the neighborhood, but instead of walking through it, I'd veer right and go into the town proper.

When I was on my way, I asked, "How do you know where they are?"

"The locals talk via unsecured handheld radios."

That was stupid of them but good for us.

"Are you responsible for my new 300 Blackout?"

"I know how much you love a Honey Badger."

I barely suppressed a laugh.

"So sue me, I love a good brand name."

"I remember."

There was a melancholy there I didn't like.

"Can I ask you something?"

"Sure, as long as you don't get pissed if I don't answer."

That was new. The man I remembered was open with his team. He was one of the ones who, on those long walks, would wax poetic about growing up in Nebraska. He told stories about working on the ranch, getting drunk by the 'crick,' as he called it, the high school shenanigans he got up to, and a whole slew of other things besides. He'd never not answered a question, personal or otherwise.

I hated that he now sounded closed off and closed down.

"Are you doing okay?"

"I'm alive."

I hated that more, because him being alive and the undertone in which he said it meant something ugly.

"Shawn—"

"Shawn Miller is dead, Catarina."

He wasn't. He was very much alive, talking to me.

"Right."

"He died in that cave with the rest of his team."

My heart bled for my old friend. A good man, a loyal teammate, a skilled soldier. A man I never thought I'd see or hear from again. Not because I didn't know if he was alive. I'd heard he'd been rescued, but after he was pulled from the bowels of hell, he'd done what he was good at doing and dematerialized.

"Okay."

"Not being a dick, Cat." He softened his tone. "But the man you knew is gone."

I'd bet Shepherd Drexel was exactly the same person as Shawn Miller.

Now was not the time to tell him that.

"Got it, Shep," I told him, even though I didn't.

And God willing, I never would *get it.* Getting it would be to understand what it was like to be captured and tortured and witness the same happening to my team before they were executed in front of me. Only then would I truly comprehend what Shawn went through and why he'd needed to leave the name behind in a cave with his fallen brethren.

I continued on in silence.

Shep broke it. "Shep sounds all kinds of wrong coming from you, Sphynx."

"I could call you Phantom, but you know Mason is a nosy bastard, and he'd recruit the rest of the guys to dig into my past and find the squadrons I worked with until they found a Phantom. Though, hate to tell you, but the name's not very original. I'd bet there are like five hundred Phantoms out there between the Teams, the Unit, and the SF groups. Not to mention, Rangers love their cool nicks. I'm sure there are a bunch of Ranger Phantoms running around out there."

I heard Shawn-slash-Phantom-slash-Shep chuckle.

In front of me the road forked. Before I could ask Shep which way to go, he told me, "Go right. The south street is a direct line in. Five hundred yards down there's a stand of trees and a pathway between two houses to get to the beach. Head north and hold at the light-blue cabana. You'll have a direct view of the yellow cinderblock boathouse where Pete is being held."

"Do you have eyes on Jack and Mason?"

"Negative."

Shit.

"How close are you?"

"I'm at your six, and close enough."

That could mean anything. Shep was a sniper. He could be a mile away and he'd think he was close enough.

"Can you call them and tell—"

"Tried that. Jack's not answering."

Double shit.

He's busy finding a way to get Pete out of a jam, I reminded myself.

I silently crept between the houses Shep had guided me to, careful not to trip over any of the children's toys that were scattered in the sand and dirt. I hit the sandy shoreline and took off in a dead sprint to the blue hut that Shep had called a cabana, but it was more of a dilapidated structure that should've been demolished twenty years ago, if the half-missing roof was anything to go by.

"Movement at your eleven," Shep called in.

I slowed to a walk, swung my rifle left—and stopped dead when I found myself on the business end of a rifle.

"Goddamnit." A familiar growl came from the man holding the M4. "Sorry, Kitty Cat."

Mason lowered his weapon.

I lowered mine and reported to Shep, "Found Mason."

"Copy."

"Who are you talking to?" Mason inquired.

I pointed to my ear. "Shep."

"How in the . . . never mind . . . good to see you. Do you know what's happening?"

"Tom, then Shep, filled me in on the basics." Mason's head jerked, then he looked around, belatedly realizing Calista wasn't with me. "She went with Tom. I'll tell you about it on the plane."

"She left with Tom?" he incredulously snickered.

Interesting.

I'd probe him later about why that seemed to bother him.

But first . . .

"Where's Jack?"

"Covering the east side of the building. Pete's inside with one tango. Six guards surrounding the building."

"There's a former SAS soldier who stayed behind when the others went out to the island to get Calista."

"Fuck," Mason clipped and pulled out his phone.

He angrily stabbed at the screen before he lifted it to his ear.

"Shep? Do you have a good copy?" I asked, making sure he could hear Mason and I talking.

"Yep. Confirmed six men. The two on the north side are sitting on their asses catching a smoke break. The other four are amateur at best, more like four dudes who could use some extra cake and agreed to roll out of bed to stand outside a building in the middle of the night. My guess is the SAS soldier got word his buddies back on the island are dead and he's pissed as fuck, taking his frustration out on Pete."

That was my guess too. Obviously Mason was of the same mind, since he was on the phone with Jack, giving him an update.

". . . yeah, she's here and good. We hit in thirty, count down now."

Mason lowered his phone and glanced at his watch.

"Tell Mase I've got overwatch," Shep radioed.

"Shep has overwatch," I relayed.

"He's here?"

"He's my backup."

Mason let out a low whistle and shook his head.

"Twenty seconds to go time. Follow me."

"Copy," Shep acknowledged.

With my left hand on Mason's shoulder, I followed him to the side of the hut while counting backward from twenty.

Three men stood by a door looking like they were having a natter.

"Is that the only entrance?"

Mason nodded.

Easy day, as the guys would say.

A shot rang out, then a second.

The three men in front of us went on alert.

Mason charged forward, popping rounds off, easily dropping the guards at the door.

"Clear," Shep announced in my ear.

"We're clear," I told Mason as I ran after him.

The door to the building swung open. Mason zigged right, I zagged left and caught sight of a big-ass bear of a man taking up almost the entire frame of the door. Too big to be Pete. I fired a round. The wood next to the man's head splintered.

It was now a game of who could pull the trigger the fastest.

Luckily for me, I was damn quick on the draw *and* trigger.

My second shot landed. The man pitched to the side and fell out of sight.

Mason veered back center and hit the door first, pointing his rifle down and to the left. He double-tapped the man I'd already put down.

I heard Shep chuckle in my ear, proving he was close enough to see what Mason had done. He followed up with, "Jack's rounding the building now."

I glanced to the side just as Jack appeared. I did a top-to-toe examination and saw he was unharmed and in one piece. He did the same and nodded.

"Go help Mason," Jack ordered. "I'll keep watch."

"Shep's got watch," I told him but offered no other explanation before I stepped into the building. It was one open space with a single light bulb hanging from a wire in the ceiling.

Pete was hanging by his rope-bound wrists from a metal hook fastened to a chain, which was anchored into the ceiling next to where the wire hung down for the light bulb. I was pretty sure that was an electric-shock accident waiting to happen.

Pete's murderous gaze came to me. Mason was next to Pete, digging in the front pocket of his cargoes. For once I read the room, which was filled with Pete's felonious vibes, and did not comment on Mason playing pocket pool in Pete's pants.

Mason's hand came out of Pete's pocket with a knife.

"You don't carry a knife?" I asked Mason.

"Left mine back on Cedros embedded in some asshole's throat."

"Well, now I know what to get you for Christmas. Unless you like playing where's the knife in Pete's pants."

Mason chuckled. Pete did not.

Other than Pete being restrained and hanging by his wrists, I didn't see any blood or injuries—he was supremely pissed but unharmed.

"What the hell happened?" I queried.

"I'm gonna kill Tom," Pete growled.

That explained nothing, I was pretty sure none of us would mind taking a swing at the man. His duplicity knew no bounds.

"Why now?"

Pete tipped his head to the side like I was dense.

"You smell like . . ." Mason trailed off and leaned closer. "Spicy. You smell spicy."

"Bear spray in the face leaves a lasting scent," Pete sniped. "Where's Calista?"

"Long story, but she left with Tom."

Mason sawed at the rope around Pete's wrist until enough of it was frayed that Pete Hulked his wrists apart, breaking through the last strands of rope.

Oh yeah, Pete was pissed.

"Let's get the fuck out of here."

I had just enough time to step to the side before Pete barreled me over.

Mason was right, he did smell spicy.

"Is it too soon to change your nickname from Pete to Chili Pepper?"

Pete grunted. Then followed up with "Fuck off, Kitty Cat."

That meant when I exited the building, I was smiling.

That smile grew when I saw Jack waiting for me.

"Ready to go home?"

Yes, please.

"Yes, and when we get there we're turning our phones off and not leaving your house—"

"*Our* house," he corrected.

"Our house for at least a week."

"Anything you want, baby."

Yeah, anything I wanted, Jack would give me.

"What is it that you want?" I asked.

"A week in bed with my woman naked—"

"My ears are bleeding!" Shep moaned.

Oops.

"Shep's on comms," I told Jack and pointed to my ear. "He heard about our plans for a naked week in bed."

"With that, I'm signing off," Shep told me.

"Wait. How are you getting home?"

"Don't worry about me, Kitty Cat."

Shep calling me Kitty Cat instead of Sphynx hit me square in the chest.

It was like with that, he'd erased our past.

I wasn't sure I liked it, but I did like having Shawn back, and if that meant calling him Shepherd Drexel and him calling me Mason's ridiculous nickname for me, then I'd take it.

"Be safe, Shep."

"The proper send-off is 'stay dangerous,'" he reminded me.

That hit my heart too.

I was right, somewhere deep inside Shep, pieces of Shawn remained.

"Stay dangerous." I repeated the end-of-transmission farewell we used to use in the sandbox.

"Good copy. Out."

My earpiece crackled before it went silent. I took it out of my ear and shoved it into my pocket.

"You good?" Jack asked.

I tipped my head back and caught Jack's gaze.

I didn't need to assess my feelings or my surroundings, or the last twenty-four hours, or even the last week to know my answer.

I didn't care where I was or what I was doing as long as I had Jack at my side.

"Never better."

Jack hooked me around the back of the neck, dipped his head, and took my mouth in a searing kiss.

It tasted a lot like triumph. But it felt like the once-crumbled foundation of my life had just been rebuilt. Strong. Steady. Solid.

With Jack, I had it all.

Chapter Twenty-Nine

Calista Ventura
Three weeks later
Abu Dhabi, United Arab Emirates

"It's time for you to call Saint and his team."

Even though Tom couldn't see me, since he was three thousand miles away and we were speaking on the phone, I still rolled my eyes at his use of Pete's real name. For some reason—and I hadn't asked—Tom didn't like calling Pete 'Pete.'

"I already told you, Mason Hughes is going to be a problem. I don't want him involved."

That was the lie I'd told Tom on the plane out of Mexico, when I'd adamantly turned down his suggestion to ask Mason and his team to help me. The lie *wasn't* that Mason was going to be a problem because he was going to dig through my past, my present, and he'd find out who I really was and who I really worked for.

The true problem was I found him attractive—in the I-wanted-to-jump-his-bones kind of way. And the more he irritated me, the more I wanted to bang him. Which in my estimation was the definition of insanity. Or maybe it was unhealthy. Though I wasn't sure I even knew what healthy was. After Liliya was taken, my life had spiraled into a tangled mess of dysfunction and grief.

"There's nothing for him to find."

"Be that as it may, Tom, I don't want—"

"I'm not asking, Calli," Tom interrupted me. "Your choices are call Saint or I'm pulling you."

The asshole would pull me out of some foolish sense of obligation to my father.

"I think you've paid your debt to my father tenfold. You don't need to keep riding in to the rescue every time you think danger's close." I'd shocked the man into silence. I took a second to savor the moment. "And just as a reminder, I didn't need help back in Mexico. I'd gotten myself out of that situation just fine and got us the authorization to go after Ahmad Sindi."

Still nothing.

"Tom, did I lose you?"

"How long have you known?"

"Since my father confessed all on his deathbed with a warning and instructions what to do if I was ever approached by the Irish."

Tom had nothing to say to that.

"How's Diane?"

Thankfully, Tom had something to tell me about my friend.

"She's in Upstate New York with a friend of mine who's taking care of her."

Thank God for that.

"And the charges against me? Where are you with that?"

"We're not done discussing your current situation."

We were.

I wasn't calling Saint.

"Tell me what you're doing to clear my name?"

"They have your DNA, Calli."

I knew they did. I'd stupidly broken a window.

"Don't feed me some line of bullshit. The rich and powerful have been getting away with murder since the beginning of time. The Agency cannot expect to send me out to do their dirty work but turn it off when I'm stateside. He was raping her, Tom. What did they expect me to do? Stand outside and call nine-one-one? Wait for the police to arrive while she endured more? Then watch him get off on some bullshit technicality because he's *rich* and *powerful*, which means he gets a free pass? I call bullshit on that. I saved the taxpayers money on a trial, and if by some miracle he was convicted, I saved them money housing and feeding that monster. They owe me a thank-you, not murder charges."

"I don't disagree, but . . ."

I stopped listening. My attention was pulled to the street below and the silver Maybach rolling to a stop at the valet stand. I would've preferred a sea-view room at the Park Hyatt, however, the room I was in with the view of the parking area was tactically the better option.

"I have to go. Amir is here."

"Twenty-four-hour check-ins," he demanded. "No excuses."

I swallowed my snarky retort.

I had work to do.

"Bye, Tom."

I disconnected.

Checked my hair on the way past the mirror and left my hotel room.

I did this wondering what Mason was doing, and if I called him to ask for his help, if I could keep my hands to myself.

Probably not.

I'd be begging him for a quick and dirty romp before the first twenty-four hours was up.

Damn.

◆ ◆ ◆

Mason Hughes
Four weeks home from Mexico
Downrange Ranch

"I think you're cheating," Ryan groused as he handed over three ten-dollar bills to Cat.

"Loser!" Fallon called out from the chair next to me.

I took a swig from my beer and for once kept my mouth shut. I was enjoying the show too much to interject.

The day was warm, the sun was shining, the sound of rapid gunfire *not* aimed at me was the perfect lullaby to help me relax.

"Rematch?" Cat offered for the fourth time.

Ryan nodded, and the shooters moved away from the match stage to the table with their ammo. Pete ambled out to the targets and placed stickers over the holes in the paper target while Jack reset the steel.

"What's up with you?" Fallon asked.

"Nothing, why?"

"You've missed numerous golden opportunities to bust Ryan's balls, and you're sitting quietly."

"You've got it handled," I reminded him.

My friend narrowed his eyes.

"Are you sick? You never miss an opportunity to flap your gums."

"What are you, seventy-two? No one says that anymore."

"That's not an answer," he pointed out.

Maybe not, but I didn't have an answer for him. At least not one that made sense. Something had felt off since we'd come home from Mexico. Like there was a disturbance in the Force. Like there was unfinished business out there, and it was making me antsy.

"Just enjoying watching Ryan embarrass himself."

Fallon didn't look like he bought my excuse, but thankfully he dropped the subject.

Pete and Jack came back from cleaning up the range just as Cat was making her way to the starting box. The stage was simple, with a mix of paper and steel. Ryan should've been running circles around Cat's time. But true to her word, the woman was damn fast and accurate.

Jack stopped behind Cat, glanced behind him, taking a visual account of everyone.

One could never be too careful when playing with guns.

"Range hot," Jack loudly called out. "Shooter ready?"

Cat's hand hovered just above her holster.

"Ready," she confirmed.

"Stand by."

A moment later, the beep of the timer Jack was holding went off. A millisecond after that, Cat pulled her Glock from her Kydex holster—the draw so smooth and so fast, if I'd blinked, I would've missed it.

She double-tapped the first paper target, ran to the next station, leaned to the side to get a clean sight picture of the steel, and plinked each of the five down lightning quick. Without lowering her weapon, she released a mag, let it fall to the dirt, tipped her Glock to the right while her left hand pulled a new mag from her belt. She shoved it in, straightened the gun, and resumed firing, executing a perfect combat reload.

"Damn, that reload was quick," Fallon mumbled my thought.

Watching her move through the stations was impressive as fuck. Every step she took purposeful, there was no wasted movement or breaths, and she counted her bullets like a pro, making sure she was never without ammo for the shots she needed to take.

Cat knocked down the last steel target and Jack stopped the clock to call out her time.

"Fastest run yet," he proudly announced.

Cat tipped her head back and beamed a megawatt smile at her man.

An emotion I'd never felt before slithered up my spine and made my gut uneasy. An emotion that felt a lot like jealousy. It wasn't that I'd never had a woman look at me like that. It was that one had never looked at me with so much love and actually meant it.

Love was a bullshit farce unless it was Catarina Keys beaming a smile at her man. Then I believed it. Or it was Mia smiling at her man, Cole. Then I trusted it. Any woman beyond those two, I didn't trust or believe. Women were lying and manipulative and only loved a man until they got what they wanted, then they bailed.

My phone vibrating in my pocket pulled me from thoughts that were really memories I'd done everything I could do over the last two decades to forget. And I'd done a damn fine job of forgetting her but remembering the lessons she taught me.

Never again would I be someone's fool.

I yanked my phone free, glanced at the screen, and frowned.

A text from a number not programmed into my contacts.

I positioned the phone to read my face and opened the text.

What do you say about a trip to Abu Dhabi? I could use some backup.

The left side of my chest started pounding.

Just to be sure, even though I was fairly certain I knew who that was from, I texted back, Who is this?

CV

Calista Ventura.

Fuck me.

I shot back another message.

Are you safe?

Define safe.

Give me five minutes to get the team together. Answer me when I call.

Do women always bend to your orders?

I felt my lips tighten.

And just like in Mexico, I had an overwhelming urge to kiss the fuck out of her to shut her up. Unfortunately she was on the other side of the world.

> That's a show not tell, sweetheart. And I'm happy to show you when I get there.

What the fuck was wrong with me? I'd never in my life had the urge to kiss a woman to shut her up. Moreover, I was never happy to show a woman *anything*.

The feisty blonde with gemstone eyes and a death wish was a temptation I didn't need. A temptation that stirred something inside me that was better left dead. A temptation that would test my control in ways I wasn't sure I could best.

Fuck.

I stood and shoved my phone back in my pocket.

"Yo, Pete, we need everyone at the big house. ASAP."

My best friend looked over at me, read my tone, and pulled out his phone to gather the rest of the team.

Looked like we were headed to Abu Dhabi.

Author Note

Are you curious about Pete's sister, Mia, and her husband, Cole? Their book is *Dangerous Mind*—Takeback, book 5 (https://www.amazon.com/dp/B08WC69MNM). You'll also get your first taste of Pete and Mason in that book. Catarina and Jack first meet in *Dangerous Affair*—Takeback, book 7 (https://www.amazon.com/dp/B08WC69MNM).

Jasmin and Lincoln Parker, as well as Zane Lewis, are from the Z Corps Universe. If you're interested in starting that journey into the fast-paced and action-packed world of Zane and his team, check out *Nightstalker*—Red Team, book 1 (https://www.amazon.com/dp/B07G8RQ3X7). Be warned: Zane Lewis is highly addicting and full of sarcasm. As Zane says, insults are his love language.

About the Author

Riley Edwards is a *USA Today* and *Wall Street Journal* bestselling author, wife, and military mom. Riley was born and raised in Los Angeles but now resides on the East Coast with her fantastic husband and children.

Riley writes heart-stopping romance with sexy alpha heroes and even stronger heroines. Her favorite genres to write are romantic suspense and military romance.